THE BOOK OF SIGNS

From the Case Files and Personal Journals of Cheyenne Bruce, Private Investigator, Book Three

Lella Rae

MasterPieces Unlimited

ISBN-ebook: 979-8-9858206-4-5
ISBN-Paperback: 979-8-3863573-8-2

Cover design by Gale Peck, Iceberg Strategic Creative
Printed in the United States of America

To Barbara Holtz Sullivan. Without her creativity and generosity this book may never have been written. Thank you, dear friend, for giving this book a "life beyond the pages." Those were the days, weren't they?

Prologue

Before the Whalesong murders, a writers' colony seemed an ideal setting; a lovely island in the Strait of Juan de Fuca, comfortable cabins in the woods, the companionship of like-minded men and women who loved books and writing.

After my previous case which had taken me to San Francisco and then to Hawaii, I had foundered into a bog of depression that threatened to pull me under. When I had returned from Hawaii the previous month, I had found myself in an unfamiliar world. My case there had almost finished me and the events haunted me over thousands of miles and came to rest on my doorstep. I had caused a death. My emotions lived in a horrible dark place that winter and sometimes I was terrified that I would never be able to climb out.

I had hoped that the familiarity of home, the comfort of friends and the daily routine of work would somehow weave enough magic to pull me out of the quicksand. The Whalesong case was waiting for me and I viewed it as my salvation. I planned to immerse myself in it. I wanted to plunge into it as though it were a cooling, healing pool and the work a powerful medicine. From the moment I stepped into the case, though, and became a part of the population of its world, I knew that something was very wrong. There seemed to be darker forces afoot that were not immediately visible.

Little did I know that behind the idyll of Whalesong, lurked something much more sinister than I had imagined. It was a case full of dangers, deceptions and threats that I didn't yet understand. I didn't know that in the woods of a dark island in the San Juans, I would meet people who had secrets and desires that when exposed, would have lasting tragic repercussions for us all.

ONE

Mid-February-Mid April, 1984

When you are facing a man who means to kill you, all of your ideals go out the window. The person you thought you were seems not to be the person you actually are. The pacifist suddenly becomes the warmonger, the dove becomes the hawk, the kindest, gentlest soul becomes a killer.

Of course, the man I was battling that chilly day in February wasn't out to kill me or harm me in any way. He was, in fact, my best friend. Easy Radford was a classmate in my quest to fight the demons inside me.

My name is Cheyenne Bruce. My detective agency, The Sign of the Cross, had been in existence for six or seven years by then. I had worked scores of cases and knew my way around, so I really wasn't a newbie in the self-defense game.

I had always been proud of being able to defend myself with my own body, not resorting to the false security that a weapon affords. But a brief attack in

San Francisco and a more serious one in Hawaii had severely undermined my confidence and I knew that I had to make some changes. Besides, after those unfortunate incidents, I had promised Easy that I would hone my self-defense skills so I had enrolled in a class optimistically called Keeping Yourself Safe.

Easy had volunteered to attend the class with me. He was as opposed to violence as I was and though he worked in law enforcement, he, like me, refused to carry a gun.

E.Z. Radford was the kind of guy you liked on first meeting. He was the perfect man for his job as Chaplain for the Seattle Police Department. Kindness and good humor poured out of his lovely denim blue eyes. His height, upwards of six feet, and his muscular body gave him a power that he rarely had occasion to use. A gentler soul you would be unlikely to ever find. We had been having what you could loosely describe as a relationship for several years.

"The ready stance," our instructor called. "Remember your ready stance!"

I knew he was aiming his warning at me. I had moved aggressively forward. Again.

Easy waved his forefinger at me and winked.

I resumed my ready stance and Easy aimed a blow to my face, which I successfully blocked, then a kick to the knee which I blocked as well. Then I aimed a kick at him. He blocked it and shuffled back, ready with his own feint to the left, then a swing to the right. I blocked him and lunged with an elbow toward his chin.

Besides the practice, the most valuable lesson I had gotten from that day's class had been the realization that my habit of walking for exercise, while good, was no longer enough. I needed to build strength and practice balance as well. In order for me to be more controlled and therefore more effective, I realized I seriously needed to whip myself into shape. My muscles were screaming in their own self-defense.

When, at last, the instructor signaled the end of class, there were more than a few sighs of relief from the other participants. That day had been our first of physical defense. Until then we had sat in a classroom learning, I thought, more about how to be paranoid than how to avoid a confrontation.

"Do you think you might be pushing yourself a little hard?" Easy asked me when we had dashed through the late winter rain to his car.

I glanced at him. "I don't think so," I said. "Why?" Easy had a tendency to be somewhat overprotective. I fought it, but I never seemed to make much headway.

"Nothing. I just noticed that you seemed a little fierce."

"That's what we're here for, isn't it?" I dug my icy hands deep into my jacket pockets.

He looked at me while the defroster on his old Ford struggled with clearing the windows. “Well, no,” he said. “This is a defense class, not a kick-his-ass-when-he-gets-in-your-face class. How many times did Mr. Barth have to tell you to get back into ready stance?”

“What are you talking about?” I shrugged deeper inside my jacket and shivered.

“I mean that you seemed to be fighting, aggressively fighting, something more than just the hapless guy standing in front of you.”

“Hapless, nothing,” I said and laughed. “You were aiming plenty of aggression toward me, too.”

“I think you were fighting more than just me, Chey.” He pulled out into traffic so I couldn’t see his face. “It was as if you were fighting something else. Maybe some*one* else. Like you were lashing out at someone or something you couldn’t quite reach with your fists and feet.”

I didn’t say anything. I knew he was right. Each of my strikes, each kick, each jab, each block seemingly was not aimed at Easy, my opponent, so much as at the phantoms which haunted me. It often seemed his insight into me was as good as mine was into him.

I might add here that I’m psychic, though I never mentioned that in my business literature. It always pushed people off the track. If I told the client I was psychic, they thought that I could do anything when, in reality, I couldn't. I can get feelings from most people and places. I can tell, generally, if someone is lying to me or not by touching them. That's about it. It isn't much, but I had consulted with the Seattle Police a time or two and I used my ability when I could. It often helped.

"It seems ironic, doesn't it," I said after a moment, "that we, peace lovers that we are, are taking a class where we are learning to kick the ass of the guy who gets in our face, as you so elegantly put it?"

"I think you're missing the point. It isn't a class in kicking ass. It's a class in not getting your own ass kicked."

I conceded that he was right again. I felt the familiar depression threatening to intrude on the thin veneer of self-control the activity in class had given me and didn't want to talk about it anymore. I stared out into the February rain and wished that I was somewhere else and that the whole miserable winter was over and forgotten. As soon as spring arrived, I knew I would feel better. I always did. Winter was and still is my least favorite time of year, though, that year, it seemed, the season wasn't the reason for my problems.

* * *

Eventually the month of February did end and so did our defense class. I still struggled with my sour moods and sleepless nights. They continued, pitiless and persistent, into March and then April. It didn't help that I was between cases. For once in my professional life, I didn't need the money, but I would have welcomed the activity, the keeping busy.

Instead of investigating, I concentrated on working at the local stained glass shop. Earlier in the winter, Ab Eberstein, the owner of Avenue Art Glass, had made me an apprentice. I helped in the shop while Ab taught me the craft. It had nothing whatever to do with my private investigation business, but that was probably its appeal. It was relaxing, creative work that left me with a wonderful feeling of accomplishment, not to mention a beautiful piece of artwork or two. In the summer, Ab would be attending an art show that would take him from the shop for four or five days. I would be in charge of the shop during his absence, so I needed to feel confident enough in my abilities to do a good job for him. I owed him much. But that was another story altogether.

It was during this time that I began to write a journal. At first, it was self-therapeutic, I thought. At least, it seemed so as I jotted down my day to day activities and feelings. Gradually, though, I began to think about including some of my past cases. Not all of my job was looking for cheating husbands and doing background checks. I've had a few noteworthy cases that might be interesting for others to read. This is definitely not to say that I planned to become a writer. I liked what I was doing just fine. But it couldn't hurt to put down some of the things I had done and seen in the past six or seven years. It helped when the hours seemed to drag and I felt that I couldn't escape my own thoughts.

I thought with increasing anticipation about my upcoming case. On the surface, it promised to be fascinating and I looked forward to it. I was sure it would give me relief from the relentless nightmares that had been plaguing me since the last one. How was I to know that the world I was entering would put me in a different kind of nightmare?

TWO

Mid-April, 1984

My newest clients, the Mercer family, had provided me with some of the background and a wealth of printed material I would use in the course of the case for which they were hiring me. In January, a large box full of manuscripts had been delivered to my door. In it, I found stories, fragments, even the notes and the manuscript of a completed novel. I had been eager to get started, almost desperate for something new, and had begun reading the moment I was home from Hawaii.

I didn't yet know all the particulars of the case. The Mercers had given me some indication of what it would entail. I knew that it involved going undercover, that I would be investigating the writers' colony that their son had attended for the past few years. Beyond that, I knew very little.

The idea of becoming someone else, even if only for a short time, appealed to me. Not surprising, considering that I was something of a nervous wreck most of the time in those days. I knew that the case would take me out of Seattle as well. The prospect of that appealed to me too, though I couldn't have said why. Looking at it from this remove, I understand that leaving the city was a further futile attempt to get away from myself.

The meeting with the Mercers was scheduled in my office on a bright morning in April.

Stella Mercer was a small woman who looked like the world had taken its turn with her. She was dressed beautifully in a flattering blue jersey dress and her warm honey colored hair looked breezily expensive, but there was something in her demeanor that let me know she had been abused by circumstance. Her tired looking eyes seemed full of sorrow and as I shook hands with her, I could feel her bone deep distress.

Stella's husband, JW, carried himself with an air of self-assurance. His clothes, too, were impeccable. He did not smile and I could read nothing in his face. When I shook his hand, however, I felt his depthless heartache too.

Claire, their daughter-in-law, smiled at me tentatively as though she had been in a dark room for a long time and had only recently emerged. She seemed to be a brace for the older couple. Her strength, it appeared, was a crutch that Mrs. Mercer leaned on. I felt the same weary sadness, the same sense of helplessness when I touched her. I understood it. I had been feeling something similar in myself.

As the three of them sat in my office, the April sun streamed in through the double glass doors, making the room cheerier than it should have looked under the circumstances.

The Mercers' son, Kegan, Claire's husband, had committed suicide the previous winter. I understood that they were looking for some kind of closure. Some, if not justification, then an explanation for the inexplicable.

"You indicated you had received the box of manuscripts we sent," JW said. He sat on the edge of the sofa and seemed unable to relax.

"Yes," I told him. "I've read some of Kegan's work. He was a wonderful writer. I'm certainly not an expert but I believe he was very talented."

Mrs. Mercer raised a tissue to her mouth and nodded. Claire looked down at her lap and JW rose to pace the room for a few seconds before stopping near the door. He gazed out at the front yard.

"Yes," Claire said. She looked up and nodded eagerly. "He was. Everyone said so. Every writing teacher he ever had. They knew he had promise and I knew it too. That's why we think that something... something strange was going on at Whalesong. The man who runs the colony, Russell York, told Kegan that his book was not worthy of his talent. That it was not sellable. He went so far as to say that Kegan was wasting his ability!"

I nodded my understanding. I failed to see how that opinion could possibly be justified. From what little I had read of his work, I could tell that Kegan had definitely been a gifted writer. I stayed silent, though. Sometimes it was best to let the client explain in his or her own way.

"Writing was so important to him," Claire said. "It was the only thing he wanted to do. I worked so that he could stay home and write." She looked as though she had gone over this sentence again and again. "I know our friends thought he was taking advantage of me, but that wasn't the case at all. I believed in him." She looked down at her lap again and I saw a tear fall onto her hand.

"Why don't you tell me more about Kegan?" I said. "How long had he been writing?"

"Since he was a child," Stella said. "He used to write his own bedtime stories when he was just a little boy." Her voice stumbled over the last word. She moved the crumpled tissue to her eyes.

"I've known him for five years," Claire said. "He was always writing. Always. It meant everything to him."

I saw JW nod. He continued standing near the door gazing outside.

"Had he ever shown signs of depression?"

"None," his mother said instantly. "Never."

Claire leaned over and put her hand on her mother-in-law's. "He got...*down* sometimes when his writing wasn't going well, but that's natural, I suppose," she said. "The longest that ever happened was a few weeks. He would keep plugging at it and all of a sudden, it would be flowing smoothly again. Depression, though? No..." She sounded so unsure that I knew she and I needed another, more private, conversation.

"He had been going to that writers' colony for a few years now," Stella said, giving her husband a glance. "But since that last time... Since he came home last spring, he wasn't himself." She looked at Claire. "Was he? He stopped talking to us. He looked like he wasn't sleeping and he lost weight." She bent and fumbled a fresh tissue from her purse.

Claire was nodding. "It's true."

Mr. Mercer turned from the door. "Miss Bruce," he said. "We would like you to infiltrate that writers colony. Find out what you can about what's going on up there. Kegan told us some of what happens and, frankly, it doesn't sound right to us. Those people are supposed to be encouraging writers, helping them, not driving them to suicide."

Stella made a little sob and pressed the tissue harder to her mouth.

"What makes you think that they 'drove' him to it, sir?"

Claire looked at her father-in-law who had turned

his attention back to the outdoors. "We don't believe that Kegan would have done that unless they had completely broken his spirit," she said. "He said they had told him that literary fiction was all wrong for him. They said he should write adventure stuff. He wasn't interested in that! His work is...well, it's beautiful. And I'm not just saying that because he was my husband. He won awards for his writing in college. I *know* he had talent." She looked as though she would burst into tears herself. "Of course, he did and I know they recognized it too, yet they discouraged him from writing what he wanted to write." She did begin weeping then.

"Claire said that he told her they had burned his manuscript," Stella said while Claire seemed to gain control of herself.

I said nothing and, though I was shocked, I kept my face expressionless.

Claire nodded. "They convinced him to hand his manuscript over and they burned it right there in front of the class."

"The colony is very regimented," JW said. He turned from the window and came to stand behind his wife. She seemed to gain strength from the hands that rested on her shoulders. "There are lots of rules that seem ridiculous to me, but Claire says that it's all for the writers' benefit. They don't want the writers to be distracted, apparently."

"For instance," Claire said, "They don't let them

fraternize. They don't let them wear watches. They let them know mealtimes, meetings, lights out and such by a bell, Kegan called it a gong, at the Main Cabin. They couldn't even make phone calls but once a week and," she glanced at her mother and father-in-law. "I think they listen in on the calls. It does sound crazy, I know, but the writers all go along with it."

"There's a list of the rules in the registration packet," JW said.

"We want you to infiltrate...go undercover... whatever you call it," Stella said. "Find out what's going on there. We don't think Kegan would have... done what he did if he had not gone to Whalesong. If they had not forced him to destroy his work."

"It sounds almost like it's a cult." I said, thinking that it might be even more interesting than I had first imagined.

They looked at each other. "That's exactly what we *do* think," JW said. "Though, we hadn't put it into those words. We are willing to pay whatever it takes to get to the bottom of this for our boy. We believe those people drove Kegan to kill himself and we want them stopped. My God! How many other talented writers have they destroyed?"

Stella sobbed and turned her head away.

"It's too late for Kegan," Claire said, glancing at Stella. "But he can't be the only one who has had a promising career, not to mention a life, ruined!"

"I'm certainly willing to do it," I said. "Unfortunately, they—the owners of the colony—might have other ideas. I'm not a writer. I would need to be accepted as a student. I imagine there would be little hope of that. Perhaps I could work in the main house as a domestic?"

Claire started shaking her head before I had finished. "Kegan was referred to the colony by a writer friend of his who used to attend the spring term," she said. "His place in the colony is already reserved for this spring term. There are several sessions a year apparently. Every year, the attendees in each of the sessions are given the option to reregister for the next year. There's a code. A registration code that you can use. Each spring term, for example, the colonist—that's what they call the people who attend—can register for the next spring term. If the student can't make it for one reason or another, and if there are no openings in one of the other sessions, they are allowed to give the code to someone else to take their place, either temporarily or permanently. The code makes it official that Kegan is authorizing you to take his place. It's a way for his spot to be held for him so he could return if he wanted to. If he were able." Her voice strangled on her last words.

"In fact," Stella added, "They imply that you have to find someone to come in your place or you forfeit the tuition that you've paid." She glanced at Claire, who nodded.

"I think, or at least, Kegan thought," Claire said, "that they use the codes so they don't have to screen writers and can keep the place filled without them having to do the work. They said that they relied on the colonists to refer only people they trusted to be competent writers. You designate another writer to hold your place for a term."

"But I'll be discovered as a fake the minute I open my mouth," I told them. "I'm afraid I don't have a chance of passing myself off as a writer." Unless I could overcome that obstacle, I wouldn't have a hope of believably infiltrating the colony. I felt a stab of disappointment. I had been looking forward to getting involved in the case.

"That's why we sent you the box of manuscripts," JW said. "You say you've read some of them? Read them all. Familiarize yourself with them. You don't have to know a lot about writing, just make those people think that his work is yours." He had finally sat down on the other side of his wife, but was up and pacing again a moment later.

"Won't they recognize Kegan's writing?"

"No." Claire looked at me, her eyes round. "We've given you the novel that he had finished just before he died. He had never read that one in the colony. He had only read *The Way of Wonder*." She looked down at her lap again. "And they destroyed it."

Hope started creeping cautiously back.

"We've given you some of Kegan's short stories,"

JW said. "The Whalesong people *have* heard those. You won't want to take them with you but you will want to read them to understand what Kegan... what he was about. We have also given you the manuscript of his novel, *The Book of Signs.* Read that thoroughly. That's the new one. None of them have seen or heard of it." He glanced at Claire. "Apparently, there are sessions where the writers read their work aloud."

Claire nodded. "Meeting. That's what they call it."

"And you're sure that he never mentioned this new book to the other, uh, colonists?"

Claire nodded. "He told me he was determined they would never find out about it. That he wasn't going to give them the chance to destroy that one too.

"And the people who run Whalesong don't know that he's...that he died?"

Stella continued to look into the middle distance while her husband gazed out the door. They shook their heads in unison.

"No," Stella said in a tight voice. "Considering the circumstances, we didn't announce Kegan's passing in the newspaper or anywhere, really. Very few people outside our family know."

"Do you know who any of the other writers in the colony are?" I asked Claire.

She nodded and produced a list from her purse. "I

meant to put this into the box," she said, handing it over to me.

I scanned the list. "So, nine writers altogether including Kegan…uh, me?"

"I'm not sure of the spelling of some of those names," she said. "Kegan mentioned people occasionally and I always wrote down the names thinking that someday I could find their books or stories and read them. I'm not even sure that those are the same people who will be there this term. There could be one or two different attendees, although Kegan always said that the same ones come back again and again."

"Did you ever find any of the books they wrote?" I asked while I perused the list.

She shook her head. "No. I know some of them have had things published, though. Most of them have. Kegan used to tell me what good writers some of them were. This woman—" she leaned over and pointed to a name on the list. "She had some romance novels published. I don't really like that kind of thing, so I've never read any of them." She looked ashamed, but I didn't blame her. I wasn't into romantic fiction either. I was a mystery gal, myself.

I studied the list, trying to visualize the people.

"You'll have to send the papers in right away," Claire said, a slight note of urgency creeping into her voice. "If you send in the packet today or tomorrow, it should secure your spot. As I said, Kegan had already registered, and the session is paid for but you'll have to register as his replacement."

My decision clicked into place. "I will do that," I assured her. I passed them the papers I needed them to complete for the job as well as a standard contract.

As they read and signed each page and passed them back and forth, I opened the registration packet.

There was a brochure about the writers conference that would follow the Whalesong session. I set it aside.

I browsed through the colony's pamphlet and encountered the smiling faces of Bleusette Huntsman and Russell York, the husband and wife team who ran Whalesong. They looked friendly, self-assured and prosperous.

There was indeed a list of twenty-six rules that dictated everything from a pledge to remain at Whalesong for the duration, to what would happen to you if you didn't follow the rules. There was a non-disclosure agreement. That interested me. An NDA sometimes indicated that someone had something to hide. Sure, some companies had formulas for products they would like to keep under wraps, but we were talking about a writers' colony. I couldn't imagine what a group of writers would need to keep secret. The plots of other writers' books? Hadn't I heard that there were only a few dozen plots that are rewritten over and over? Besides, the NDA mentioned the plots of other writers' works, but included a lengthy paragraph about the day to day structure and the rules. In other words, what went on in Whalesong, it seemed, had better stay in Whalesong.

Included in the requirements was proof of identification and full payment for the four weeks at the colony. In addition to the colony, attendance at the West Coast Writers Association Conference at the end of the Whalesong session was expected as well.

Mr. Mercer had given me a check that covered all expenses not already paid plus a generous retainer. Claire provided me with the registration code and I filled out the application, listing *The Book of Signs* as my designated "work in progress". In reading the part of the manuscript I had completed, I believed it to be the work of a genius. In fact, I had felt a thread of connection to the author as I read his words and wished that I could have known him in life. I would finish his novel and probably read it again.

In the course of my last case, I had procured an alternate identity. I had the birth certificate, driver's license and business cards for Sarah Noble Augustine, Freelance Writer. Sarah, in actuality, had been a little girl who was born in Portland in 1946 and had died in Medford, Oregon two years later. She would do fine as a writer attending the prestigious Whalesong Writers Colony Spring Session of 1984.

When they stood up to leave, JW took his wife's arm and, after saying their good-byes, steered her out the door while Claire lingered.

"I said that Kegan didn't get depressed," she said with a glance toward her parents-in-law, now nearing their car. "But he did. I don't think they know how bad it could get, but I thought you should know."

I nodded encouragement and she gave another glance outside. "He was very insecure about his writing. Much more than his parents know. He would get upset when it wasn't going well and his depression could be...quite...severe. He would be devastated when he received rejections. I'm not sure what you can do, if anything, but I think it would make us all feel better to have that place investigated. It seems to me that encouragement is what Kegan and other writers like him need. Certainly not discouragement."

I had to agree. "I will do my very best," I told her. She gave me a thin, sad smile and turned to follow Kegan's parents.

As I said goodbye to Claire, I felt a glimmer of hope begin to steal into my sore soul. There was much work ahead of me for the next few weeks before I boarded the ferry to the San Juan Islands. There were books and magazines to look for and read. There were the backgrounds of ten people that would need to be checked.

I was enthusiastic about the case. I felt that therein lay my salvation. I believed the damage from the events in Hawaii would never fully go away, but immersion in another life seemed the perfect antidote for the poison that flooded me.

At the time, I didn't realize that I was stepping into a world that was deceptively beautiful, falsely serene. Had I known what was ahead, would I have gone? I think yes. The paths we choose to walk almost never have destination signs. If they did, I suspect, we would cheerfully follow one over the other only to realize too late that we have not chosen wisely after all. But we are all driven by inner entities, sometimes angels, sometimes demons, which steer us along *their* chosen paths, not our own.

THREE

Mid-April, 1984

When the Mercers had gone, I took my registration packet to the post office then headed to my favorite used book store in West Seattle, Pegasus Book Exchange.

On the way from the car, the April wind gusted, blowing what grit was left from the winter into my face. April in Seattle can be glorious or horrible. That day had started beautifully but was quickly headed toward the horrible. A cold pale sun shone through clouds that promised rain by nightfall.

Pegasus was exactly the bright spot I needed in the dismal afternoon; warm, cozy and literally stuffed with books. I handed my list to Fred, the owner. He frowned.

"A romance? For you?" he said, his eyebrows almost meeting his hairline.

"It's for research," I told him.

"I know this Thornton Swift," Fred said. "That is, I know his work. I just read a short story of his in *The*

Seattle Review." He eyed me for a moment. "You may not like it. It's what you might call 'Men's Adventure'. I wasn't wild about it myself. Kind of spare, if you know what I mean." He mused over the list for another moment.

"I think I have something by Delilah Duncan. Her books don't sell real well," he said, tapping the list. "I won't accept her books for exchange anymore 'cause they sit around on the shelves. For years, sometimes."

"Well, *that* doesn't inspire me to read them," I said. I had picked up a copy of *Killer Clown: The John Wayne Gacy Murders* and was perusing the back. What a recipe for nightmares that was! But it was more up my alley than a romance or men's adventure.

He pulled a new looking paperback from the shelf then wandered over to another section while I continued to look over the True Crime area.

After a moment Fred returned with a short stack of two paperbacks. One was a slender, tattered copy of *Fighting Doctor Black* by Cyr Antonio and the other, the Delilah Duncan novel.

"I could only find two, Chey," he said. "Besides these books, of the names on this list, I've only heard of Russell York. He's been out of print for years, though, and the used copies just don't come in anymore."

"This is fine," I said. "Better than I had hoped,

actually." I regretfully put down the book about Gacy and followed Fred to the counter.

"What are you up to now?" he asked when he had rung up the books.

"Can't say," I told him. I loved to tell people that. Don't ask me why.

He nodded, as though any bizarre thing I did was totally understandable to him. And, I guess, he was used to me after all.

* * *

From West Seattle I headed to the downtown library and spent some time browsing the card catalog. I found a copy of *Deirdre's List* by Lyric Prentice, *World Without End*, a fantasy novel by Axel Meredith and a copy of *Analog Science Fiction* which carried a story by Shigeru Takano.

I gave my list to the librarian and he directed me to where *The Seattle Review* was kept. There I found the short story by Thornton Swift. He also told me that Fritha Danielsen had had a story published in *Three Penny Review* but that the downtown branch did not have that copy. He graciously offered to call the other branches and see if it could be found. I asked about the leaders of Whalesong, Russell York and Bleusette Huntsman, but the librarian was unable to tell me anything that I didn't already know. He steered me to a shelf of Books in Print where I combed through what seemed to be decades worth of books. There had been nothing by Bleusette Huntsman, though I did find the titles of two books by Russell York from the early 1960s. The library had copies of neither.

I lingered awhile in the library, browsing through the books the librarian had found for me. I looked at the dedications and acknowledgements and jotted down a few names.

From the library, I went to the County-City Building and up to the fourth floor where I spent an hour gathering sketchy information about some of the Whalesong participants. Most of them, including Bleusette Huntsman and Russell York, had no birth records whatever, which only meant they were born elsewhere. They appeared to have had no dealings with the law either. At least, not in Washington.

I found Shigeru Takano's marriage license and birth certs for each of his three daughters and that he owned a home in the Beacon Hill neighborhood.

I found an arrest warrant for Thornton Swift for sexual assault which must have been settled out of court or dropped for whatever reason. What was more interesting was the assault with a deadly weapon charge that had landed him in jail for five years. After that, I was marginally more interested in reading the story he had written.

I still had one name on my list. Lyric Prentice's book had been dedicated to Camille Bishop, with "all my love," and I had intended to look her up too. Unfortunately, my parking meter was about to run out so I decided not to dig further. At the time, I didn't think that little lapse would come back to kick me in the ass.

From downtown, I jumped onto I-5 and pointed my car north toward my friend Molly's house.

Molly's snug little home was possibly the most comfortable place in the universe. She had surrounded herself with pillows, soft fabrics, comfy chairs, thick carpets and pastel colors. She kept the temperature just a degree from being too warm and she always tried to get me to eat.

Molly herself was easily as comfortable as her home. Her loving nature had saved me from myself time and time again. She was older than I by about ten years, yet she loved to mother me. She had graying brown hair and the warmest smile of welcome I ever saw. No matter how I felt, she always made me feel better.

I have to say it isn't all that hard to persuade me to partake of one of Molly's homemade cinnamon buns or a bit of warm apple tart. On that day she handed me a plate holding two thick shortbread cookies and a mug of apple-cinnamon tea.

"So, a month," she said with a sigh, sinking into one of her overstuffed chairs. I had told her about the possibility of my taking the Whalesong case. She had heard some of the particulars but not all.

"What is Easy going to do without you for a month?" It vexed Molly no end that Easy wanted to get married and I didn't. Even more than it did Easy, I suspected.

"I think Easy will manage just fine without me," I said.

"Maybe it's a good idea to not let him get too complacent," she said. "So, tell me more about this case. A writer's colony. It sounds like it would be heaven on earth. Peace and quiet. All the time you need to work and think. I've thought about writing, you know."

I shook my head while she watched me over the rim of her cup. "I'm not so sure you would want to attend this one, though," I told her. "It's regimented to the extreme. My clients think that their son was driven to kill himself because of the two who run it." Even though my cases were confidential, Molly often had insights that astounded me with their perceptions. She was also the most honest person in the world. Not only that, she would cheerfully keep a secret even under torture.

I was surprised when she looked skeptical.

"I don't think anyone can drive you to suicide," she said and took a delicate bite of her shortbread. "Isn't it pretty much a personal decision?"

"His wife thinks they undermined his confidence in his writing and broke his spirit." I took another sip of tea. It was wonderful. It's warmth and comforting fragrance was making me sleepy.

"It must be some hard-core place. What is it? A writer's boot camp?"

"I guess I'll be finding out. I go up there at the end of the month." I suddenly felt a premature bout of homesickness. "I may not be seeing you for a while. I have a ton of work to do before I go and the twenty ninth is not that far away."

"While you're there, be sure to call me every few days and give me the scoop."

"Can't," I said around the last mouthful of shortbread. "We're only allowed to use the phone once a week and it's in the Main Cabin where everyone can hear everything you say."

"Yikes," she said. She mused a moment. "You and Easy should set up a code."

I guess I looked questioning because she said, "You know, 'The rain falls straight down,' means you miss the heck out of us and want to come straight home. Or, 'The shoe is on the chair,'" she added in a voice that sounded like someone announcing a bad horror film.

"What does that mean?" I asked, laughing.

"I don't know. That's for you to figure out." She took a prim sip of her tea.

"That really isn't a bad idea," I told her. "I could work out some sort of rudimentary message system with Easy when I see him tonight. We could use song lyrics or lines of poetry, movie titles or something."

"Oh, right. What are they going to think when, all of a sudden, you say, 'The darkness spills out with my blood'?"

"Well, I wouldn't have to use that particular song lyric, but I could tell him that I was thinking about some song or some film and that would mean that I wanted him to do something."

"Leave it to me to come up with the really good ideas," she said when I got up to leave.

"You never fail me, Molly."

"You should take along a couple of bottles of wine for those long, lonely evenings in that cabin. I think I have a few bottles. Want to take some?" She made a move toward the kitchen.

"Except we're not allowed alcohol, drugs or cigarettes at the colony. Thanks for the offer, though. At some point, I know I'll be sorry I didn't take you up on it."

"What? No alcohol? I thought writers all drank when they got writer's block. And don't all writers smoke? Besides, when did not being allowed to do something stop *you*?"

She was right, of course.

* * *

On the way home I made a detour to Avenue Art Glass.

Ab Eberstein was one of the nicest guys in the world. He was in his late fifties then, with wispy gray hair and a scraggly gray beard. I don't think I ever saw him without his green apron and a tool or two in one of his pockets. He looked like the quintessential shop keeper. He called most women "babe" and most men "buddy" because he either had a hard time remembering names or simply didn't want to take the trouble to recall them.

I told him that I would be unavailable to work at the shop for more than a month. He was eager to hear the particulars of the case but I couldn't let him in on it. I knew and trusted Ab completely. He had saved my life once. Telling Molly was different. And I never told her too much. Knowing about my cases could put the people I loved in jeopardy. In my last big case, Ab's shop had been vandalized by one of the people I was investigating.

I assured Ab that I would be home in time for me to manage the store while he attended the big art show in July. He would be displaying the wonderful stained glass pieces featured in his shop and he had an entry in the Pacific Coast Arts Collective contest as well, a lovely Tiffany-style window intricately done in gorgeous shades of purples, greens and peacock blue.

"I feel guilty leaving you for so long," I told him.

"Hey, babe, I worked this place all by myself for years. Only thing is, I'll miss the heck out of you. You're good to have around."

"I'll be back, never fear," I told him. "It just doesn't seem right for me to leave for so long."

"Well, I guess if you can spell me in the shop while I'm at the show in July, I can spell you when you go out on a big case. Don't get yourself into any trouble now. I don't want you coming in here all broken up like you were with that last one."

I laughed. "I'll take care."

We hugged goodbye and I went home to prepare dinner for Easy.

* * *

Easy arrived about six. I had dinner simmering and he eyed it suspiciously. He was firmly convinced that the things I cooked were all made of at least tofu if not twigs and grass after I once mentioned that I didn't care for red meat—although I was not averse to a good, greasy hamburger now and again. I am most definitely not a vegetarian. I love bacon, after all.

"What is it?" he asked, giving the sauce a little stir.

"It's Chicken Cheyenne," I told him. He visibly relaxed. I had fed him Shrimp Cheyenne a time or two and he had loved it, though it was a million times healthier than some of the things he ate on a regular basis. Shrimp and Chicken Cheyenne were simply my own recipes for a yogurt based spaghetti sauce which he claimed had butter and cream as ingredients.

After I had served up the savory chicken and we had taken our first bites, I said, "Molly thinks that you and I should set up a code for when I'm on Klallam Island. We're allowed one phone call a week and it's monitored."

"Do you think that will be necessary?" He raised his eyebrows in surprise. "Isn't this guy some kind of famous author? How dangerous can he be?"

"He may not be dangerous at all. But the Mercers seem to think something nefarious is going on up there. That's why they want me to investigate. It wouldn't hurt to have a few code words so you'd know that everything is okay or that something isn't right. Or," I added, "if I need you to do something for me that I don't want them to know about."

He chewed, looking thoughtful. "You could be right. How do you want to do it?"

"I thought we could set up a system based on song lyrics or movie titles. Maybe use a kind of telephone charades, I don't know. I could mention to you that I had been thinking about "our song" and you'd know that I had something to tell you that I couldn't speak freely about."

"We don't have a song," he said. "Though it's not a bad idea." He waggled his eyebrows.

"We don't have to have a song for me to say that. For instance, I could say that I have a song running though my head and then I could sing a few bars of something like, 'What a Wonderful World' and you'd know everything was fine, that I was having a grand time and we could talk normally. Or, if I said, I've been thinking about *our* song, you would know that something is wrong. Then I would sing a few words of, oh, I don't know. You'd have to help me with that part since you know several million songs. Or we could use movie titles."

He thought for another moment. "I think we could work something out. Do you know if by 'monitored' it means recorded or just that people are listening?"

"I won't know until I get there and actually make a call and maybe not then. If I could unscrew the receiver I could probably tell if it was recorded," I said, thinking aloud. "Sometimes you can tell by the sounds on the line. I seriously doubt that will be possible. Hmmm..., I'll have to let you know somehow."

"After dinner, let's get some paper and write down

some ideas to use for certain phrases and maybe we could cook up a code so you could let me know if I can talk freely."

"Good idea," I said. I put down my fork and took a deep breath. "Easy, I want your word that you will not charge in and ruin everything if you think that I'm in danger." I gave him a warning look. I wasn't kidding and he knew it.

He put up his right hand as if he were taking an oath. "I solemnly swear," he said.

I eyed him through my narrowed lids. "You say that now..."

He put down his fork too. "I noticed how you tried your hardest to kick everyone's ass in class. I feel relatively confident that you can take care of yourself."

We had had more than one argument about his tendency to worry way too much about me. We never got as far as fisticuffs and broken bottles, but we had had a few serious disagreements about it. He could be something of a sexist, and worried quite a bit about my job, which, I admit, sometimes leaned a bit to the dangerous side.

"I'm amazed," I told him. "You actually said that you now know that I can take care of myself."

He looked at me for a moment. "I do feel better that you brushed up on your defensive skills."

I shrugged. "I knew I had to do something after

San Francisco," I said. I had received a star-shaped scar on my cheek and a huge blow to my self confidence in that altercation. I had pretty much botched any self-protective moves I had made in spite of having taken a good self-defense course years before. Easy and I had had a serious discussion about it and I had promised to brush up my skills if he wouldn't be so vocal about his worrying.

Neither one of us mentioned what had happened in Hawaii. It had resulted in my assailant's death and I knew that I would never get over feeling the weight of that responsibility.

I didn't say anything and we continued with our dinner.

After we had finished and had stacked the dishes in the dishwasher, he went into the living room while I rummaged in my office for some legal pads and pens.

We settled on the sofa in front of the fire.

"You should make a rough list of some possible messages you may want me to hear," he said. We both had pads on our laps and pens poised to write. "I'll think of some song lyrics that might be useful. We'll both have to memorize these, you know."

"You won't have to. You can have a crib sheet. I won't be able to look at my list and then say "Easy, 'Send me a ticket for an aeroplane, ain't got time to take a fast train' if I need to get out of there in a hurry."

"Nah, you should be a little more subtle than that," he said.

We both got to work with our respective lists.

"Why do you think the writers keep coming back to this place with all these rules and restrictions?" he asked at one point, after I had recited all the rules I could think of.

I put down my pen. "I think they do it so they can develop discipline and so they can work without distraction. Claire was telling me that Kegan had a hard time working sometimes because at home there were always interruptions. When you work from home, people seem to think you aren't working at all. I find a little of that in my own job. If I'm home, I'm usually *at* work but it doesn't look like it to other people. At Whalesong, these writers have nothing to do but write. They're forced into it, even though it's voluntary."

We worked for a while longer, then I looked up and saw him looking at me.

"Chey, I think this case is going to be good for you," he said. "You seem to have perked up some."

"What on Earth are you talking about?" I asked, going back to my list and pretending to write.

"You haven't been yourself since you came back from Hawaii."

It was said. I had thought that I had hidden my depression damned well, and now this. I put down my pen and gazed at him.

"You noticed."

"Of course, I noticed. You've been downright depressed."

I didn't say anything. What could I say? He was right.

"I know that you feel responsible for that guy's death. No," he said, stopping me. "Let me finish. I know that you think it could have been prevented in some way but the only other outcome was your own death. He didn't have to come after you and threaten you with a gun. He brought it on himself. You did not seek him out and deliberately kill him."

I still didn't say anything. I was waiting to see what else he had gotten from the minuscule amount of information I had given him about my previous case.

"He shot that other guy too," he continued. "You both could have been killed. You know that I am just as opposed to violence, especially gun violence, as you are. But even I can see that it was nothing for you to feel guilty about."

"There are some things you don't know, Easy," I said, wondering how much more I should reveal. "It isn't only that incident."

"What is it, then, honey?" he asked when he saw

that I was not going to continue.

I can't stand it when he talks like that. It makes me want to cry and go ahead and agree to marry him.

I stood up. "It's getting late and you should probably go. I have a ton of reading to do before—"

"Sit down," he said, gently. "I want to talk about this for a minute." He watched me as I slowly sat down again. "What else happened?"

I hesitated, but not long. I think a part of me wanted to talk about what happened. "I believe I found David," I said. I couldn't look at his eyes. They were too kind and caring. I couldn't handle that right then.

"David? You mean, *that* David?"

I nodded, but said nothing.

"He's not dead," he said. It was not a question. He had accepted my statement as fact. No "Are you sure it wasn't someone who only looked like him?" or something equally inane.

"No," I said but had to try again because it came out in a whisper. "Apparently not."

"You talk to him? Approach him?"

I shook my head. "I couldn't."

He nodded. Of course, he understood. Easy almost always understood.

"Easy, he's missing an arm and a leg and an eye," I

said.

He winced. "The explosion."

I nodded.

"What are you going to do?"

I looked at him, surprised. "Do?" I asked. "Nothing. What can I do?"

He nodded this time. "I think jumping into this case with both feet will be the best thing you *can* do," he said.

I agreed.

I so rarely talked about David that it was almost impossible for me to do so. David and I had been in love so long ago. We had planned to get married, raise a family, live for many years and then die of great old age in our sleep on the same night. Our dreams were so innocent, you could almost see the rainbows and stars shooting out from them. Then David had had to go to Vietnam. There had been, as Easy had said, an explosion. It had been a mine. The Army had been unable to find anything of David except his dog tags.

I had held on to memories of David for twenty years. In my mind, he had never changed. He was still the fresh faced boy who waved at me from the walkway leading to the plane that would take him away forever.

In my last case, I had occasion to see a man who, for a while was David, then was not, then was again. At last, after not contacting him at all, I had said goodbye in my mind and had flown home. The double blow of feeling responsible for someone's death and finding my lost love was almost more than I could stand.

The man I believed to be David, the man I was convinced was David, was a writer now. A well-known one at that. His science fiction book, *Still Life: Earth* hung at the top of the best seller list. Oh, sure, the dust jacket said his name was Guy Loring and the picture of Guy Loring looked nothing like David. But I had seen David in that long haired, bearded, one-eyed, scowl-wearing man.

Easy jolted me out of my thoughts. "Chey?"

"Sorry," I said. "I was wool-gathering."

He looked at me with that patient, understanding gaze again and nodded. "Let's get this narrowed down, shall we?"

And we did. We came up with a few strategies that I could use to convey a few meaningful messages to him should the need arise.

Before Easy left for the night, we made up ridiculous messages until we collapsed against each other in helpless laughter. I was still chuckling even after I had closed and locked the door behind him. It was probably silly, I thought then.

As it happened, it wasn't silly at all. In the end, it turned out to be deadly serious.

FOUR

Saturday, April 28-Sunday, April 29, 1984

The day before I was to leave for Klallam Island, I got out my Fodor's for Washington State and on the map located the small patch of land between the Strait of Georgia and the Strait of Juan de Fuca. It wasn't very big and, in fact, it looked like there was only one town on it. Half of the island was marked 'private'. The description was short, but mentioned a hotel and convention center. I knew that the Writers Conference would be housed there. Undoubtedly, the "private" area was the Whalesong compound. The book told me little about the island beyond descriptions of the native vegetation, rainfall (not much, it seemed) and the local wildlife.

I packed for the month that I would be away from home. I knew there were washing facilities at the compound in a building called the Bathhouse. According to the brochure, a pamphlet really, there were assigned hours for showers as well as laundry. This, according to the literature, was to minimize fraternization between the Colonists. Communal showering seemed to somewhat counter the no fraternizing rule but what did I know? I had to smile, too, at the formal sounding names for the buildings and collections of people.

Since there would be laundry facilities, I decided to take minimal clothing. A couple of pairs of jeans and two or three T-shirts should suffice, with a pullover sweater, a long sleeved T and a jacket thrown in with respect for the spring weather. I did bring a decent pantsuit so I would look professional and presentable at the writer conference, assuming I was still in residence by then.

Besides my clothes, I had Kegan's manuscript, a ream of paper, the rest of the attendees'—that is the Colonists'—work that I had gleaned from the library and used book stores to bring too. I had my portable typewriter as well as my bag of detective tricks. That was an old doctor's bag that Easy had bought for me years before. In it, I carried essentials like a flashlight, swabs, vinyl gloves, evidence bags, my little camera (though there would be no hope of film development until I had returned to the mainland), and binoculars. I added my planner, my journal and the notebook I had started.

When I was working on a case, I sorted out my notes in a loose leaf binder divided into sections. Interestingly, I got this idea from taking a novel writing class at one time. I had never written the novel, but my organization system worked fine for what I did. In the one I was taking with me I had written what I had learned about the Colonists so far but nothing else. I added extra filler paper. *I may not need all of it*, I thought, *but you never know*. I would be a virtual captive for a month after all.

* * *

Weather in the Pacific Northwest is usually iffy. You never know what you'll be getting from one day to the next. We were lucky to be riding the ferry on a clear and sunny, though not warm, day. I said goodbye to Easy and walked on board. The Whalesong van would be picking me up at the end of my trip since I wasn't allowed to bring my car. Another of the many rules.

Though it was chilly, I sat outside, letting the wind bathe my face. I could almost imagine some of the negativity of the past few months washing away from my mind. I thought it might do me some genuine good to get away and plunge into the case.

Although the rules forbade fraternization and implied that staggered ferry rides were encouraged, I didn't see how that one could be reasonably enforced. After a while, I was pretty sure I had spotted three of the attendees already on board. I could tell they were Colonists because they kept sneaking looks at me and conferring with each other. I think the portable typewriter gave me away just as theirs did them. Before they had a chance to draw straws on who would approach me, I approached them.

"You all wouldn't be going to Whalesong, would you?" I asked, smiling.

"Sorry you caught us staring. We were all curious," one of them, a man of about fifty said in a faint British accent. "We hadn't heard there would be a newbie this term and when we saw you and your typewriter, we wanted to get a better look at you."

"Seriously, Art, be polite," a short woman with black corn rows and huge brown eyes said. She put out her hand and shook mine. Her handshake was strong and sure. She seemed to be no nonsense. Something like myself. I also felt something dark in her, like she had an agenda. Well, hell, didn't we all? I felt a little thrill of deception from her too. Nevertheless, I liked her. "I'm Lyric," she said "This is Arturo," she nodded to the man then turned to the other woman. "And Fritha."

Fritha held out her hand too. "Hi," she said. "Welcome." She was tall and Nordic looking with incredibly blond hair and eyes as blue as you could get. Her handshake was less firm than Lyric's, and from her came a sense of insecurity, as though she was unsure that she should be there at all. I felt a wave of guilt from her as well. I wondered why.

"Hello," Arturo said. His hand grasped mine and I immediately knew he wasn't who he said he was.

I felt deception in him too, more so than I had felt from Lyric. *Interesting*, I thought. He snatched his hand away and grabbed at his beret as a breeze rushed at us from over the water. They all had given me a sense of acceptance with a little sprinkling of curiosity and even suspicion.

"I'm Sarah. I'm taking Kegan's place," I told them.

"Ah," Fritha said and nodded. "I'm not surprised he's not coming after last year and the disast—"

"Well, we're glad to meet you, Sarah," Lyric interrupted her and gave Fritha a frowny look.

"I was wondering about all the rules," I said, choosing to ignore the slip. I could find out about "the disaster" later. "There seem to be so many. Like, why can't we wear watches?"

"Russell and Bleusette don't want us to get distracted by the time," Fritha said. Her face had gone pink either from the breeze or from Lyric's sharp look. "There's a gong that calls us to the Main Cabin for Meeting and Class and Monday Dinner and stuff. But mostly, we tell time by the comings and goings of the ferry. The cabins ring the western half of the island so I'm pretty sure you can see the water from all of them."

"Can we go inside?" Arturo asked. "I'm about to lose my hat."

"Oh, my God!" Lyric said. "You wouldn't want to do that." She gave me a look that said, "Men!" and we trooped inside. I heard her mutter, "He never takes the damned thing off."

"So, you always have the same assigned cabins?" I asked.

"Yes," Fritha said. "Although it wouldn't really matter. They're all the same. Some of them are closer to the Main Cabin and the Bathhouse, but everything else is the same." I noticed that Fritha had a habit of looking around her almost constantly. It was as though she expected someone to be spying on her. She seemed to have an aura of perpetual guilt. I always thought Easy was the guiltiest feeling person on the planet, but Fritha had even him beat.

"I, for one, am looking forward to getting to work," Arturo said, rubbing his hands together. "No distractions. Nothing to do all day but write."

"You going to completely ignore the classes?" Lyric asked him. "Not to mention Meeting."

She turned to me. "You probably read the brochure pretty thoroughly. I know I did before I came the first time. Breakfast is brought to our cabins, then we go to Class, then lunch. Then writing until dinner."

"How many of the group have been published?" I asked. I already knew the answers to most of the questions I was asking. And those I didn't know, I wouldn't be asking for a while anyway.

"Oh, we all are," Fritha said, then looked

embarrassed again. “Except Arturo.”

“I’m getting closer,” Arturo said cheerfully. It didn’t seem to bother him at all that “everyone” had been published but him.

“Some of us have only had stuff in literary magazines, but Lyric has had a book.”

“Really?” I said. I knew she had had a book published. I had read *Deirdre’s List*. It was different from my usual fare but I had found it to be quite good. I believed it was what was known as Women’s Fiction.

Lyric nodded.

“I don’t think she really likes to talk about it,” Fritha said and Lyric shrugged.

“I don’t mind talking about it, Frith. I’m more focused on my second book,” she continued to me. “That’s my work in progress for this term. I’ve only just begun it. You’ll be hearing some of it in Meeting.”

“So, tell me about Meeting,” I said. “I read in the brochure that Meeting is held every evening and that we are all required to attend.”

“Someone is designated to read their WIP—that’s work in progress, if you didn’t know,” Fritha said. “Then Russell critiques it. We all write down our critiques. Russell has his say and then we tell the writer what we thought.” She turned to Lyric. “Should we tell her about the ‘Unwritten Rule?’”

Lyric shrugged again. "I guess so, since you spilled the beans that there *are* unwritten rules. Anyway, if she's going to be in class and Meeting with us, she should probably be aware of how things work."

"See," Fritha began eagerly. "Sometimes, Russell can be a little hard on our work. Or, at least, he doesn't exactly *heap* praise on it."

"Russell isn't big on praise," Lyric said.

Fritha glanced at her, nodded and continued. "So, say I read and everyone writes down what they think. Then Russell says, 'It's far too thin, dearheart. It lacks soul. It lacks basis.'" She used a pompous, faux male voice and the rest of us laughed. Lyric was nodding. "Of course, everyone will agree with Russell out loud," Fritha said. "He usually offers some suggestions about how to fix it. Later, he gives you a written critique that's more detailed. Anyway, after Meeting, everyone turns their written comments over to the reader and they're completely different from what they said in class. They'll say, 'I loved it! Good work, Fritha! Loved the part about the snow.' We've learned to rely on the other students' comments if we need..." she turned to Lyric. "What do you call it? Validation."

"Does he dislike everyone's work?" I asked. He sounded like an ass to me.

"Oh, no, he doesn't exactly *dislike* it. He wants to see our very best work. He pushes us to be better. Sometimes he praises. Delilah gets fabulous praise and so does Axel," Fritha said.

Lyric shook her head. "It isn't exactly fabulous, Frith. But she doesn't get criticized much. And neither does Axel. Arturo pretty much escapes too." She turned to look at him.

"He's hard on us because he wants us to succeed," Arturo said.

"Tell me about the other students. Who is Delilah?" I had read Delilah Duncan's erotic romance and didn't think much of it at all. In fact, I thought that it was nothing more than pornography dressed up in a kind of tawdry Sunday best. And I'm no prude.

"Delilah Duncan," Lyric said, not sounding enthusiastic. "She writes romances." She said the word romances as though it had quotation marks around it. "Axel Meredith is fantasy, Thorn Swift, I don't really know very well. Besides you, he was the newest Colonist and he hasn't had much to say. He's been there a couple of years I guess. He's a little macho for me. I think he likes to think he's the reincarnated Ernest Hemingway."

Fritha and Arturo laughed.

"Cyr Antonio writes adventures, whatever that is," Fritha added.

"That book he was working on last year was kind of western-y, I thought," Lyric said.

"And Shig Takano writes sci fi," Arturo said.

"That's all of us. You'll get to know them."

"Except for the no fraternization thing," I said.

Lyric scoffed. "Don't worry about that. We manage. There are lots of ways of getting together without R & B finding out. They like to think we come to the island on separate ferries, but really, it's only the Entourage who does that."

"The Entourage?"

"Delilah, Axel and Thorn," Lyric said. "They follow Russell and Bleusette around sniffing at them like dogs."

"Oh, I don't think that's entirely fair, Lyric," Arturo said. "I like to think that we're all special to Russell and Bleusette."

Lyric nodded. "Yes, you're right," she said and gave me a broad wink behind Arturo's back. Fritha giggled and Arturo eyed her suspiciously.

"What?" he said.

"Looks like we're almost there," Lyric cut in. "Let's get our stuff together."

The sound of chains clanging onto the iron floor of the lower car deck drifted up to us. The ferry tenders had just loosened and dropped the heavy barriers to allow the corralled cars to escape onto the island. The motors of the ferry churned into reverse, slowing its onslaught and allowing it to creep into the harbor.

We gathered our bags and stood while the ferry squeaked against the pilings.

While we waited to disembark, I watched my companions. I liked them. I felt acceptance from them already and it was comforting considering that I would be essentially trapped with them on a small San Juan island for a little more than a month.

The Whalesong van picked us up at the dock. Lyric made a covert gesture toward the driver. "Strom Lundgren is the caretaker, handyman, driver for Whalesong," she whispered to me. According to Lyric, Strom had no love for Russell York or Bleusette Huntsman or anyone at all that she knew of, though she didn't elaborate.

The ride was surprisingly short. Had we not been carrying our bags plus portable typewriters, it seemed we could have easily walked, although, when the van came to a stop, we were in a clearing next to a large rustic house and civilization seemed miles away. Before we climbed out, Lyric just had time to whisper to me, "Remember the no frat rule." So I was ready when the front door opened and a couple stepped out onto the porch.

I thought I did an admirable job of acting completely disinterested in Lyric, Fritha and Arturo. They, too, said nothing when Russell stepped off the porch to greet us.

"Welcome to Whalesong!" he said. He spread his arms grandly and solemnly shook hands with each of us. He was a tall, slender man in, I would have said, his early sixties. He had a moustache and a magnificent mane of silver hair. His smile was wide and friendly, and white against his tanned skin. The picture I had seen of him and his wife in the brochure had likely been taken several years before, but Russell was still handsome in a dignified, distinguished sort of way. He looked each of us straight in the eye as he shook hands with us all. When his hand touched mine, though, I was immediately flooded with an onslaught of sensations that were hard to sort out. I felt a bit of hauteur, a smidgen of foppery and a surprising dollop of defeat, grief and even anxiety. Charming as he appeared to be, I thought he was most likely extremely insecure and I didn't think I was going to trust the man, though I couldn't have said why. At least not then.

Bleusette followed her husband down the porch steps and greeted us as well, though not quite so grandly. Her gaze skimmed briefly over Lyric's face, then Fritha's, then mine. She seemed to scrutinize me for a moment before her attention turned to Arturo. She looked to be in her early fifties, maybe late forties. She wore a sapphire blue dress and matching embroidered jacket that was made of something light, like linen. At any rate, it looked expensive. She was slender and had long, red hair. Her features were sharply defined and accentuated with artfully applied makeup. She carried herself in a somewhat arrogant, royal way.

"I cannot, I'm afraid, shake hands," she told us focusing her attention on me. "I am so very allergic to many things and have to be careful. Lyric, Arturo and Fritha understand. We're old friends. You must be Sarah." Her voice was low and possibly came across as sultry to some.

"Yes," I said. "I'm Sarah Augustine. I hope that we can be friends as well."

"Yes," she said, but I got the completely unreasonable idea that she had left "but I don't think so" unsaid. "I trust you'll all forgive me. I'm terribly busy today. Russell, will you please check them all in. I must get back to my duties." She smiled at us and gave a friendly enough wave on her way back into the house.

I was surprised at my reaction to her. Allergies or not, I would have liked to shake her hand. It's an easy way for me to tell what people believe they are successfully hiding from the world.

"Certainly, my dear," Russell said, his eyes and smile still on Fritha. Then his gaze slid over to me. "Lyric, Fritha and Arturo, you know where your cabins are. I will check you in myself. We can dispense with the formalities this one time. Right now, I will take Sarah in and we'll complete the registration process. Then I'll show her to her cabin myself."

Just before he ushered me into the house, I saw

Arturo start onto the right hand path. Lyric and Fritha gave each other a look before Lyric followed Arturo and Fritha took the left path leading away from the porch. The paths seemed to disappear into nothing more than a deep, dark wood.

Inside, the cabin was lovely and hardly a cabin at all. I couldn't get enough glimpses of the warm reds and rich cream furnishings before I was led into a study that was obviously the writer's private lair. The walls were lined with books. Not just your ordinary paper and hard backs, either. Those books were bound in leather and gold and looked like jewels nesting deep in the teak bookshelves. A huge desk sat in the middle of an oriental rug and a ruby and amber stained glass lamp glowed on top.

"Sit down, please," Russell said and indicated a carved chair near the desk. He sat behind it and picked up a pen that looked to be made of mother of pearl.

"I assume you have been over the rules, Miss Augustine?" he asked, startling me with the unfamiliar name. I probably should have gotten Easy and Molly to call me that a few times before I had left Seattle, just to get used to it.

"Yes, I read them thoroughly," I told him.

"We take the rules very seriously at Whalesong," he said. Again, he was smiling, yet I thought there was a small hard, cold glint in his eyes. Either that or I was misreading him. A second later it was gone. I wondered if the Mercers' suspicions were influencing my reactions. "Our rules may take a bit of getting used to," he continued. "but you'll soon find that here you will do your best work. Do you know why?"

"I would assume it's because there is nothing to distract us," I said.

"The point of the rules is you, Miss Sarah Augustine. You are the only writer here." He was smiling but he sounded pompous and dramatic. I was sure he had given this speech to newcomers countless times over the years. "You are the one you will concentrate on for this month in the Colony. For you, none of the others exist. We want you to focus."

I nodded, I hoped sagely. At any rate, he seemed satisfied. I wondered how I could completely ignore the other writers when I would soon find myself living among them. I was expected to react to their writing and offer my comments. I would be eating with them at dinner once a week and in class with them every day. It seemed like a tiny flaw in his plan to me.

"Your first task is to memorize the rules," he said. "Internalizing them will make it much easier on you." He eyed me over the top of his glasses. "The rules are strictly enforced."

I nodded as though I agreed completely and he looked down at my registration form again.

"I see that you have a work in progress.

Mmm... *The Book of Signs*." He paused. I hoped he wasn't going to ask me about its inception or my inspiration for it. "Is this a novel?"

I nodded.

"Excellent! Now, may I see your identification? It's a formality, of course," he said. I presented the driver's license I had acquired the previous winter and sat quietly while he rustled among some papers and eventually got up to copy the card.

"How well do you know Kegan," he said from the copier.

"He and I go back a long way," I said. I hoped he wouldn't ask me about Kegan's schooling or his home town. I didn't have the slightest clue.

"We expected to see him back at Whalesong this term." I didn't say anything. He came back to the desk.

"Now," he said and handed back the license. "I will escort you to your cabin. You are assigned to Number 8. That is Kegan's usual cabin."

We both stood and headed for the living room.

Just then, Bleusette appeared in the doorway. "Russell," she said. "May I speak to you?"

"In a moment, my dear. I'm going to escort Miss Augustine to her cabin."

"I'm afraid I need you rather urgently," she said, sounding miffed. "I'm sure she can find it herself."

She turned to me.

"I'm sure I can, if you will point me in the right direction." I smiled at her, and she returned it. In a second, though, it was gone.

"Take the path to the left and when you reach the trail, turn left again. You will pass Number 7. Continue on the trail until you come to Number 8." With that, she turned from me, faced Russell once more and began conferring with him in low tones.

I stepped back into what sunshine was left and could filter through the thick trees. I lugged my suitcase, typewriter and doctor's bag along the path. In a very short time, the Main Cabin was no longer visible and I could have been alone on the island. Since there was nothing to do but continue, I did, stopping now and again to shift the heavy cases. At last, I arrived at what I assumed was the trail. It was a bit wider and better travelled than the path, though just as covered with pine needles and last fall's leaves. I turned left and continued. On my right, several yards from the trail, I saw a cabin through the trees. A small weatherworn sign at the edge of the trail indicated it was Number 7. Farther on, I found another, marked 8 and turned toward my home for the next five weeks.

My cabin was small. Apparently they all were. Fritha had said that they were all alike. It was quite charming really. It was only one room and full with a futon, a wood stove, a desk and a chair.

On the futon I found a backpack emblazoned with the Whalesong logo. Inside was another package of paper, a laminated list of the rules, a flashlight, two ball-point pens also bearing the Whalesong logo and some energy bars.

A small alcove held a toilet and a sink. Bathing facilities were in the Bathhouse. There was nowhere to store clothing other than a row of hooks on the bathroom wall. I was glad I hadn't brought much. I found a kerosene lamp on a shelf in the bathroom and a box of matches, possibly in case of a power blackout.

There was a small table next to the futon with a lamp and another lamp on the desk.

I set up the desk with my typewriter and the notebook. I stowed my doctor's bag with my investigation tools under the futon-side table. I had brought the books by the other students that I had not yet read and lined them up on the window sill over the desk. I put "my" work in progress next to the typewriter. The reams of paper would have to go under the futon.

When everything had found its own place, I felt a little at a loss. There I was, literally in the middle of nowhere, isolated and in the midst of an entirely unfamiliar life. I wondered for a moment if I was up to the task ahead of me.

I realized with a not-unpleasant start that the thoughts which had been plaguing me since my return from Hawaii had been absent for a couple of hours. Maybe the wind off the straits truly had washed away the past. It gave me a thrill of hope to look ahead to working the case. To finding out what I could for the Mercers.

A light tap on my door interrupted me and when I opened it, I saw Strom walking away. He had left a covered metal container on the porch.

"Thank you," I called to him. Apparently, he hadn't heard me for he continued on his way without turning. He dragged a red wagon behind him that carried several more trays with metal covers.

I brought the container inside and lifted the lid. The savory aroma of spaghetti sauce drifted up to me. I noted the presence of meat balls and realized that there had been no questions on the application pertaining to food choices. While I don't consider myself a vegetarian, I rarely eat red meat, but I wondered if there were any of the Colonists who *were* vegetarian. There was a dish of buttered asparagus as well as a garlic-cheese roll and a cookie. It looked delicious and, in spite of the meatballs, I ate every bite.

FIVE

Sunday, April 29, 1984

Meeting began that night, as it did every night at 7:00. We, of course, had been forbidden watches, but I didn't think that I was the only Colonist who had a timepiece smuggled in among my clothing. We were summoned to the Main Cabin by a gong that sounded all through the compound at 6:50 and I could believe that after five weeks, I would be thoroughly tired of hearing it.

I had packed my backpack with the first two chapters of the manuscript I would read were I asked to, a sheaf of blank paper, my case notebook and a pen.

I found a seat next to a tall woman whom I knew to be Delilah Duncan. I had seen her photograph on the back of the paperback copy of her book. She had unnaturally blonde hair, a wide, thin-lipped mouth and cold, ice blue eyes. Her clothes looked expensive and she wore them well. Her shoes, however, were gold and, in my mind, looked cheap.

I was tempted to comment on them but knew that I was not allowed such liberties, at least in the presence of Russell and Bleusette. While they were not yet in evidence, I didn't want to be caught engaged in the dreaded fraternization this early in the game. Besides, Fritha and Lyric had told me that Delilah was one of the Entourage. I would have to tread carefully with her. I doubted that she would welcome the interest of a newbie like me.

When we had entered the room, the sound of chanting was already filling the space. The room was stark, with white walls and a hard tiled floor and there was little in it besides our chairs and a lectern. At the front of the room, on a window seat, sat a brazier which did nothing to warm the air. I resolved to bring a jacket to next day's Meeting. The chairs, equipped with their own desktops, were arranged in a U configuration. I had heard from the Mercers that Bleusette was superstitious and believed that nine was a lucky number which was why the number of Colonists was nine. Never more, never fewer.

We sat silently, awaiting I wasn't sure what. But in a moment, Russell and Bleusette entered from a side door. She positioned herself behind the lectern while Russell stood nearby.

Bleusette stood for a moment with her eyes shut as if she were praying. The chant was the only sound in the room. I had an almost irresistible urge to cough or shuffle my feet to see what would happen, but I restrained myself.

After a moment, Bleusette turned to a lacquered box next to the brazier and lifted a thin stick from it and a small white candle from a second box on the other side of the brazier. She used exaggerated arm movements as if she were performing some sort of ritual. If she was, its significance was lost on me. She lit the candle in the flames and positioned the incense in a holder. Then she lit the end of the incense stick with the candle. When she had done that, she turned and, holding the candle in her left hand, she slowly pinched out the flame with her right index finger and thumb. She held her fingers long enough on the wick that I realized that the candle snuffing was part of the show.

When she had finished, she moved to a comfortable looking chair near the brazier and sat down.

Russell stepped forward and took his place behind the lectern.

"Welcome, Colonists," he said, his smile at its widest and most becoming. "It's wonderful to have you returnees back for another term at Whalesong. And we welcome our newest Colonist as well. I trust that this term will be fruitful for you all.

"As I said, we have a new Colonist. Sarah Augustine is here taking Kegan Mercer's place." He nodded in my direction as though the other writers had not noticed a stranger in their midst until that moment. "Sarah, your first duty to Whalesong, as well as to yourself, is to memorize the rules.

"Axel," he said. "Tell Sarah what Rule number 23 states." Russell had a surprisingly strong voice. For some reason, I had imagined him a soft spoken man. To me, writers were quiet introverts. I imagined that was not the only myth that would be dispelled by the end of the Whalesong term.

Immediately, seemingly without a thought, a tall balding man wearing an ascot spoke in a soft voice, just right for a writer, in my mind. "Everyone is required to accept critiques gracefully and professionally."

"Thank you," Russell said. "Lyric, please tell us what Rule number 9 instructs us to do."

"Once a week, on Monday evening, dinner is served for all Colonists in the Main Cabin. Everyone is required to attend," Lyric said smoothly.

"Sarah Augustine." I looked up. Good luck to him if he expected me to recite a rule. I had read them but that was all. "You are responsible for knowing and following our rules. Is that clear?"

I *so* felt like saying, "Is what clear?" but I said, "Yes, sir," and he seemed more than satisfied.

"We have these rules for a reason," he announced to the room at large, as though we had never given the purpose of rules a second of thought. "The rules are about trust. They are about focus and about discipline. I must know that you, the Colonists, will trust me. I am a published writer. I have worked at my craft for decades. You," he swept his arm around the room, "are only just beginning. As a successful writer, I know what I am talking about. If you wish to succeed, as I have, then you must trust me. You must do what I ask of you, even if you don't agree with it."

Most of the others looked bored. I was sure they had heard some version of this speech each term. I thought he sounded more than pompous, but the others seemed to be taking it all in stride.

After a few more minutes of the same, he turned toward Bleusette and said, "My dear."

Bleusette stood then and took the lectern. She had changed her clothes since that afternoon. She now wore a pair of tailored black pants and a magenta blouse. Her jacket, which looked hand painted, had splashes of color that matched the blouse and looked *tres* expensive.

She stood before us for a few long seconds and looked at her audience as though we had all been chatting and she was waiting for the noise to quiet. At last, she spoke.

"Hello, Colonists, and welcome," she said and bowed her head. I resisted the urge to bow back, though I saw one or two of the others do it. Or, perhaps they were simply nodding. "Welcome to the spring session of Whalesong. Most of you know me, and, as most of you know, I am clairvoyant."

I thought this was an odd opening, but I had to admit my interest in her was, at last, piqued.

"I know who is going to succeed and who is not. I know who is going to give up and go home." She looked at us a long moment, then said ominously, "I know more than you think."

She let her gaze sweep over us again. "I, too, am a successful writer and have had my work published."

Okay, I knew that was a lie. I had searched decades of Books in Print and she had appeared nowhere.

"I will do my best to make you successful writers as well. Those who come to Whalesong are in a unique position to learn writing from a master." She turned and gestured to her husband who nodded. "And then," she continued, "to have their finished manuscripts represented by a successful and respected agent. As you are undoubtedly aware, I was Lawrence Fawcett's agent when he was completely unknown."

I remembered seeing in the Whalesong brochure that Bleusette had once represented Lawrence Fawcett who was possibly the most famous historical thriller fiction writer of the century.

"As I look at each of you," Bleusette was saying, "I only see one or two who will not succeed in their current work. But, if you follow my advice as well as Mr. York's, we will make successes out of even you."

She moved again to her comfy chair near the brazier. She didn't seem at all aware that her last two sentences had contradicted one another.

Russell rose again. "Let's get down to business, shall we?" he asked, smiling.

"Tonight, we will ask Delilah to read for us," he said, then. "I believe you have begun a new novel."

I crossed my arms. It was chilly in the room. I envied Bleusette's position near the brazier.

Delilah nodded and opened a folder on her desk. "The story I am making this term is called, *Barberta Unbound*."

Her arch voice and her habit of holding her head high and looking down her nose made her words sound as serious as hell. She began reading in a low, throaty voice.

If I had not read her book, *Felicity's Freedom*, I might have thought that this manuscript was meant as a joke. I looked around at the others' faces and they all had polite but rather blank expressions. I wondered if they were listening or perhaps hearing their own inner dialogs.

The story was of a servant girl who had been captured by a bandit who had waylaid her coach. The sex began almost immediately and seemingly never stopped. Poor beleaguered Barberta didn't seem to mind in the slightest.

I listened for a while longer, waiting in vain for

some sort of plot to develop. Finally, I let my mind wander as I watched the other Colonists.

Axel of the ascot didn't seem to be listening either. I was sure that I saw something passing between him and Bleusette. It was nothing tangible but he kept watching her and she was fully aware of it. There were looks exchanged and tiny, almost imperceptible gestures. I began to think that maybe they were having an affair, or, if not, soon would be. I tried to remember if I had learned anything about him from the background check. My notebook was in my backpack and I thought it would be rude to rustle around in it while Delilah was reading. I was pretty sure, though, that he was one of the students about whom I had found nothing but a marriage certificate. That meant little, since he probably had been born elsewhere and had never been in trouble with the police.

Russell seemed to be enjoying Delilah's story very much. He smiled and nodded throughout. I had found out little about him as well. I hadn't even been able to locate either of his books in the short amount of time I had had available before leaving.

Bleusette, when not sending covert signals back and forth with Axel, seemed almost bored with Delilah's work. And, after all, there really wasn't much substance to it. It seemed to completely lack any sort of plot. I began to wonder what I would say if I were forced to give an opinion.

Delilah read on, taking obvious pleasure in reading about Barberta being subdued again and again by the tireless bandit. I began to get a sense of her aloofness to the other members of Whalesong. I had found out nothing about her either except that she owned a home in the Wallingford District of Seattle. She had been married and divorced but that had been all I could find.

Fritha was writing furiously in her notebook. I wondered if she was taking this time to work on her own writing or if she were actually making notes for Delilah. About Fritha, I had found a birth certificate and that was all. If she were married, she had tied the knot elsewhere. She did not appear to own a home or rent an apartment in Seattle, though she had been born there. There was literally no record of her in Seattle beyond her birth. Of course, she could live in Idaho for all I knew. I had no idea where some of these people hailed from nor anything about their personal lives. That was a situation I would have to remedy.

My gaze found a handsome Asian man whom I knew to be Shigeru Takano. He was about forty. His flawless face was virtually unlined and his dark hair hung boyishly into his eyes. Fritha and Lyric had told me that he wrote science fiction and I wished that that was what we were listening to then. He continued to look at his desktop with no expression whatsoever. I didn't have a clue what he was thinking, but I did see a dull red begin to creep up his neck.

Lyric, too, stared at her desktop. But she seemed to be concentrating on her own thoughts. Perhaps she was working out a plot or a character profile.

Arturo was listening raptly and even seemed to be enjoying himself. He nodded occasionally and smiled now and again. I wondered at what he found to amuse himself.

A younger man who had to be Cyr Antonio, seemed to be listening as well. He looked to be in his twenties, and I knew him to be, in fact, twenty-eight. He had a pleasingly imperfect smile, dark hair which he wore in a shaggy, youthful cut. He had brown eyes and the beginnings of a moustache. He made occasional notes on a pad of paper but otherwise, his demeanor was neutral. A surprise, considering what action was happening on Delilah's pages. Cyr was another about whom there had been little record. I had found a birth certificate for him. Beyond that, nothing.

The other man, a blond, muscular guy of maybe thirty-five - he must be Thornton Swift, I decided - seemed to be getting more entertainment out of Delilah's reading than any of them. He periodically leered, frowned and grinned as he listened. He made no move to write anything down but seemed swept up in the action, so to speak. Thornton was the one about whom I had discovered the most. I knew he had a police record and that he may be a somewhat dangerous character. I planned to keep a close eye on him.

At long last, Delilah stopped reading and closed her folder with a satisfied sigh. The blond, Thornton, gave her a small flurry of applause. Russell frowned at him.

"Thank you, Delilah," Russell said. "I believe you have a good start there."

I thought I probably should have listened more attentively because I had caught nothing about it that sounded "good". But, then, I was not a writer. Maybe all new books started out terrible and got better as they were worked on. But I didn't think so. I had read Kegan Mercer's work from first to final draft and it had been noteworthy all the way along. I determined to reserve my judgment, though. I was, after all, a little out of my element.

"I believe that your characters are solid," Russell said, aiming his comments at Delilah. "I was intrigued by Jacobeau's audacity and Barberta's insouciance. I do think a bit of backstory would benefit. You did begin with action, which is good, but a word or two about background would be in order. Nevertheless, I'll look forward to hearing more in future Meetings. Any comments?" His gaze wandered over the class and landed on me.

Bleusette stood and moved to the lectern, saving my bacon for a few minutes at least.

"I thought that it was fine, of course," she said.

"It is, after all, our Delilah's writing and we all know what a fine writer she is." She wore a tight smile which implied that she didn't believe Delilah a fine writer at all. There were murmurs but no one volunteered anything. "I too, would like a bit of backstory and a few fewer adverbs. Your story does begin with action, but farther in, as Mr. York has stated, it could use some background."

Delilah was nodding and making notes.

"That is a valid suggestion," Russell said, as though she had not parroted almost exactly what he had said. "Fritha, what did you think, dearheart?"

"I thought the characters were well rounded," she said and I swear I saw Lyric cover a smile.

"Sarah, would you like to contribute?"

Sure, I thought. *Love to.* "I was impressed by the variety of description," I said. I truly had never heard the male sex organ described in so many different ways before. Someone had once told me that there were over 800 terms for that particular item and I believed Delilah had used most of them. "It had a lot of energy, feeling and penetrating insight."

Russell nodded. "It's something with which Delilah is very skilled."

This time I did hear Lyric stifle a snort which she adeptly turned into a cough.

The other writers all offered tentative, if rather vague comments. When the verbal suggestions and remarks had been completed, Russell asked that Delilah hand in what she had read and the rest of us were to pass our notes to her so that when her work was returned to her, she could follow up with further changes. As everyone passed sheets of paper to Delilah, I fumbled the pages that were handed to me and, in picking them back up, I neglected to add my own contribution. I didn't think anyone had noticed. I needed to interview each of the writers here at some point and I wanted to do it in a friendly, non-confrontational way. The notes I had made about Delilah's work were less than complimentary and I had determined to rewrite it with something more, if not praising, at least vague, in case she questioned where my comments were. I would have to learn how to write diplomatic comments so that I could survive the five weeks without antagonizing anyone.

I knew that two people usually were chosen to read at each Meeting. I hoped Shig Takano would be next. I was a big sci-fi fan as well as a mystery junkie. Lyric had told me that he was a very good science fiction writer and I was eager to hear his work.

I had brought the first two chapters of *The Book of Signs* with me, so I was ready to read, but not willing at that stage. As I gazed at the manuscript in front of me, I realized with a start that each page still carried the name Kegan Mercer in the upper left hand corner. I quickly put the cover of the folder over it and tried to look everywhere but at Russell. If

I was asked to read and had to hand in a manuscript with Kegan's name on it, I was doomed. My cover would be blown completely on the very first day. I was about to plead nausea and go back to my cabin, when Russell asked Arturo to read. It was all I could do to keep from heaving a huge sigh of relief.

At the end of Meeting, the others handed their comments to Arturo. I easily found good things to say about his work and handed my assessment in along with the rest. His book, a mystery, had captured my interest. I would look forward to hearing more, I decided.

At last, we were released to return to our cabins for the night. I knew that I had some work to do. I would have to retype all of Kegan's manuscript with my own name in place of his. The task was daunting, but it would, after all, give me something to do.

The night air was cool and crisp and redolent of the pine trees all around us. We silently followed the path, Fritha, Axel and I. At the trail, Fritha turned right while Axel and I went left. After Axel turned off to his cabin, I still had several yards to reach my own. The darkness was profound. We had been instructed to carry the flashlight in our packs and I now understood why. I heard the rustling of woodland creatures to my left and wondered what I had gotten myself into.

SIX

Sunday, April 29, 1984

I had been "home" only moments when there was a light tap on my door. It was Fritha. She looked both ways before stepping into the cabin, then breathed a sigh of seeming relief. For some reason, I felt a surge of relief too although I don't know who I had expected it would be.

"I hope you don't mind my dropping in," she said, breathlessly. "I'm not supposed to be here, you know, but I remember how scared I was on my first night here." She kept her voice barely above a whisper as though she thought someone was lurking just outside the door.

"I'm glad you came," I told her. "I *was* feeling a little overwhelmed."

"I knew you would be." She looked around at the cold wood stove. "Do you want me to help you bring in some wood and get that started? It's going to be downright cold tonight. These islands are pretty chilly in the spring."

She showed me where there was a stack of wood on the far side of the cabin and how to light the stove. Apparently, Strom, the caretaker, kept us supplied with wood as well as delivered our food. I began to hope he earned a hefty salary.

When the fire was rapidly warming the room and we had settled on the futon, I rubbed my hands together. "The Meeting room could have used a little heat," I said. "My feet are never going to warm up."

"Oh, Bleusette keeps it that way on purpose," she said. She sat perched on the edge of the seat as though to be ready to spring up and flee at any second. "She says that the cold is good for creativity. I suggest you wear a sweater to Meeting if you brought one. And a couple of pairs of socks."

"Thanks," I said. "I will. Is that the way Meeting always goes?"

She shrugged. "Pretty much. Someone reads, we comment, someone else reads, we comment. Except...once in a while.... when Russell and Bleusette decide you're not working up to your potential." She shook her head. "That can get bad."

"How so?"

She opened her eyes wide in surprise. "I would have thought that Kegan would have told you."

"Do you mean the burning?"

She nodded.

"Tell me more about that. He...he didn't tell me

too much."

"In a way, I'm not surprised. It must be terribly humiliating to the person it happens to. First, they told him that he should be writing something else. A different genre. That what he had been working on was not the right thing for him or it would have been better." She shrugged again. "I have no idea why. *The Way of Wonder* was...well, it was wonderful." She laughed a little sadly. "They told Kegan that he should settle on adventure novels, but he wasn't interested in that at all. Did you ever read his work? Of course, you did," she continued without waiting for me to answer. "He writes wonderful stories and I was so excited about his book. It was beautiful. I knew it would be published. But they convinced him to give it up."

"But how could they convince him? He could have refused, couldn't he?"

"The rules," she said, looking startled. Her blue eyes opened wide.

"But, he could have...He could leave the group and go ahead and write whatever he wants."

"Well, you know him, don't you? You know that he is insecure about his work. We all are. Maybe Delilah isn't, and maybe Axel isn't, and Thorn probably, but the rest of us are. Kegan and I are probably more so than anyone else. We need encouragement and instruction and..." She waved her hand. "We need this."

"Not if they tell you that the work you are doing is trash when you know it isn't."

"But we don't know that. Do you know that about your own work?"

I shook my head, uncertain how to answer. "So, tell me how it works," I said. "This burning of the manuscript thing."

"I've only seen it done once," she said. "So, they convince you to give up on your novel or whatever you're working on. Once you've made the decision, you hand in all copies of it. Bleusette turns on the chants and lights the incense and then puts the manuscript, page by page into the brazier and we watch it burn. You have to literally watch your work go up in smoke." Fritha's hands fluttered around while she talked. I thought it was nervousness.

"So, that's never happened to you?" I asked. *My God*, I thought. *Were these people all masochists*?

"No, not me," she said. She seemed to think for a moment. "Arturo said it happened to a friend of Lyric, though. I think her name is Karina or something. Maybe Kamilla. I didn't know her. It was before I came here. But I guess she went on to other things. Lyric says that she's in New York right now negotiating a contract on her next book."

"But they don't criticize *your* work too harshly?" I asked, wondering if "Kamilla" was the Camille that Lyric had dedicated her book to.

"Not really. Although they told me at the end of last term that Nordic folktales aren't going to go anywhere."

"Doesn't that alone make you question writing Nordic folktales?"

"No," she said, seeming to think the question over "See, the other Colonists like them. That's what we rely on. The others in the group. Besides, I…It's what I want to write. I'm not interested in romance or mystery or any of the other genres."

"But, Fritha, surely there are other writers' colonies that you could attend. I'm sure there are. You could find a group that supports you. Helps you. Lots of people belong to groups of other supportive writers."

"The other writers here do that." She shook her head. "We need this place. We need to get away from our families, our work, other distractions and spend one whole month out of the year just writing. Learning and writing. Ask any of them. You'll get hooked on it too."

I doubted that. I wanted to keep her talking, though.

"Tell me about yourself, Fritha. Do you have a family? A husband? Kids? What do you do when you aren't being a writer?"

"I work at an advertising agency," she said. The corners of her mouth tuned down ever so slightly and her gaze found the wall behind me.

"That sounds interesting," I said. "Do you do any writing in your job?

"No." She looked forlorn. "I hate it."

"Why don't you get something else, then?"

She looked at me as though the thought had never occurred to her before. "Oh, my father would have a fit."

Her father? How old was this woman, anyway? I had seen her birth certificate and I was sure she was around thirty. She was young, but not *that* young.

"He put me though college and insisted on a Business Degree. Marketing. 'That's the big thing of the future' he told me. And, he was paying for it, after all."

"How does he feel about your writing?"

"My mom and dad both want me to quit. They think it's a waste of my time." She looked at her lap and I thought I saw a sparkle of a tear in her eye. "They think it's foolish of me to save up all of my vacation for this session once a year. I get three weeks and have to take a week of unpaid leave. This year It's two weeks."

"Maybe you shouldn't tell them." I tried to sound gentle. I was hoping to get a smile out of her.

"Oh, I have to." This time, I really did see the tears. "I live with them."

I put my hand on hers and she gave a big sigh and dragged a tissue from the pocket of her jeans.

As soon as I touched her, I knew her story. She was an open book. Some people are like that—I can see everything about them right off the bat. She had an overbearing mother who suspected her of wrongdoing at every turn. Her father thought she was just a ditzy little girl who had to be told what to do. I was very sorry for her and thought the best thing she could do was get away from those toxic influences. Clearly, they were affecting her.

"I'm sorry, Fritha," I said. "I didn't mean to pry into your life."

"Oh, that's okay," she said. "I should go. It must be getting close to ten. Lights out, you know."

I fished around in my pocket and came up with my watch. "Nine forty-four," I told her. She looked so surprised I wondered if I had made a mistake.

"Don't ever, ever let anyone see that. You'll get a mark against you and you're only allowed three."

She stood and we went to the door together. "Before I go, I want to say that I'm glad you're here," she said. "Lyric and I thought your comments about Delilah's work were priceless."

"Speaking of Delilah, I have a question," I said. She stopped and looked at me. "Why does Delilah say 'the story I am making'? I thought that was a very odd thing to say."

She laughed softly. "She thinks it sounds smart. She never says 'writing a book' ever. She always calls it 'making a story.'" She laughed again. "I think it sounds silly too."

She opened the door and leaned out, carefully looking both ways. Then she silently waved and disappeared into the darkness.

* * *

After Fritha was gone, I realized that I was going to have to start working on re-typing Kegan's manuscript immediately. I would need at least the first chapter by the next day in case I was asked to read. I unwrapped the ream of paper I had brought and took the cover off my typewriter.

I had only been working for a few minutes when the lights went out. I suspected that the power stayed on in the big house but, since none of the cabins, including the main one, were visible from any of the others, I couldn't tell for sure. I had brought out the kerosene lamp and set it up on my desk. I lit it and wondered if anyone patrolled the place to make sure we were all tucked up in our little beds but that seemed a little over the top even for Russell and Bleusette. At least I hoped it was.

The more I typed, the more I realized what a remarkable book Kegan Mercer's *The Book of Signs* was. I had read it, but going through it very slowly and, in a way, savoring the words, it stood out more and more as a work of genius. Occasionally, as I typed, I would stop and reread a sentence, marveling at the sheer beauty and aptness of it. It gave me a feeling of awe, and I truly felt honored for the opportunity to represent the marvelous author Kegan had been.

I had a lot of work ahead of me. I still wanted to finish reading the rest of the works that the other writers had done that I had collected from bookstores and libraries before coming to Whalesong. I had Kegan's whole manuscript to transcribe as well. Briefly, I thought about the coming criticisms and that I would be expected to make corrections and alterations. I was not looking forward to it. I had written my share of reports, but any change in the beautiful manuscript seemed nothing less than sacrilege.

It was after midnight when I finally stopped typing. My back ached as well as my head. I had completed the first few chapters with my new name appearing on each page where Kegan's had been. It was a relief to put out the lamp and go to bed.

Sometime during the night, I awoke to absolute darkness. Outside, I could hear the forest murmuring in the breeze and an occasional call of an owl. Around me, inside the cabin, I heard the faint whisperings of those who had come before me. Every structure holds the imprint of those who have lived and worked in it. For a moment, faint breaths of hope and despair swirled and dissipated in the dark. Among them, Kegan's voice whispered to me too. Then I slept again.

SEVEN

Monday, April 30, 1984

Class the next morning was held in the Classroom, a room in the Main Cabin next to where Meeting was held. There was a large window behind a mammoth desk where I presumed Russell York would preside. As in Meeting, the chair/desks were arranged in a U configuration. This time I sat next to Lyric with Shig Takano on my right.

Russell strode in and self-importantly half sat on the corner of the desk. His smile that morning seemed a few watts dimmer than the day before.

"Normally, I would address this problem in Meeting," he began without any good-morning preamble whatsoever. "However, this is urgent and must be dealt with immediately. The rules at Whalesong are extremely important," he said. "Mr. Antonio, will you remind the class why the Whalesong rules are important?"

Cyr, seemingly taken unawares, answered slowly and somewhat hesitantly. I thought he looked like he had been caught reading porn when he was supposed to be reading King Lear in English class.

"The rules are important so that the Colonists are not distracted by anything outside of the normal routine," he said. "And they are about trust," he added as if he had just remembered it. He sounded as though he were trying to convince himself.

My thought was that, unfortunately, he was young and hadn't developed any really good rude answers yet. I could have thought of several much less banal things to say.

"Correct." Russell's stare bored into me. For once, his smile had disappeared altogether. "Ms. Augustine, will you kindly recite Rule Number 18?"

I would have been utterly delighted to recite Rule Number 18 if I had had a clue as to what it was. Lyric, next to me, dropped her pen on the floor. As she bent down to retrieve it, I heard her whisper, "Lights out."

"Rule Number 18 states that lights out is at 10:00pm, I said promptly.

"I see. You are conversant with the rules after all. May I ask you, then, why there was still a light burning in your cabin at 10:30?"

My immediate answer would have been, of course, "None of your damn business," but I was at Whalesong after all, and I knew I had to behave myself for at least another four weeks. At this rate, I wasn't at all sure I could manage it.

"I was finishing something," I told him.

Maybe he had expected defiance from me, or fear. At any rate, he seemed a bit disappointed.

"You have broken a rule. Therefore, you will receive one demerit on your record. This is your first. You are allowed three," he said. "Three infractions will get you expelled from Whalesong. You will not receive your tuition back, nor will you be allowed to return." He continued to stare at me and I wondered if he truly was trying to stare me down. If he was, he was in for another, even bigger, disappointment. I have held the undisputed staring championship since the third grade.

Russell gave up after a ridiculously short time and picked up a book that had been lying on his desk.

"Today, I'm going to read a portion of a short story, 'Stillness Instead.' In it is a classic example of setting.

He began to read and instantly I understood what he was trying to tell us. The setting of the story, a small town in Ohio, was so vivid and so seemingly important to the story that it was almost a character unto itself. I fell under its spell and was disappointed when he broke off the story before it was finished.

As he put the book on the desk, I leaned forward trying to get a look at the author's name on the spine.

"Miss Augustine," he said. "Do you have a question?"

"I was trying to see the author's name. Does that say 'Bailey Attwood?'

"That story, dearheart, was written by me. Bailey Attwood is one of my pseudonyms."

"It's a wonderful story," I said. "Why on Earth would you use a pen name for it?"

I caught a glimpse of Fritha's horrified face. Even Lyric looked startled.

"There are many reasons why authors use pseudonyms, Miss Augustine." Russell looked nettled. "Suffice it to say that I used one because I had one of those reasons."

I tried my hardest to look contrite, but I think I failed. I could tell that he was asking himself if he was going to have difficulty with me. I reminded myself once again that I had another four weeks to go at Whalesong. It wasn't going to be easy keeping out of trouble long enough to be allowed to remain.

I paid little attention to the rest of the lesson that day. I believe he continued to talk about settings, but my mind had its own questions to deal with.

I was going to have to speak to each of the Colonists. And I would like to get a look into their cabins as well. I knew there was little hope of walking into Delilah's or Axel's, or Thorn's. The others seemed friendly enough that I may be able to wangle invites into their cabins but not those of the esteemed Entourage. And what about the main house? Did Russell and Bleusette ever leave the island? If they did, would Strom be about to watch the place? I knew that I had to bide my time. I was new and, apparently, being watched. But I suspected everyone was watched, not just me. We were under a tight rule and it would take some ingenuity to enable me to engage in a little of my usual snooping.

* * *

It was later that afternoon, after we had dragged ourselves from class and carried our box lunches to our cabins to begin our long afternoons of working, that I escaped into the cool forest for a walk. I needed one. As I walked, I shredded the ham from my sandwich and dropped it along the path for woodland creatures to devour or scorn. Either way, it would go back to nature quickly enough. I hadn't thrown the last few strips away when I encountered Lyric, Fritha and Shig sitting silently on logs just beyond the path. Fritha, when she saw it was me, breathed out a long sigh of relief.

"I thought we were caught," she said. She fanned her face with her hand.

"No, I heard her warning," Shig said.

"Warning?" I was baffled. I had been tossing

fragments of ham into the woods, nothing more.

"No one told you about the warning?" Shig said. "When we go for walks, we mutter to ourselves or sing, recite poetry, whatever. That way, it warns anyone else who is out walking that it's a 'friendly' approaching. Someone not saying anything could be one of the Entourage, Strom or Russell or Bleusette. If it's one of them, we silently scatter."

"Why didn't you scatter this time?"

"You were muttering," Lyric said, laughing quietly. "I distinctly heard you say, 'Come and get it.'"

"Ah," I said. "I was talking to any potential wildlife who might be interested in the ham from my sandwich."

Lyric scooted over on her log and invited me to sit. "You were wise to get rid of it that way and not leave it in the box to be collected. They frown on food left behind."

"Seriously? Do they think we are children? I haven't had to clean my plate since I was eleven."

Shig seemed to think for a moment. "In a way, we are children." Lyric and I snorted softly. Fritha looked baffled. "We *are* like children," he insisted. "We're stumbling around in the writing world, barely knowing how to walk. We need their guidance. That's why we're here and that's why we put up with the rules and the discipline. Like children, we need to have direction and someone like Russell to give it to us."

"What makes you think that he's the only person who can give you direction?" I asked. "You could get perfectly fine instruction from someone else who wouldn't watch every move you make."

"He's had several successful books published," Shig said. "He knows the ins and outs of writing, getting published. He knows what he is doing."

"He's had two books published and they are no longer in print," I said.

"He's had several things published under pseudonyms," Shig said. I could see that he was irritated, though he kept his voice calm and patient.

"We may not agree with his methods, but we have agreed to them all the same," Fritha said. "And we're breaking one of them right now." She looked around, then shivered, though the afternoon was not chilly. "I'm always antsy when we get together like this."

I wasn't so sure they were right, but I was a newbie. So far, I hadn't found out much. Getting to know these people would help with that. "Are there any other rules that you all routinely break that I can get in on?"

"Actually, yes," Lyric said. "We regularly meet in one another's cabins after Meeting."

"I don't always go," Fritha said. "I don't need any marks on my record." She shuddered again.

"You seem to have caught on," Shig said to me,

seemingly no longer nettled. "Kegan must have given you a few hints. How is he doing, anyway?"

I had debated about when to tell them about Kegan. At first, I had thought I wouldn't say anything. But I wanted them to be honest with me, and I have always found that being honest in return was the best way to gain trust. "I'm so sorry to have to tell you this," I began. "I'm so sorry, but Kegan is dead." I tried to say it as gently as I could.

Fritha's hands flew to her mouth and she emitted a small sob.

Lyric stared at me with her eyes round.

Shig shook his head. "What happened?" he asked.

"This is to be kept quiet," I told them. "Kegan's parents haven't let anyone know beyond the family." They all nodded. "He committed suicide," I said. "I'm so sorry."

"I was afraid of that, after last term," Fritha said, sobbing softly.

"Oh, God," Shig said. "I'm…I don't know what to say."

Lyric, so far, had said nothing.

"What happened last term, Fritha?" I asked finally when she had subsided.

They all turned to look at me and I knew I had made a mistake. "I know they burned his book but did something else happen that he didn't…tell me about? He wasn't talking to his friends much after he came back from Whalesong."

"They trashed Kegan's book," Fritha said. "I told you that. Isn't that enough?" She started crying again.

"I hate them," Lyric muttered. *Interesting*, I thought. I wanted to hear more about that.

Shig said something quietly to Lyric and she frowned and turned her head away.

"Do you think he did it because of them, Lyric?" I asked. "Because of Bleusette and Russell?"

"Oh, who knows?" Lyric said. "He wasn't in very good spirits when he left here. I'm not surprised he didn't want to talk about it. He wanted to keep working on his novel and they wanted him to work on something else. They said literary fiction wasn't for him. That he had talent, just not for that."

"Lyric—" Shig said, but she interrupted him.

"Oh, let me talk, Shig! You know as well as I do that Kegan was talented. I don't care what Russell said. Kegan's book was wonderful. I hate Russell," she said again.

"We should get back to our cabins," Shig said uneasily. "Let's get together after Meeting tonight. We can talk more then."

"Ugh! It's Dinner night," Lyric said. She said it as though she was referring to an execution instead of a meal.

"My place?" Shig asked.

I wanted to stay. I wanted to hear more about what happened to Kegan last term.

Lyric nodded sourly and Fritha shrugged but said nothing.

"I'll be there," I said and we all went in different directions through the thick trees.

* * *

Dinner was awkward. Fritha could barely restrain her tears and Lyric continued to stab Russell with covert looks.

If I had not felt that I was being treated as a child before, the dinner made me realize what a hold the couple had over their students. I felt watched from the moment we sat down. When I had been served, I was relieved to see that scallops were on the menu. I love almost all seafoods, but I know that many people don't. Russell and Bleusette didn't seem to realize that others might not share their tastes. Bleusette had managed to mention her many "allergies" more than once but she seemed to believe that no one else had any. Lyric whispered to me that she couldn't eat shellfish and was going to have to suffer the wrath of Russell and Bleusette for not eating and being ungrateful for what she had been served. I quietly slipped the three large scallops from her plate when Russell was in the kitchen and Bleusette seemed engrossed in something Axel was saying. I don't know if Delilah or Thorn saw me do it or not, but I didn't care. I would rather get in trouble than see Lyric die on the spot from something that could easily kill her.

"So, does Russell actually cook? It said in the brochure that he makes the Monday Dinners," I asked Lyric quietly. "That's hard to imagine."

"I, personally, don't think he does," she said, finishing up her au gratin potatoes. She glanced up at the couple who were again deep in their own dinners. "I always thought the mysterious 'woman from the village' who makes our other meals makes the Monday dinners too, and Russell just pretends he does. It sounds like him."

"Ladies," Bleusette's voice rose over our murmurs. I looked up to see her watching Lyric and me. "If you have something to say to each other, say it out loud so we can all hear." She was smiling beneficently, but there was a slight cold edge to her voice.

Oh, brother! I thought. I knew that we were allowed "polite conversation" at dinner with the other Colonists, but it was generally expected to be public. Apparently, whispered confidences were not allowed

"I was just saying to Sarah that the scallops were particularly well cooked," Lyric said smoothly.

"And I was agreeing," I said, amazed to see Bleusette look satisfied and return to her own food.

In Meeting that night Axel was asked to read first. He read a short story, which I didn't understand. He had declared it to be "new-age fantasy" and the character and place names were apparently only pronounceable by Axel himself. I'm ashamed to say that I lost interest almost immediately. I wrote him some vague comments and knew that I was failing miserably at this writing thing. It would be a wonder if I came through this without being found out.

Next, Shig read some of his novel, *Baka na Warriors*. I had been looking forward to hearing his science fiction novel but this one was about medieval Japanese hoods who seemed to do nothing but roam the countryside looking for people to torment. Russell and Bleusette both praised it. In Meeting I praised it as well, repeating almost word for word what Russell had said. My written comment to Shig was, "What the hell?" but I didn't hand it over to him.

As we walked out after Meeting, I murmured to Lyric: "Are you coming to Shig's cabin later?" She looked at me for a moment then nodded.

I stopped at my cabin first to make sure my briefcase/doctor's bag was locked and to grab a jacket. Also, I had to make sure Axel had gone in so that I could creep past his cabin on the way. At Fritha's I stopped to make sure she was coming too.

When she opened the door, she peered into the darkness to the right and to the left then motioned me in. "Come to Shig's with me," I said.

She shook her head. "I've been breaking the rules too often. I don't think I should risk it tonight."

"Oh, come on, Fritha," I said. I could tell she wanted to. Sure enough, after another moment of persuasion, she nervously joined me. I suspected that she waged an inner war with herself most of the time. Half of her was intent on obeying the rules to the letter, while the other half craved the company of like-minded others.

Shig's cabin was what I would have expected. Meaning, it was just like mine. I immediately felt a sensation of contentment, purpose and self-satisfaction. He was happy here, I knew. He had his desk set up the same way as I had mine. It looked like he had been using his kerosene lantern too but had been smart enough to shade it plus pile books up on the window sill all the way to the top in order to block the light. He picked up a few stray items of clothing and tossed them over the desk chair.

We all sat on the floor, leaning against the futon or the wall.

"I'm sorry I didn't hand you my comments on

your work tonight, Shig," I told him. "I honestly didn't know what to say. I thought you wrote science fiction."

"Shig gave up sci-fi for Samurai adventures, didn't you, Shig?" Lyric said.

I could tell something was going on that I didn't know anything about. I looked from one to the other.

"She's kidding," Shig said. "I gave up reading my sci-fi in Meeting last year because they started trashing it and I didn't want it to go the way of all decent novels and get burned. They told me to write Samurai adventures, so I did."

"But you still work on the science fiction, don't you?" I asked.

"I write that during the day. By night I read *Baka na Warriors*." He looked at me. "You don't have to like it. I don't."

"Tell her what *Baka na* means, Shig," Fritha said.

"*Baka* means 'stupid'. So pretty much, the title is *Stupid Warriors*."

"Last year, Russell asked him what it meant and he said, 'It means warriors with superpowers,'" Fritha said. "I thought we were all going to choke holding in our laughter."

"The miracle is, he doesn't even speak Japanese,"

Lyric said.

"I don't have to. I do have a trusty English-Japanese dictionary, though, which comes in very handy. I've forced my stupid warriors to do all kinds of things."

"Once he had them pole-dancing," Lyric added.

"In Japanese, of course," Shig said.

"So, tell me something," I said after the laughter had died away. "How do they handle mail around here? It says in the brochure that we get mail at the Main Cabin. Does Strom deliver that too?"

"Yes," Lyric said. "If you get it at all."

"What? Do you think they don't deliver it?"

Lyric and Fritha turned to look at Shig, but he said nothing.

"My mother claims that she sends me things and then gets mad when I don't thank her for them," Fritha said. "She swore she sent me a letter about my dad's illness but I never got it. In it, she said I should come home and I would have too, but I didn't get the letter. It turned out he was okay, though."

"My wife sent me a letter from an agent once that I never got," Shig said quietly. "She had opened it and had seen that this agent was interested in *Saturn Blaze*. She sent it to me right away. Later, when she found out I never got it, we looked up the agent and

I contacted her. Nothing came of it, though, and I always thought it was because I never got that letter and had responded too late. Who knows?" he said. "The mail is spotty here on the island."

I personally thought he was making yet one more excuse for the antics of Russell and Bleusette.

"So, basically, they restrict our phone calls, screen our mail and make us clean our plates," I said. "And we have to be in bed by ten o'clock. Is there anyone here who likes being treated like a 10-year-old?"

Shig shrugged but said nothing.

Fritha looked frightened. "We did agree to follow the rules," she said.

I decided again to back off. I had agreed to follow the rules too. I didn't want to badger anyone. I needed these people to help me get to the bottom of what had been happening in Whalesong.

"I hate them," Lyric said darkly. "I feel like calling on Moki." The others laughed, but I noticed Lyric didn't.

"Moki?" I said. "Who's Moki?"

Shig turned to me. "Moki stands for *Murder on Klallam Island.*"

"It's a book title we made up years ago. We invoke Moki whenever one of us gets so pissed off with Russell and Bleusette that we want to kill them,"

Lyric said.

"Well," Shig interjected. "Not *actually* kill them. We were thinking about writing this book and killing them *in* it. We were all going to take turns writing chapters. We never did it, but now and then we 'call on Moki' to make us feel better."

"I don't blame Lyric," I said. "They tried to kill *her* after all."

"Oh, I wanted to thank you for that, Sarah," Lyric said, her humor seemingly restored. She turned to Shig and Fritha. "In case you didn't see, she ate my scallops for me. They wouldn't have killed me, exactly. I would have gotten sick, though. I may have wished for death."

"I thought Bleusette was all uber-conscious of allergies and then she serves shellfish to someone who's allergic," I said. "What's up with that?"

"Maybe she thinks she's the only one with allergies," Shig said. "She's told us she's allergic to tomatoes, peanuts, cucumber, bees, cinnamon. Is anyone really allergic to cinnamon?"

"Actually, I knew of a woman who died from eating cinnamon," Lyric said.

"Whoa! Death by snickerdoodle! That's harsh!" Shig said, eliciting another laugh. "Talking about Moki does give us a good release valve, though. It does relieve the tension."

"Oh, *I'll* relieve the tension," Fritha said and they all laughed again.

I looked from one to another, again at a loss.

"Wow," Shig said. "I'm not sure it's fair to inundate Sarah with all of the in-jokes in one night." He turned to me. "Lyric once said that you can repeat something innocent someone says and make it sound like a threat."

I felt gratified that they were becoming comfortable enough with me to let me in on their secrets and their jokes.

"I still want to call on Moki," Lyric said. "We really should write that book."

"I don't know about you, but I've got enough to do without working on Moki," Shig said. "Let's just leave Moki alone, shall we? We've all got other work to do."

"Oh, *I'll* leave Moki alone," Fritha said and we laughed. All but Lyric. She didn't seem to think it was funny at all.

EIGHT

Tuesday, May 1, 1984

That night I dreamed about Kegan. Small wonder, since his presence was everywhere in his cabin. I was aware that others used the cabin during the other sessions on the island, but somehow, I felt more of Kegan than anyone else.

I had never seen Kegan nor a picture of him. Nevertheless, I knew that he was the young man in my dream. He was sitting at the desk and doing nothing, only looking at me with large gray eyes. I felt that he approved of my being in his cabin and that he was grateful. In another moment, the dream faded. I wondered briefly, even in my sleep, if I had been visited or if my tired mind had conjured up a physical manifestation of my purpose for being immersed in Whalesong.

Early the next morning, I awoke before the wake-up gong and slipped outside for an early walk. Before I had left for the island, I had begun working with light weights and diligently doing stretches and a few simple yoga poses. At Whalesong, the only option for exercise was walking and the only place to walk was in the woods.

Breakfast would arrive at 7:00 and I had to be in my cabin to receive it or I would have another mark against me. I laughed to myself. What did I care if there were ten marks against me? Were they going to go on my 'Permanent Record'? Oh my gawd! What a dreadful thought! But, after all, I didn't want to get myself kicked out of the compound when I had basically found out nothing useful.

I had tucked my watch into my bra and consulted it. I had a good thirty minutes before I needed to be back and acting like I had never left. I followed the trail past Thorn's cabin and around to the Bathhouse, then doubled back through the woods toward the path that led from the left of the Main Cabin. I didn't want to get too close to the big house.

Just before the turn onto the trail, I encountered Arturo coming the other way. We both stopped.

"Looks like we both had the same idea," I told him. "We're not supposed to talk, are we?"

He shrugged and adjusted his beret. "I always wondered what they think we do if we encounter each other on the path," he said. "Ignore each other? Besides, Sarah Augustine, I'm still curious about you."

"Curious about me?"

"Of course. We all are. You're the new girl." He grinned at me. "You throw the rules out the window. And, we haven't heard your writing yet, either. Of course we're curious about you."

"I enjoyed hearing that piece from your book on Sunday night. I'm a big mystery fan," I told him.

"Really?" The word came out "Reh-ah-ly". As I had heard him speak over the past few days, I had gotten the impression his English accent was fake. Sometimes it was more pronounced than others. This was one of the times.

"Would you like to read my book?" he asked, eagerness giving him an almost boyish look. I thought he was at least fifty, maybe even closer to sixty, though his hair, what you could see of it under the beret he perpetually wore, was still dark.

"I thought that wasn't permitted either," I said with a smile.

"It isn't, but who cares? Let's throw one more of those rules out the window. I'd love for someone who's keen on mysteries to read it." He pushed up his sleeve to reveal a watch worn far up on his arm. "We have time to get to my cabin. I'll give you a recent draft. I'd love to hear what you have to say about the whole thing. It's so difficult when you can only hear it in pieces that are read days apart."

I followed him to his cabin which was all the way

on the other side of the compound. I knew I would have to jog to get back in time, but I was eager to see his work. I knew that he had only written the one book, that he kept revising and reading parts of it at Meeting. From the way he spoke in class and from what I had heard, it seemed that he was more in love with the idea of being a writer than actually being a productive published author. He loved to talk the talk but really wasn't interested in doing the work. Oh, he had written his book but he didn't seem willing to go any further. I liked him though. He seemed very comfortable with himself and the persona he had cultivated.

We talked a little on the way to his cabin. I should say that Arturo talked. It turned out he had a fetish for gossip. It seemed he knew the scoop on everyone. Or at least he thought he did. Nevertheless, he was willing to tell all. I personally thought that some of his tales were more fiction than reality. I fervently hoped not all of them were true. For instance, the one where he said he saw Russell York hanging around the Bathhouse trying to get a look in the windows.

I did manage to get him to talk about himself a little, though I had to wonder if his story about having an uncle in England with a large country estate was true. He implied that he didn't have to work and was free to be a writer.

While we walked and chatted, I had managed a

light touch to his arm. I knew without a doubt that he was going to remain a mystery to me. His name was not Arturo Kuppendapper. He was not English. I had no idea who or what he was. It was no wonder I couldn't find anything about him in my background check. He had completely invented himself. I could hardly judge him. After all, wasn't I doing the same?

After Arturo had handed me his manuscript, I hurried back through the woods, avoiding the trail in order to keep from being seen by Strom. I didn't know if he was at all sympathetic to us writers but I didn't care to find out. I thought he most likely had reported my late night to Russell and Bleusette.

I had had to wolf my breakfast then rush to Class. I made it in time, but barely. I had only just slid into my seat when Russell came in and strode to the desk where he placed a gun.

No one said anything, but I saw Thorn nod. I saw Fritha look positively terrified and I saw Delilah smirk.

The lesson that morning was about weaving your plot either tightly or loosely depending upon the length of the story. He dragged in anecdotes from his book, *Velvet Wings and Mud* which were lost on me since I hadn't read it. He talked about chaos versus order in both life and fiction. I don't think any of us, though, could keep our attention off the gun.

"Woven into this tapestry we call fiction," Russell

said, “are many bits of the story. Small details, like beads and ribbons, give the work interest. Give it flavor. Give it”—and here, he made his voice low and sepulchral—"foreshadowing.”

At last, Russell picked up the gun. He moved it from his right hand to his left and back again.

“Anton Chekhov told us that if a gun is going to go off in the third act of a play, it must have been on the mantle in full view during acts one and two. Conversely, if you have a gun sitting, say, on a desk, it had better be used in your story by the third act. What he was telling us is that critical characters and important developments *must* be present all through the story for it to be believable. You cannot drag in a previously unintroduced character to save the day at the end. The savior must have been there all along. Disguised, perhaps, but there, present, visible. No Deus ex Machina will get past any modern editor.”

“I brought my gun in today, not to use it, so I am breaking Chekhov’s rule. I brought it to make a point. I believe that you will all remember this point. When my gun is back safely in my desk, not one of you will forget the lesson here today.”

* * *

After class I felt drugged and bleary-eyed. I picked up my lunch and, giving Fritha and Shig a tired wave, I turned off the path and onto the trail to my cabin. Axel, as usual was nowhere to be seen. I sometimes wondered how he managed to get back and forth from the Main Cabin to his own. We were neighbors, so to speak, but I rarely saw him except in Meeting and Class.

My cabin was cold even though the day seemed to have started out warm. I hurriedly ate my lunch then headed over to the Bathhouse to do a load of laundry.

In the Bathhouse, Cyr Antonio was finishing up his own pile of clean clothes, folding it on top of one of the small tables.

"Sarah," he said, looking at me for only a second before returning to his t shirts.

"Cyr."

After a moment, I laughed. "It seems too silly to be standing in the same room with someone and not feel free to speak to them. I realize we aren't supposed to fraternize, but it's probably okay if we talk about writing, isn't it?"

"Oh, no," he said solemnly. "They don't want us to talk about our writing. It would contaminate our concentration." His voice was serious until he broke into a charming grin. His teeth were crooked in the front and it gave him a sweet, boyish look, but then, he really was a boy. His twenty-eight years seemed a far cry from my thirty-nine. "Hey, I don't mind breaking the rules if you don't."

"I've never been one for obeying the rules," I told him.

"I'm eager to hear your work," he said. "What are you working on?"

I told him a little about *The Book of Signs*. I always felt a bit self-conscious talking about it since I had nothing to do with writing it.

"I read *Fighting Doctor Black* before coming to Whalesong," I told him.

His eyes immediately sparkled with pleasure. "What did you think?"

"I liked it! I normally don't read adventure, but it was fun to read." That was true enough. I had read it and it *had* been fun to read. Something like watching a corny horror movie. You aren't really in it for the culture.

I felt like we were two teenagers trying desperately to conduct a normal conversation but lacking the skills.

"Thanks," he said. "What I'd really like is for someone to 'discover' my books and want to make movies out of them." He made finger quotes at the word "discover".

"I would think they would be great for that," I told him. I really didn't know how good a writer Cyr actually was. I didn't feel that I could judge fairly by his first novel. He wasn't very old now and he had been even younger when he had written *Fighting Doctor Black*.

So far, we had been in the Bathhouse together for several minutes and had said a whole lot of squat. I would have liked to get to know this man and find out what his agenda was. All the writers here had agendas, including me. I didn't feel that I could adequately evaluate this place and its people unless I could speak freely with them and invade their spaces. Being one of the drones wasn't going to help at all.

"How long have you been coming to Whalesong?" I asked him, thinking that was a safe enough question.

"This is my fifth year," he said, gathering a handful of socks and piling them onto the t-shirts.

Again, the conversation faltered.

We talked for a few more minutes, barely touching on any one topic. It seemed that he was keeping himself pretty well bottled up. I wondered if any of the Colonists knew him very well.

When he was finished, Cyr picked up his load of clothes. A pair of socks slid from the top and we both bent to pick it up, our hands touching on the way down. From Cyr, I instantly felt that there was something more to him than I had first perceived. That, of course, was perfectly normal. Everyone has more than one persona. Just listen to how a man talks to another man versus how he talks to a woman. It's like two different guys. But, from Cyr, I felt ambition as well as something devious. Likeable and boyish as he seemed, I felt that he was someone of whom I needed to be careful.

When I had finished my laundry, I walked slowly back up the path. I had things I could do but the birds singing in the trees made me long for an afternoon picnic with Easy.

Lyric was just coming from her cabin when I turned onto the trail. She waved, indicating I should wait for her. We walked toward my cabin together.

"I was just coming to see you," she said. "I wanted to thank you again for rescuing me at dinner last night." I must have looked blank. "The scallops," she said. "You didn't have to do that. You risked getting in trouble yourself."

"Oh, the scallops. I love scallops," I said. "I'll steal them off of the plate of anyone who is nearby. Besides, I owed you for the save about Rule Number 18." I put a grim emphasis on the last three words.

She laughed again. She was quite pretty when she laughed. Her brown eyes sparkled and her teeth looked extra white against her brown skin. "We have to stick together, I guess. Anyway," she said, "I just wanted to tell you thanks."

"Come on in and we can talk awhile," I said.

We settled on the futon and I mentioned seeing Cyr in the washroom.

"He talk to you?" she asked me. She seemed surprised. She played with the beaded end of one of her braids.

"Oh, yes. We laughed for a minute about what constitutes fraternization and why we shouldn't talk and then we talked anyway. Mostly about his… our books."

"Hmm. He usually doesn't talk to anyone much. He sticks to the rules. I think he respects whatever Russell says. He thinks Russell is the greatest writer in the world." She flipped the braid behind her and folded her hands in her lap.

"I kind of got that impression." I looked at her. "And is he? I couldn't find any of his books before I came to Whalesong. I wanted to read some and familiarize myself with the man."

"He hasn't written anything for a long, long time. He says he's 'too busy shaping minds and shit like that." She stopped. "Sorry," she said, looking sheepish.

"Hey, you can say anything you want around me," I told her. "He must have made a ton of money on whatever he had published. That cabin and this whole Whalesong thing has to have cost plenty of bucks." I had wondered about that more than once since I had been in residence. The Main Cabin was lavishly furnished and keeping half of an island running had to be expensive. "He, apparently has been writing under other names."

Lyric nodded.

"That's a bit odd, don't you think?" I asked. "Why would he use other names when he already had made a name for himself?"

She shrugged. "Who knows? All I know is, they get money from somewhere. I know, I've always wondered how they could do it," Lyric mused. "I always thought Bleusette or maybe Russell had family money."

"Someone has some, at least. It's not cheap to come here and spend a month but it isn't that much. Not for board and everything. They do this, what? Four times a year?"

"Four," she said. "There's one for every season. I have always wondered how they get people to come up here in the winter." She began to inspect her fingernails. They looked like she bit them but I had never seen her do it.

"Do you know of anyone who comes more than once a year?" I asked.

She shrugged. "I don't, no. There doesn't seem to be a lot of turn-over in the Spring session. That's the only one I know about."

"I would think that the classes would get old after a while, though," I said. "Don't you get tired of hearing the same lesson every year?"

"Actually, Russell is very good at making it interesting," she said, putting her hands in her lap again. "I've been coming here a few years and I've never heard the same lesson twice. I have to give him that," she conceded with a shrug. "He's a good teacher. I learn something different from him every year."

She stood up. "I need to get back. The longer I stay here, the more likely it is that we'll be caught." She sighed heavily. "If you run into Cyr again, be careful. He would very much like to be Russell's—what do you call that?—teacher's pet. I know of a few times when he's tattled on the other colonists thinking he can get in good with Russell. He would like very much to bc part of thc Entourage. He doesn't know that it's only the Entourage because we—the others, the outsiders—have made it so."

"I'll take care," I told her. "Is there anyone else I should look out for?"

"I wouldn't pay too much attention to what Arturo says." She thought for a moment. "And Thorn. That man scares me. Axel and Delilah are pretty tight with Russell and Bleusette." She looked right into my eyes. "I'd say, pretty much everyone."

I wondered then if Lyric meant to include herself.

NINE

Wednesday, May 2, 1984

By the fourth day, the chant and incense show at the start of Meeting was beginning to wear thin. Each time, Bleusette made a spectacle of lighting the candle, then the stick and pinching out the flame with her fingers. Besides, the smell of the incense was starting to worm its way into my sinuses and sometimes I could still smell it when I awoke in the morning.

Fritha was chosen as the reader that night. She read at length from *Hildra the Queen*. I thought it was charming and it gave me an appreciation of a folk culture I had never given thought to at all. I said so in my notes to Fritha. Frankly, I was surprised. This was the first time I had heard any of Fritha's writing. She had a way of making an ancient tale fit seamlessly into the modern era. I could see that her book had potential with audiences of all ages. I was impressed.

Russell and Bleusette seemed less pleased than I.

"Fritha," Russell began and I knew at once that it wasn't going to be good. "I'm rather surprised at you."

Fritha looked stricken. She had read strongly, almost proudly, as though she sensed that her work had some merit. It only took a few words from Russell to knock her back into her place.

"Technically speaking, I thought your sentence structure was strong, as was your characterization. The imagery was commendable as well, if a bit wordy. But, I'm sure you realize that these older tales have no place in our culture today." He looked us over, as he always did. "Any comments?"

"Yes," I said. "I thought it was delightful." I heard a little gasp from someone but I couldn't tell who. I thought Delilah, most likely.

"What did you find so amusing about it, Sarah? I didn't see you laughing."

"I didn't find it amusing," I told him, wondering too late, if I should have kept my mouth shut. "I found it pleasurable. I enjoyed the strong characters and I thought that Fritha did a good job with her descriptions," I wanted to add, "You asked." But I didn't.

"I thought it was rather tame," Axel said, looking and sounding bored. It seemed to be a perpetual look for him. That expression and his eternal ascot gave him an air of aloofness. He rarely spoke and the only time I had ever heard anything like emotion in his voice was when he was talking to Bleusette. Arturo had told me that Axel was married and that his wife supported him by working as a nurse. According to Arturo, Axel liked to keep his "professional and private lives separate." I didn't know how much of that was Axel and how much Arturo.

"Anyone else agree with Axel?" Russell asked. There were one or two inarticulate murmurs but no one actually said anything.

Shig was looking at his desk, which it seemed he did most of the time when he was in class or Meeting.

Lyric was writing in her notebook.

Delilah looked pleased. "I agree with Russell," she said. "I don't think fairy tales have any place in adult literature."

"I liked it," Arturo said.

I saw Thorn shake his head. He sat back in his chair, stuck his legs out straight and crossed his arms. His demeanor conveyed that he thought the rest of us a bunch of clowns.

"Thornton," Russell said. "We would like to hear your opinion."

"It's not my kind of stuff," he said, suddenly looking self-conscious at being pinned down to an actual point of view. "I think it's more for kids. Girls, maybe. Men wouldn't go for it, that's for sure."

"So, it seems we have a debate here," Russell

said. "Fritha, dearheart, hand in your chapter there and I will get it back to you after I have made my suggestions. I must warn you, they may be rather extensive. The rest of you, please pass your comments to Fritha."

Russell's gaze wandered around the room. At last he said, "Cyr, let's hear what you have been working on."

When Cyr began to read from his newest novel, *Deadly Duels*, I kept my focus on Fritha. She didn't look as upset as I had expected. She sat, without moving, staring at the collection of comments that had been handed her. I saw a light pinkness creep over her face but it was impossible to tell if it was embarrassment, anger or simply from having been forced, however briefly, to be the center of attention.

When he had finished reading, I wrote my comments to Cyr. He had loaded lots of fighting, sex and action into his book. It was a sort of western, really, I thought, though he called it an historic adventure. It wasn't my cup of tea, but I believed it was reasonably well written, as was his first book, *Fighting Doctor Black*. I commented truthfully that I could see improvement from his first book and that he had a good start. I then suggested that he use more color and more of the other senses. There was lots of fighting going on but no one ever got hurt in the slightest. I thought a bit of blood would be in order at least. Actually, I felt completely at sea and wasn't sure about my comments at all.

By the time I handed my notes to Cyr, Fritha had disappeared. Lyric seemed to have left as well. Shig whispered that he would go find them and try to convince Fritha to come to his cabin. I told him I would be along later. I had business elsewhere in the Main Cabin that night.

It was my phone night and I was ready. Immediately after Meeting I was admitted into what I had to assume was Bleusette's office. As with the other rooms that I had seen in the Main Cabin, this one was lavishly appointed. The desk was made of shining cherry wood and looked hand carved to me. I wondered again where these people came up with the money for such gorgeous furnishings. Who knew? Maybe running a writers' colony was the best kept money making secret in the world.

The phone was one of those French jobs that looks like it would fall apart if you slammed down the receiver in a rage. Even so, I could see that there were at least four lines which minimized the chances that Russell was somewhere else in the house listening. If it had been a single line, all he would have to do is pick up an extension to listen in. With the four lines, that would be difficult if not impossible to do.

Bleusette sat at her desk, not four feet from me and made herself look busy shuffling through papers, perusing some of them and shuffling a little more. The whole room had the smell of stale incense.

Easy answered on the first ring and I breathed a prayer of thanks that he hadn't been called out on an emergency.

"Hi, Easy," I said cheerfully, keeping my eye on Bleusette.

"Sarah," he said. "The Seattle Police are on your trail. Perce O'Dell is looking for you."

"I don't want to talk about that right now," I responded. Bleusette looked up from her work. I smiled at her, hoping I looked a tiny bit guilty.

"Well, I didn't tell them where you were," he said

This was all according to plan. I figured that if Russell were listening and thought the police were after me, he would call the Seattle Police Department and ask to speak to Perce O'Dell. He would certainly be curious to know the reason why the police were looking for one of his students. If he did call, Perce would then tell Easy, since Easy had warned him of our plan. Perce was an old friend from long ago and he was always happy to cooperate in my shenanigans. He knew what to say if anyone should question him. If Russell mentioned it to me at all, I could tell him that I had just broken up with my boyfriend, Perce, who was an officer and that's what Easy had been referring to. I would know then that Russell or Bleusette or both had been able to hear what Easy had said.

"Good," I said and sighed with convincing sounding relief.

"Everything going okay, otherwise?"

"Oh, yes!" I said. "This is a wonderful place. I'm getting so much work done."

"That's what you're there for."

It was pretty much a non-conversation from then on. We neither one of us could talk normally and it felt stilted and awkward. Bleusette had seemed to lose interest and had gone back to pushing things around on her desk, but I still felt she was listening carefully.

I so wanted to tell Easy that I was homesick and how bizarre everything connected to this place was. But I settled on describing the lovely settings and the comfy cabins and the superb guidance we were all getting.

When I left Bleusette's office, I felt that I had been released from an uncomfortable audience with the principal. Thorn was hovering outside the door awaiting his turn at the telephone. I badly wanted to do some hovering myself and listen in on his call but it would have been too risky at this point. Maybe on another Wednesday.

Russell seemed to be nowhere about and I had to resist the urge to snoop, too. I left and headed straight to Fritha's cabin.

Fritha opened her door, then turned back into the room. I looked at her carefully trying to gauge how Russell's comments on her work had affected her. She appeared to be calm enough, considering someone was in her cabin with her doing the forbidden fraternizing.

"Come on over to Shig's with me, Frith," I said.

"We aren't supposed to fraternize," she said. She sounded impatient, as though I simply was not getting the point.

"Well, 'aren't supposed to' shouldn't stop you. It never stops me," I said.

"I'm not you. I have to follow the rules." She did her characteristic glance around the room as though she expected someone to be spying on her from the corner.

"No, you don't!" This woman was not the lighthearted Fritha I knew after all. She seemed more nervous than she usually did. "You're an adult. You can do whatever you like."

"They'll kick us out of Whalesong if we break three of the rules. You already have one strike against you. I would think you would be more careful." She didn't look at me as she spoke.

I moved to the futon and sat, then patted the seat next to me. "Sit down. Let's talk," I said.

She sat, then folded her hands in her lap. She looked for all the world like a scolded little girl. I wondered what had so cowed her that she would allow herself to be so intimidated.

"We'll both get kicked out," she said.

"No, we won't."

"What did *you* think of my book?" she asked. "Russell didn't like it, I guess."

"He didn't say he didn't like it. In fact, he had some good things to say. It was more than good. I enjoyed it very much. You told me the first time I met you that the unwritten rule was that you go by what the others say and not Russell."

For a long moment, she said nothing. "You don't understand," she said finally.

"Tell me."

"I...everything hinges on this book. Everything. If it fails, then..."

"Then what? If it fails, you write another. But I don't think it's going to fail." I watched her for a moment. I put my hand on her arm. I felt a stark, cold fear emanating from her. It took me so by surprise that I almost gasped. Before, when I had touched her, I had seen deeply into her. I knew that her parents intimidated her as much as Russell did. Maybe even more since they were her parents.

"Why are you afraid, Fritha?" I asked her gently.

For a moment I thought she wasn't going to answer. "If I fail, then I will have nothing but a job that I hate to look forward to day after day. I might as well...do what Kegan did." She looked down into her lap as though she was ashamed of what she had said.

"I think that would hurt your family very much," I said. "I know Kegan's family is having a terribly hard time dealing with his death."

"Well," she said, sighing. "I don't think I *really* would. But I would want to. There would be nothing more to live for."

"There would be other books. This isn't the only book you will ever write."

"You don't understand," she said again. "If I fail with this book, my parents will demand that I stop wasting my time and concentrate on getting promoted in my job. I don't want a promotion. I want to write."

We sat quietly for a moment. I honestly didn't know how to reply to such a statement.

"How old are you, Fritha?" I asked her finally.

She sniffed, got up and found a box of tissues on the desk and brought it back to the futon. "I'm thirty-one," she said.

"Then, you know what? You don't have to quit writing. You don't have to try for that promotion. You don't have to do anything you don't want to do. You don't like your job? Quit and get another one doing something you *do* like. Or stay in it and write in the evenings. You can move out of your parents' house and not tell them your phone number if you want. You are an adult and you can do anything you want to do."

She looked at me as if I had suggested she get a wild tiger for a roommate. “I know, but...”

“No,” I said. “There is no ‘but’. You *can* do these things. You could take a hike to Nepal. You could swim the English Channel. You could get a tattoo of Ringo Starr on your butt if you wanted to. You can do whatever you want.”

“I couldn’t do those things,” she said. I was gratified to hear her laugh, though it was a weak imitation of her normal one.

“Yes, you could. Sure, you might fail at one of them. Two of them. The tattoo should be easy enough...Then you could try something else. It’s okay to fail.”

“Not at far as my dad is concerned.”

For a moment, I wished her dad were actually standing right there. I had a few things I would like to say to him too, before I threw him out of Fritha’s cabin, that is.

I stayed with her for a long time that night. I talked and she talked and I talked some more. The cabin became dark and it seemed to release something in Fritha. She told me anecdote after anecdote and, sometimes, I thought I was actually getting through to her. At others, I couldn’t see how I or anyone else could break through thirty-one years of the relentless subjugation her parents had heaped upon her.

It was long after lights out before she realized that we were breaking more than one of the rules. I helped her unfold her futon and crept away to my own cabin.

TEN

Friday, May 4, 1984

Friday afternoon was cloudy, cool and threatened rain. I pulled on a heavy sweater and picked up my lunch so I could grab a walk before it started.

The woods were dark and quiet. I hummed quietly in order to warn my fellow Colonists of my presence should any of them be brave enough to venture out on such a forbidding afternoon. I hadn't gone far before I found Lyric, Shig, Fritha and even Arturo sitting on logs, huddled deep in their jackets.

"Hi, Arturo," I said, surprised. He rarely joined us. I didn't know if he was as fearful of disobeying the rules as Fritha or if he simply wasn't aware of the regularity of our gatherings. "If I had known you would be here, I would have brought your manuscript."

He moved over on his log so I could sit next to him. "No rush," he said. His British accent was almost non-existent that afternoon. "I gave you a draft."

"He let you read his book?" Lyric said. "I thought the words of Arturo Kuppendapper were sacrosanct. He *never* lets anyone read his work. How do you rate?"

Fritha giggled but Arturo peered at me and ignored Lyric. "So, what did you think?"

"I liked it very much," I said truthfully. My real thought was that he should quit dinking around with rewriting it and try to get himself an agent. "I'm surprised you think it isn't ready to send out."

"Artie's book will never be ready," Lyric said. I watched her scowling into the woods and wondered what had put her in a mood.

"I've thought that for a while," Shig said. "I think it's ready, too, Arturo."

"Oh, I still have work to do on it," Arturo said. His manner was breezy but I thought he looked a little miffed.

"Of course, no one but the author knows how close to finished his work is," I said, surprising myself. As if I knew what it was like to be a writer.

"Shh!" Fritha said, her big blue eyes growing even larger. "I thought I heard something."

"You're always hearing things, Frith," Lyric said. "You hear ghosts and goblins every—"

"No," I said in a whisper, holding up my hand. "I

heard it too. Someone is coming."

We all stood, but before we had a chance to do anything else, Strom strode into the clearing and stopped short.

"Oh!" he said, obviously startled. Apparently, he hadn't heard our bantering.

"Strom," Shig said.

We all nodded to him. I don't think anyone knew what to say.

"You people aren't supposed to be here," he said. His frown made deep creases next to his mouth. "I go now. You should go back to your cabins." His Scandinavian accent would have been charming if his expression had not been so forbidding.

"Yes," I said. "You're right. We will."

Strom turned and marched away, back the way he had come.

"What do you suppose he was doing in the woods?" I asked in a whisper, though it was a bit late for that by then.

Fritha had started to cry. She had one hand to her mouth and the other on the top of her head.

"Who knows?" Shig said. "I guess we can all count on a speech in Meeting tonight.

"Oh, no! Oh, no," Fritha groaned. "I cannot get a demerit! I just can't."

"It will only be one," Lyric said. She was trying to

sound nonchalant but I could tell she was shaken too. "You won't get kicked out for one demerit. Look at Sarah. She already has one."

Even Shig was frowning.

Arturo cleared his throat and adjusted his beret. "I'll be taking myself off to my cabin now, if you don't mind." His accent was back in all of its English richness.

"Me too," Fritha whispered with quivery lips. "I'll see you guys later."

"Well, I guess the party's over." Lyric gathered up the remains of her lunch and stood. "Later," she said.

I walked with Shig as far as the path where we turned left and headed for the trail.

"I guess we should all be a little more careful," he said.

"Do you mean we should stop meeting? I personally think interaction with the other writers is helpful to us all."

"No, I don't mean stop meeting. I need the interaction too," he said. "I just think we should be more careful. We should have been listening. He wasn't sneaking up on us or anything. We should have heard him a lot sooner and scattered, or gone quiet at the very least. Oh, well, one demerit isn't going to kill us." He gave me a glance. "You certainly will have to be careful."

He was right. I hadn't even completed a full week

of my investigation. It wouldn't be helpful at all to get kicked out of Whalesong at this point.

* * *

That evening Meeting began like all the others. The pomp and circumstance with which Bleusette opened all of them had worn so thin you could read through it. Though I didn't dare, I honestly considered pulling off a great, loud, tearing yawn right in the middle of it.

As we gathered in the chilly room, Shig, Lyric, Fritha, Arturo and I all kept exchanging glances. We knew what was coming. I wondered what Russell and Bleusette would do if the five of us all accumulated the fatal number of three demerits. Would they kick all of us out of Whalesong? That would play hell with Bleuestte's superstition, if only four of her writers were in attendance.

Russell strode in, put his hands on the edges of the lectern and took a deep breath. A sigh, really, as though what he had to do next was extremely onerous.

"I've been told by...someone, that two or three of you were seen out of your cabins this afternoon."

Everyone in the room glanced at everyone else. Fritha looked terrified, Lyric's lower jaw was jutting out just the slightest bit. Arturo looked unconcerned, Shig stared at his desk, Cyr looked startled, Delilah smirked, Axel appeared not to hear what Russell was saying and Thorn looked guilty. I wondered what *he* had been up to that afternoon.

"Now, the person who told me this couldn't see who it was, but I'm going to warn you all…" He looked at each of us in turn. "There are rules to be followed in this colony. I should give *all* of you demerits, but that wouldn't be fair to those of you who are innocent. Henceforward, I expect my rules to be followed. Does everyone understand?"

We all nodded solemnly. Oh, yes, sir, we certainly understand, sir.

"Now, Shig Takano," Russell said. "We would like to hear more of the Samurai adventures."

Shig looked up at last, taken unawares. He quickly opened his folder and in a moment was reading about the Stupid Warriors.

I gave Lyric a covert glance. She caught it and shrugged. Fritha's face had gone red and she didn't look at me. Neither did Arturo.

Shig's work was given its usual mild praise accompanied by equally mild suggestions for improvement. As always, Shig nodded and dutifully made notes, though I knew they would be thrown into the wood stove the moment Shig was back in his cabin.

I was more than ready for my turn. I wondered,

in fact, why I had not yet been called on. I was eager to read aloud the last book Kegan Mercer would ever write. I was confident that it was a genuine work of art and was eager to share it with the class.

When he had finished with Shig, Russell at last looked my way. "Sarah," he said. "We have yet to hear from you. I'm sure everyone would like to hear the first chapter of your novel.

I cleared my throat, gave the title and started to read. As usual, Kegan's words began to weave their spell. His sentences had a cadence very much like poetry and it was easy to read aloud. Each time I read them, I noticed something new and found them thrilling. There was no sound in the room besides my voice reading the splendid words of a great writer.

When I finished, I looked up at Russell. I thought I heard someone – I couldn't tell who – whisper "Wow". For a moment, no one said anything else. Then Russell cleared his throat.

"Very nice," he said. "I see a few problems. Quite minor ones, such as some weak spots in the characterization, but on the whole, I would say, very nice."

Both he and Bleusette seemed surprised. The sense of astonishment was so strong that I could feel it without touching either of them. I wasn't sure why they were startled. Was it shock that I, Sarah, had written something worthwhile? And it *was* worthwhile. I sensed their interest in it as well, though Russell had given me a thin smile that indicated he felt rather tepid about it and Bleusette seemingly concurred. That was fine with me. I didn't really care what they thought. As far as I was concerned, their opinions simply weren't valid and didn't matter anyway.

"I thought Declan stepped out of character a bit toward the beginning. You will want to address that for sure," Russell said. "There are a few more minor issues that I will address in my written evaluation. Does anyone else have anything to say?" Russell asked. "Come now, let's give Sarah some comments."

"I thought the names Declan and Dixon were too similar," Deliah said. "I got them mixed up sometimes." A lukewarm, non-comment if I had ever heard one. I knew Delilah's pattern well enough by then to know that she hadn't hated it. She didn't seem to love it either, but she, apparently never loved anyone's work but her own. I was beginning to get the impression that the most important thing in Delilah's life was Delilah herself.

Axel, the man most known for no comments at all, actually made mildly complimentary remarks while he agreed with Russell's vague assessment of the characterization.

Fritha, Shig and Lyric essentially parroted Russell too, but I would know what their real feelings were later when I read their written comments. Arturo had nothing to say but was writing furiously. Cyr made some banal suggestions but otherwise hadn't weighed in much. The one response that I had thought was interesting was Thorn's. He was quite vocal about it, calling Kegan's work 'women's fiction' and saying that he could tell a man hadn't written it. Interesting, since a man *had* actually written it.

ELEVEN

Monday, May 7, 1984

I worked at getting more of Kegan's manuscript typed so that I could have another few chapters available to hand in that did not carry Kegan's name on every page. And, when I got the first chapter back from Russell, I reworked it following some of his suggestions, which seemed, surprisingly valid. I wondered if I was blowing my cover by my inept writing, but the only thing I could do was wait and see.

At Dinner that Monday, Bleusette had an announcement to make. She stood at her place while we all looked at her expectantly. She waited for a moment too long, as if we had all been chattering and she wanted us to calm down before she began.

"As you are all well aware," she said. "The West Coast Writers Association conference follows the term here at Whalesong." Some of us nodded. She waited another couple of beats before she resumed. I knew the others were excited about the conference, but I didn't care one way or the other. It was all I could do not to make that hand rolling gesture that means, "let's get on with it."

"I have been given a great honor," she said at last.

Most of the faces around the table registered at least some interest, polite and perfunctory as it was. Only Delilah seemed to look delighted. She nodded as though she already knew what the 'honor' was, though I doubted that she did.

"I have been asked to introduce," Bleusette stopped, presumably to let the tension and excitement build around her announcement. "I have been asked to introduce Lawrence Fawcett."

She let the author's name hang in the air. Everyone, of course, had heard of the historical thriller writer who had received numerous awards. His books lingered on the best seller lists for weeks and sometimes months.

"He's to be a keynote speaker on the first night of the conference," she continued. "And I will introduce him. I know him, of course," she said with a little depreciatory laugh. "He and I go back...oh, goodness...a very long time. People will tell you that I made Lawrence Fawcett who he is today." I could tell by her demeanor that she was firmly in that camp.

There were some polite murmurs and Delilah

stood and began to clap. The rest of us offered light applause but it wasn't until Shig said, "Congratulations, Bleusette," that the rest of us followed suit.

"Oh, *I'll* introduce him," Fritha whispered to me. It was all I could do to stifle a laugh.

I had joined everyone in the mild applause, wondering how a writers conference on a small island stuck in the very corner of the country had scored Lawrence Fawcett as a speaker. I wondered how long Bleusette had represented him. She wasn't a prominent agent. In fact, I was beginning to think she wasn't even a very good one. Lyric, even Fritha and Shig had all told me that they would be shopping for agents at the conference. The whole point of Whalesong was that authors could be taught by the great Russell York and then, when they were ready, be represented by Bleusette Huntsman, the agent who had represented Lawrence Fawcett. I wondered how the couple would take it if three of their loyal writers defected to other agents.

At Meeting that evening, I was ready to read again, but Lyric was called upon this time. *Pauline's Red Hat* was about a young black woman living and working in Seattle. Lyric had accomplished exactly what every writer would like to do. She had nailed the perfect opening and successfully hooked the reader. I had been impressed by her novel's beginning. I had thought it was expertly done. I had never thought about books' beginnings until I had heard Russell speaking in class about engaging the reader. I thought Lyric had done an admirable job. As she read the subsequent chapter, she managed to keep the interest alive. Her characters came to life for me and I was sure that the other Colonists felt the same.

I was writing my comments when Russell stood up. "Dearheart," he said. We all stopped and put down our pens. "I know that you do not mean to so extremely limit your audience."

No one moved.

"I don't believe that the world wants to read about lesbians and most assuredly, black lesbians." The words lay there in the air, almost visible. It had not occurred to me that the woman in the story may be gay. I wondered why Russell had come to that conclusion. And, seriously, it had not occurred to me either that Russell was racist.

"I see what you mean," Thornton said eagerly. "No one wants to read about that Women's Lib stuff."

"I must agree with Russell, dear," Bleusette put in. "There are very few people who want to read that kind of thing. I doubt very much that I would have any success in selling it at all."

I felt a hot disappointment as though I myself had written it. I knew that the chapter had merit. I considered myself a typical reader and I was eager to hear more.

Lyric listened to the comments, nodding occasionally. She knew the rules. She knew that everyone would echo Russell and Bleusette's opinion and then provide her with their more heartfelt evaluations and those would be the ones to be believed.

"Why don't you try a mystery, dearheart?" Russell asked her. "A cozy mystery."

Lyric cocked her head to one side with feigned interest, but said nothing. I could almost see a neon sign blinking on and off over her head that said "Kiss My Ass".

Arturo cleared his throat and the class turned toward him. "I think it was pretty good," he said. This was huge praise. For one thing, it had come verbally. Almost all of the verbal comments were in tune with Russell's. Arturo might as well have said, "You're full of shit. This story was great." I wanted to think that I had started Artie on this road of contradiction when I had disagreed with Russell's assessment of Fritha's book the previous week. When she had read the second time, the comments had been similar to those at her first reading. At the time, Arturo had chimed in with a positive, though tepid opinion. *Way to go, Arturo*, I thought.

"Mr. Kuppendapper, I really think that I am a better judge of what the reading public is willing to buy and what they are not willing to buy," Russell said. Bleusette nodded. "Stories about lesbians are not saleable. Stories about colored people are not saleable." I don't think I was the only Colonist to wince at his words, but Russell seemed not to notice. He tried his staring technique on Arturo who turned out to be an amateur. His head seemed to retreat back into his turtleneck and he said nothing further.

Russell gazed at Arturo a moment longer to make sure that he had completed the kill and then turned to Axel.

"Mr. Meredith, we would all, I'm sure, like to listen to your work tonight."

Axel proceeded to tell us about a short story he had just finished. He would read it, tonight, he said. But after tonight he would be working on a new novel. He had, he said, developed a sure-fire plot.

"Tell us about this wonderful plot," Russell told him

"I don't want to reveal anything yet," he said, his mild voice sounding somewhat pompous. "But you can believe me when I say that this plot can't fail. I'm surprised that no one has come up with it before. It's so good, it almost guarantees a best-seller if done by the right man."

One would have thought that Russell would be happy with this revelation but that didn't seem to be the case. He frowned. "I doubt very much that—.

Bleusette intervened. “I don’t think we should question the ideas of a man like Axel, Russell,” she said. “Axel has shown himself to be a genius in the past. We mustn’t question what geniuses do.”

While Axel basked in the praise, I chanced to glace at Thorn. He sat sprawled in his chair, his arms crossed and his tongue planted in his cheek. His whole demeanor seemed to cry out that he didn’t care and thought this exchange highly amusing. I believed that Thorn thought he was successfully hiding his scorn, but he wasn’t. He clearly did not like the attention Axel was receiving.

Russell, still not happy, conceded to Bleusette. He sat down and let Axel proceed with the reading of his story. As usual, the names were nearly unpronounceable and it seemed that even Axel sometimes had trouble with them. The story itself wasn’t any more remarkable than the last one he had read. At least not after having heard the chapter of Lyric’s book.

What was remarkable was the almost palpable waves of dislike that seemed to emanate from Russell York. Not surprisingly, perhaps, I didn’t think it was all for Axel.

TWELVE

Monday, May 7, 1984

As I walked back to my cabin, I heard someone behind me and found Shig seemingly trying to catch up with me. I stopped and waited for him. By then we were far enough from the Main Cabin that no one would see us. Axel had apparently gone ahead or else had done his normal disappearing act and the only other person who used that particular path was Fritha, so we were in little danger of being discovered doing the dreaded fraternizing.

"Where are Lyric and Frith?" he asked when he had caught up.

"It's Lyric's phone night," I said. "I didn't see Fritha go on ahead." I turned and looked back through the trees, but didn't see anyone. "I hope Lyric wasn't too discouraged about Russell's reaction to her book."

"Lyric's a pro," he said. "She knows that disparagement, coming from Russell, almost counts as praise."

When we reached the trail, I turned to head toward Number 8, but Shig said "Come on over to my cabin. I think Lyric will stop in. Maybe Fritha."

"I don't think Fritha will be along. She's getting more and more skittish about breaking the rules," I said. "Sometimes I can talk her into it, but I'm always surprised when it works."

"Interesting what you said about Russell's disparagement almost counting as praise," I said when we had settled on the futon in Shig's cabin. I felt the same aura of contentment as I had the first time I had been inside Shig's living space. He was a man with purpose and he was fulfilling it to his self-satisfaction.

He thought for a minute. "It's a pattern, really," he said. "Last year, Russell started tearing down my work. The onslaught was slow at first, just minor comments that meant he wasn't liking it much. Then he began to mention that I should be writing something else." He laughed. "Hence, the Samurai adventures.

"The stupid Samurai," I said, laughing.

"I began to think that my work was on the way to being burned on the sacrificial altar, so I started writing something else. The stupid guys I read about the other day...That thing is horrible but who cares?"

"Shig, why do you come here? I heard you read in Meeting. Granted the plot sucks but the writing is good. And, I read that story you had published in Analog. You're very talented. Why do you let them push you into something second rate?"

"I come here for the time away from home," he said. "I have a wife and three daughters. I love them all dearly but it's hard to get anything done when everyone is there. My wife and I both teach and when we're home, it's pretty much chaos all the time. Liz is very generous with letting me have time to write but I can't get the same kind of concentration at home that I can get here. All I want is to stay under Russell's radar and work on my novel."

"So, you haven't given up on it?"

"Oh, hell, no! I know it must be good or Russell wouldn't have started trashing it." He looked at me for a moment. "You...uh...wouldn't be interested in reading it, would you?"

"I would love it!" I told him.

He moved over to his desk and picked up a thick stack of papers which he handed to me.

"It's called *A Light In the Sky*. It's not the latest draft so you might find a few typos, but it's not too different from the current version. And that's a working title so if you think of a better one, let me know."

"Shig, I'm thrilled," I told him and fluffed the pages, glancing at a word here and there.

"I hope you like it. Russell and Bleusette didn't so..."

"Why would Russell trash work that's good and then praise stuff like...well, like Delilah's? It isn't that she writes romances. I respect all of the other genres even if I don't read them. There's certainly room in the writing world for romances just as much as for any of the others. I'm no expert, but..."

He laughed. "You don't have to be an expert to know that Delilah's work is...shall we say 'less than good?'"

"But Bleusette seems to think it's wonderful and so does Russell." I thought for a moment. "We really shouldn't be talking about the other writers. It's not very professional."

"You're right," he said with a mock frown. "Shame on us. But, it is strange, isn't it? Russell and Bleusette praise her work and then brush off Lyric's and Fritha's."

"And yours," I added.

"And yours. I don't get it either," he said. "I guess I've never really noticed that pattern until now."

"I don't understand the whole manuscript burning thing," I said. "What would happen if Russell and Bleusette pushed someone to submit their work and they simply, absolutely flat out refused? What could they do? That isn't against the rules."

He shrugged, then paused. “I knew a guy who used to come to the spring session years ago. I haven’t seen him for about five years or longer now. He wrote a damned good novel and Russell and Bleusette were adamant that he should be writing thrillers. This guy was very literary and wanted nothing whatsoever to do with thrillers. He hated them in fact.” Shig grinned at some memory. “They pushed him and pushed him to give up his book one year but he dug in his heels and refused.”

“Was he still working on the same book the following year?” I asked.

“You know,” he said “He never came back. I thought it was because he got fed up with them harping on his work but I talked to him a year or two later and told him that we missed him at the session. He said that he had sent in his registration code and they had returned it with his tuition saying there were no openings. He said he applied more than once after that but could never get back in.” For another moment, he seemed lost in concentration.

“So you’re saying that they saw to it that he didn’t return?”

“No,” he said, then more definitely he said it again. “No. I’m sure that wasn’t it. It was probably more because they didn’t have any openings like they had said. He laughed and seemed to brush the whole question aside. “I only know that I’m here to write and when the conference starts, I’m going to be looking for an agent."

"What, not Bleusette?" I said, only half joking. I really wanted to know what he would say.

"She's a second rate agent at best, Lawrence Fawcett or no," he said. "And, of course, she got Lyric and Delilah published." He shook his head.

"And Axel, I understand," I said.

"Well, I'm going to see if I can pitch to Janet Jeffries. She's Guy Loring's agent. You're a sci-fi fan. You've heard of him, of course."

I nodded, stunned into silence by the name that kept cropping up in my mind and wouldn't leave me alone. I had hoped not to hear it again. Especially not here.

"You ever read any of his work? Guy Loring's? He's a genius," Shig was saying.

"I read *Still Life: Earth* during the winter," I said.

"That's it?" He rose and went to a short row of books on his window sill. "You should read this one. It's his first, but I think this is one of his best." He handed me a paperback copy of *Last Train, Leaving Now*. I stared at it, but wasn't seeing it.

"Thanks, Shig," I said, speaking on auto pilot. "I'll take care of it and get it back to you."

"No, you can have it. It's a gift. I have other copies of it." He smiled a sheepish grin. "I have it in every edition. I read one paperback so many times, it started to fall apart. I'll get another copy. I'm excited as hell that he's going to be at the conference. That's another reason I'm here. For that conference. It makes all this worthwhile."

I stared at Shig. "Guy Loring is going to be there?" I said. "Here?"

"He sure is. He's leading the sci-fi seminar on Sunday. He almost never does speaking engagements. Never travels. I don't know why he decided to do this conference, but I'm thrilled." He looked at me. I don't know what he saw in my face. "That's one of the reasons some of us come to Whalesong for the spring session. We get a chance to rub elbows with the big writers, we can talk to agents and publishers...I know I look forward to it all year and I'm sure the others do too. You take that book and read it. If you don't think it's one of the best you've ever read, I'll..." he trailed off trying to think of something appropriate for his side of the bargain.

"While you're thinking, I probably should be getting back," I said in a passably normal voice although I felt anything but normal. "Thank you for the book and for the opportunity to read yours."

He laughed again. "You're going to get a reputation around here if you aren't more careful."

I waved as I left his cabin and headed to mine. The night was dark and silent. I felt the familiar nausea of dread creeping into me. I had thought I had left Guy Loring—David—in Hawaii, but no. Here he was, haunting me again. I felt a desperate urgency to run. To get to the ferry, call Easy from the nearest phone booth and get the hell out of this place. But I knew I could do no such thing. I had a case to finish. I was determined to finish it before the writers conference started and get off the island.

I had seen the conference brochure in the registration packet for Whalesong, but I had put it aside. I wasn't interested in the conference. Apparently, though, everyone else was. I realized then that it was an important part of the Whalesong experience. At least for the spring session. Arturo had told me that the spring session was the most sought after but I hadn't asked him why. The conference was far more important to the Colonists than I had thought. Had I known, though, that David would be there, would I have accepted the case? I would have, probably. I would have thought, as I did now, that I could be finished and gone before the conference even began.

As I neared Fritha's cabin, I thought I heard voices and ducked behind a tree although the night was so dark, there hardly seemed a reason to hide. From my secluded spot among the trees just off the trail, I saw Fritha's door open and Russell loom in the doorway.

"I think you'll wish you had made a different decision, dearheart," he said in a hushed, almost threatening voice, then he almost stumbled down the path and I realized that he had probably been drinking. Quite a lot of drinking, it looked like. I crept after him for a bit to make sure he was headed back to the Main Cabin then made my way back in the dark to Fritha's.

"Frith," I said, tapping quietly on her door. "It's me. It's Sarah."

She opened the door and I could see that she had been crying.

I hustled her into the cabin and shut the door. The last thing I needed was for Russell to double back and find me wandering around outside.

"I swear," Fritha was saying. "I thought it was Russell coming back to finish the job and I was going to kill him." She looked at me, her blue eyes round and furious. "I was, Sarah."

"Finish the job? What did...What happened?"

"He has been working on me since last term. He thinks all the women are just itching to climb into bed with him. Well, I've got news for him, they're not. I'm not!"

"Of course you aren't," I told her, trying to sound soothing. "Tell me what happened."

"After Meeting, he said he wanted to talk to me. I thought he wanted to talk about my work. Well, he did, sort of." She balled her hands into fists and pounded on her thighs. "I hate him!" She jumped up and began pacing around the small room. "I told him I was tired and maybe we could make it another time. Sometime when there were other people around, I was thinking." She appealed to me. "You know?" I nodded. "So, he insisted that he walk me to my cabin and I couldn't get out of that. On the way, he took a big drink out of that stupid flask of his and actually offered me a drink." She shuddered. "As if! Anyway, he pushed his way in and then he tried to kiss me. Not only that, he pushed me back against the door and… and groped!" She shuddered again.

"Damn!" I said. "There's got to be a rule against that."

She smiled shakily. "Don't I wish. He pulled something like that last term but this term he's gotten worse. Delilah must be turning him down or something, although I can't see her doing that. She would cheerfully step over Bleusette's cold dead body to get to Russell if she had the chance."

What was it about this place and these people that made them think they were so dependent on Russell and Bleusette? I wondered, not for the first time.

"You know," she said, frankly appraising me. "If you aren't careful, he'll come after you too."

"I think I could handle Russell York, all right. Would you like me to teach you some self-defense moves in case this happens again?"

She sighed. "No." Her voice was tired and dispirited. "I don't want to fight him. I don't want to make trouble in the colony. If Bleusette finds out, she would see to it that I never published anything for the rest of my life. If she thinks I'm after Russell, I could get kicked out of Whalesong and my father..."

"What would your father do, Fritha?" I asked when she didn't finish her thought.

"He would win," she said. She had squeezed her eyes shut and I knew she was watching some scenario running inside her mind.

"Well, you can't put up with Russell harassing you like that! He has no right to do that. And, Fritha, Bleusette doesn't have that much power, no matter how much she would like to believe she does. She couldn't prevent your book being published."

"I know," she said. I could see that she really didn't know, yet the fire seemed to have gone out of her.

I wanted to kick her butt and tell her that she was better than that. That she didn't need Russell or Bleusette. None of them did.

"There will be a big fight in the main cabin tonight." She looked at me. "Your cabin isn't too far away to hear it, especially on a night like this when they might have the window open upstairs. Bleusette gets furious with him when he drinks."

"Will she kick him out" I asked, thinking that if she did, I would see to it that Fritha spent the night in my cabin. The two of us would be no match for Russell.

"No. She always lets him sleep it off. Things will be all fine tomorrow."

Fine? I didn't think so. Nothing was fine.

THIRTEEN

Wednesday and Thursday, May 9 and 10, 1984

Things were relatively calm for the next couple of days. No one's manuscript had been burned. No one had gotten a demerit. No one had said a word to me about the SPD or Perce O'Dell, so I felt relatively confident when I headed into my turn at the telephone. I was sure that only my end of the conversation could be heard. Inconvenient though it was, at least it made communication a little easier. This week, I had another plan to test.

This time I was ushered into Russell's study and not Bleusette's office. The phone itself was located on Russell's desk. I was told to sit in a chair next to it and make my call. The whole time, Russell worked at his desk. Occasionally he would get up and rummage in his file cabinet, but mostly he was right there, listening. Not for the first time, or even the second or third, I felt like I was in prison.

"Hi Easy!" I said, sounding as delighted as I could.

"You're okay," he said. "Perce didn't hear anything from the island. They aren't listening except on your end."

"Good to know," I told him. "I've had this song running through my head. I can't remember the name of it."

"You want me to do something?" he asked.

"Yes, let me hum it for you." I sang a couple of lines from a Royal Blue song. We had worked out that those particular lyrics meant that I wanted him to send something to me.

"Okay," he said. "I got that. Is it a paper? A report?"

"No, that's not the one. It's something about a book."

"You want me to send you a book?"

"Yes. 'I'm so close to him,'" I sang. That wasn't a song lyric, Royal Blue or otherwise, but I was pretty sure Easy would understand. He did.

"A book by Russell York?"

I laughed. "Okay," I said.

"What one? He's probably written several."

"No, only a few that I know of. I think the last word is it." I knew that to Russell I wasn't making much sense and I probably sounded drunk to boot, but I didn't care.

"The last book he wrote?"

"Uh huh. But it doesn't look like it."

"You want…I'm not sure what you want. Another hint?" he asked hesitantly.

"Yep. A cover band did it."

"Do something with the cover?"

"Yes! That's the one. I had that record but the cover was so worn I thought I would get a new one."

"Ah. You want me to send you the last book that York wrote, but put another dust jacket on it."

"Exactly!"

"My God, do they open your mail, too?" He asked. He must have been appalled. He doesn't use the word God lightly.

"I believe so, yes."

"I will be so glad when you are back home."

"Me too!" I said.

After that, we had a fairly normal conversation. I don't know what, if anything Russell thought about my side of the phone call. If I were him, I would have been instantly suspicious as hell. But maybe Russell was so used to being in control that he couldn't conceive of anyone getting by with something right in front of his nose.

* * *

On my way to Meeting the next day, I saw Delilah on the trail in front of my cabin. As hers was all the way across the compound on the other side of the main house, I wondered what she was doing so far out of her way. I thought this might be a good opportunity to speak to her. Since I never saw Delilah beyond Class and Meeting, I hadn't spoken directly to her at all.

"Hi, Delilah," I said, trying to sound my friendliest.

She glanced back, as if checking that no one was about. I followed her gaze and thought I saw someone duck into the forest by the side of the trail.

"I know that you are relatively new here," Delilah said, "but we all know the rules. We have them for a reason." She literally looked down her long nose as though to intimidate me. She turned away and I saw a piece of paper flutter to the ground.

"Delilah," I called, bent and picked up the twenty dollar bill she had dropped.

She turned. "You *are* a trouble-maker, aren't you?" I wondered if she was parroting Russell. "I know you realize that you are flaunting the rules," she continued.

"You dropped this." I walked toward her and handed the money to her. Our fingers touched for only a second but not too short of a time for me to get a good impression of the woman. The main focus of her mind was not Delilah herself, as I had thought, but Russell. She wanted him. I would have said 'pure and simple' but there was nothing pure about her desire.

Without saying a word, she took the twenty and walked in the other direction, deliberately, I thought, taking the longer way around.

"You're entirely welcome," I said. "By the way, the word is 'flout' not 'flaunt'. I'm surprised that a woman who considers herself a writer doesn't know that." Then I spotted Thorn watching me and subsided. I gave him a non-verbal greeting in the form of a wave, wondering if he was as prickly as Delilah.

He caught up to me after a moment and seemed eager enough to talk.

"Hello, neighbor," he said. His gaze travelled all the way from the top of my head to the tips of my shoes and back again.

I smiled. I had not spoken to Thorn at all, either. Like Delilah, I had only seen him at Class, Meeting and Dinner. I needed to speak to each one of the colonists if I could manage it. Now seemed like a good time to take on Thorn.

He tagged along with me and we headed in the direction of the Main Cabin. Usually, he went along the back trail. It was shorter for him. I wondered if he and Delilah had been spending a little unauthorized time together. Undoubtedly, it had been him I had seen duck behind that tree.

I thought about saying "What's up?" but was afraid he would tell me. I settled for "How's the writing coming along."

"Pretty fair," he said. "Pretty damn fair."

"That book giving you any problems?"

"Nope. It's coming along great. Oh!" he turned and aimed an imaginary rifle into the woods and allowed it something of a kick as he "shot at" whatever animal he had seen. "Got me a deer," he said. "Wish I'd been able to bring my gun. I could have bagged that 'un."

He caught my look and laughed. "Oh, hell, you're probably one of those bleeding hearts who hates hunting," he said good naturedly. "Don't worry, I got all my permits and everything."

I doubted that. He was a felon, after all. Any gun ownership on his part would be illegal.

"I guess you're not as much a stickler for the rules as Delilah is, are you?" I said.

He chuckled. "Naw. I've never been much of a man for rules. I do what I want, when I want." He performed one of those fake nonchalant yawns and stretches he had a habit of doing. "Yeah, there aren't many rules that I haven't broken I guess."

Oh brother, I thought. I had known guys like him before. Everyone has. They're the men who are so afraid that they will be thought of as less than men, they actually turn maleness into a caricature. It isn't a good look. I heartily wished I could get a read on him without touching him, but that wasn't very likely. Normally, I had no trouble touching people. Just a quick hand on the arm or even an accidental nudge will give me quite a lot of information, but I was in no hurry to touch this guy. I was sure that any move I made toward him would be misinterpreted to my detriment. Nevertheless, I decided to take the plunge.

I pretended to stumble and made a grab for his arm. In that second, I saw that he had great disdain for women and that he was not terribly smart. *I knew that without even touching him,* I told myself. I wondered if that was all there was to him.

We walked on without speaking. I suspected he was shyer than he wanted me to know. Either that, or he did care about the rules. Either way, though I knew that at some point I had to talk to him, right then was not the time after all.

* * *

That night I was asked to read again. I had noticed that, while there was no regular rotation, we each read about twice a week. Every day, I made sure that I was prepared. I had re-typed all of Kegan's manuscript with my own name listed at the top. When I was critiqued and offered suggestions, it was on my own copy that I made the changes. Kegan's intact manuscript rested in the bottom of my briefcase/doctor's bag and that was locked.

The criticism was harsh from Russell and harsher still from Delilah and Axel who were seemingly unable to find anything at all about it to praise. Russell's suggestion was for me to give up "literary works" and try a romance. Delilah actually preened when he voiced that opinion as though she carried proprietary rights to the genre. I was once again amused by how touchy I felt about the criticisms considering that I had not actually written the work myself.

Walking out of Meeting, I saw Fritha, Lyric and Shig all give me covert winks and reassuring smiles. I knew there would be a gathering at one of their cabins that night. I raised my eyebrows at Shig and he cocked his head toward Lyric, who nodded. We were getting quite adept at communicating without talking.

It truly amazed me how grade-school all of it was. It seemed that much, much more could be accomplished by open communication between all of the particulars.

The wind had picked up and it felt like a spring storm was in the offing. So far, we had had reasonably decent weather for the Strait at that time of year. I stopped by my cabin to put on my sweater under my jacket.

When I reached Lyric's cabin, Shig and Fritha were already there, looking windblown. I settled on the floor with Lyric while Fritha and Shig sat on the futon.

"If I was polite, I'd let one of you ladies sit on the futon and I'd take the floor," Shig said without making a move to rise.

"If you were sexist, you mean?" Lyric put in smoothly. I reached over and high-fived her.

"We men can't win, you know," Shig said. He was trying to sound put out but he didn't fool any of us. We all knew what an easy going guy he truly was. "We're doomed no matter what we say. And I'm doubly doomed because I'm Asian and male."

"I'm triply doomed because I'm Black, female and short," Lyric said, sounding pleased with herself.

"I'm doomed too," Fritha said, looking affronted. I was surprised to see her so animated. I think we all were. She had been more than usually vigilant since Strom had caught us in the woods. It was my opinion that contact with the rest of us was the best thing for her, despite Russell and Bleusette.

"Why are you doomed?" all three of us asked.

"I'm blonde. No one takes blondes seriously." We all scoffed and snorted.

"Are you saying that the only one here who isn't doomed is Sarah?" Shig asked. They all looked at me.

"She's doomed because Russell and Bleusette trashed her work tonight," Lyric said.

"That's not doomed," Shig said. "That means it's good."

"This is the second time," I said.

"It was great," Shig said. "I'd say you have one more chance, maybe two, before you're asked to turn it in for ritual sacrifice at the Sacred Altar of Defeat."

"So you liked it?" I asked them. "I haven't read your comments yet."

"Yes, we loved it," Fritha said. "Before you came in we were all talking about it. It was wonderful. It was so wonderful that they will probably make you get rid of it and write something awful like Sci Fi-Romance or something." Her face went pink and she turned to Shig. "I'm sorry, I didn't mean that Sci Fi is bad! I only meant—"

"It's okay, Frith," Shig said. "I know what you meant. I don't think I would like sci-fi romance either."

"Why would they destroy only the good manuscripts, though, do you think?" I asked, really puzzled. "I just don't understand that reasoning at all."

Shig shrugged. "Who knows what goes through the inscrutable minds of R and B? I could see the writing on the wall, so to speak, after the second time they trashed my book. I knew what was coming so I set it aside and did one of those Samurai adventures they were always trying to get me to do. It's terrible, but that seems to satisfy Russell. I haven't heard any talk of trashing one of those." He shrugged again. "I don't get it either. I only know that during the day I work on my novel and when it comes time to read, I drag out one of the Samurai things to get through it unscathed."

Lyric turned to me. "What did Russell tell you that you should be writing? Romance?" I nodded. "My advice to you, then, is to write one. It doesn't matter if it's bad. Or, better yet, write a good one. They can just keep giving you suggestions to their hearts' content and you can keep writing it, like Arturo. Or let Bleusette sell it, but don't stop work on *The Book of Signs*. I expect that to be on the best seller list someday.

"But once you stop reading the good stuff in Meeting," I began, thinking, "they, or at least Russell, seems to dismiss you. They treat you like they treat Arturo. They treat him like his work doesn't matter. The only time you matter to them is when you're working on the *real* writing, the stuff that matters. It's like they want you to hand it over to Bleusette for the—how did you put it, Shig? The 'ritual sacrifice on the sacred altar of defeat'? Once they think you've stopped working on that, they tend to ignore you. Not you, Shig. Well, yes, I guess I do mean you. They don't give you the careful thought and constructive criticism that they gave you before you started working on the Samurai stuff, do they?"

"Now that I think about it, no," he said. "They pretty much leave me alone. Which, I might add, is fine with me. When I need critiquing, I have a good group of people back home. We read each others' work and get and give solid feedback."

"And, Lyric," I continued. "They seem to have started in on *Pauline's Red Hat* too. Because it's good. It's well done."

"I don't think they'll be too likely to trash that one, though," Shig said.

"Why not? I think they will," I said. "Russell said it wasn't saleable and told her to write a cozy mystery."

"I think he said that more because he's a racist homophobe than anything else," Shig said.

"Hear, hear!" Lyric said. "Anyway, I don't care what he says."

"You were talking about how they treat Arturo, Sarah," Fritha said. "How do you think they treat him? He reads too. Just like the rest of us. And his book is good."

"Oh, yes, they have him read," I said. "But the criticism they give him is superficial. Arturo's been working on the same manuscript for years, he says. He gave it to me to read. It *is* good. Not Agatha Christie, but good. Russell and Bleusette don't seem to be interested in his work at all, even though I think it's definitely publishable. My feeling is that

Arturo isn't all that interested in getting his book published. I think he likes the idea of being a writer but not actually doing the work and becoming one. Do you understand what I'm saying?"

"I think so," Shig said. "Arturo wants people to know he's a writer. It doesn't matter to him if he actually has published a book or not."

"Exactly," I said. "And Russell and Bleusette aren't interested in his work because it's a bit pedestrian. If it were truly outstanding, they would ask him to turn it over for sacrifice and steer him to something else. I see it happening, but I don't understand why."

"Jealousy?" Lyric offered.

"Because Russell hasn't had a book published for a long time, you mean?" Fritha asked.

Lyric nodded.

"Have any of you actually read any of Russell's work?"

"I read *Velvet Wings and Mud,*" Lyric said, reaching to pull her sweater across her shoulders. I stretched to help her and touched her arm. "I thought it was genius. It's what made me apply to Whalesong in the first place." I knew, with a little jolt of surprise that she was lying. *Interesting,* I thought. *Why lie about that?*

"I read *The Sailors All Go Home,* Shig said. "Not exactly my thing, but it was well done. Brilliant, in fact."

Fritha did one of those reflexive gestures and looked at her wristwatch which wasn't there.

"Cyr told me that he thinks Russell is one of the best writers ever born or something like that. He idolizes the man," I said. "If he's so good, why would he be jealous of other writers' work? And why isn't he still writing? Anyone know when the last time he was published is?"

"He told us that he's had a few novels published under a pseudonym," Lyric said. "And a couple of volumes of short fiction."

"Oh, right. And that short story he read part of in class. Bailey Attwood was his pseudonym. I have to wonder why he would use a different name," I murmured.

"Oh, my gosh!" Fritha suddenly stood. "It must be late. We should be getting back." She stepped to the door, opened it and carefully looked both directions.

"Wait, Fritha," I said. "I'll walk with you." I fished my watch out of my pocket. It was five minutes until 10:00.

"That's okay," she whispered and stepped outside then disappeared into the dark.

"Was it something we said?" Lyric said. "Or does she think she'll turn into a pumpkin at ten o'clock?"

"It doesn't take her long to get fidgety," Shig said.

"I guess I should follow and make sure she makes it back to her cabin okay," I said. "Russell has been paying her what you might call unwanted attentions."

"Ugh!" Lyric said. "Yes, make sure she's safe. You'll have to continue your detective work another day, Sarah."

Just for a moment, I was taken aback by Lyric's comment. But, I realized, it was just talk, after all.

The wind whipped my hair on the way down the dark trail to my cabin. I thought about Bleusette ritually burning manuscripts. I hadn't actually witnessed it yet, but I had already decided to continue submitting Kegan's work. It seemed only a matter of time before it would become smoke on the altar. I wanted to see how it worked. Of course, it would be my copy that burned, not Kegan's. His was waiting patiently in my briefcase to be returned to the Mercers. More than ever, I was convinced that *The Book of Signs* was destined for something big.

Before I reached Fritha's cabin, I thought I heard someone following me. I turned but didn't see anyone.

"Shig?" I called softly but the wind carried my voice away. The trees overhead waved frantically as the air moaned through them. Instead of continuing, I stepped off of the trail. No one came by. It was impossible to hear anything other than the gale and so dark, I could see nothing at all. I waited a moment then returned to the trail. It was deep dark but I was reluctant to use my flashlight and announce my whereabouts in case there was someone following me. Through the thicket of trees, I saw a glimmer of light from Fritha's cabin. Then it went out. I didn't know if it was because the electricity had been turned off or if she had done it herself. I heard nothing from inside though. Reassured that she had gotten in safely, I continued my trek to my own cabin.

I stopped again when I was sure I had heard the crunch of shoes on the dirt trail. This time I stayed in the middle intending to face whoever was following me. It would have been suicide to run in the total darkness anyway. An exposed root could break a bone in seconds. I tried to peer through the blackness but could see nothing.

I didn't even feel whatever it was that hit me. Only after I awoke, disoriented and somehow lying on the ground, did I realize I had been struck by something. I felt a lump on the back of my head, and my knees burned. I got to my feet and spotted the glow of my flashlight in some nearby underbrush. Its reassuring light helped me get back to my cabin.

FOURTEEN

Monday May 14

On Monday, the rains came. I had read that the islands didn't get much precipitation, but that Monday made up for all of the previous dry days. The trail was an obstacle course of puddles. The trees dripped and the clouds seemed to have gathered among them. I thought I was not the only Colonist who had not brought a raincoat.

As I entered Class that morning, I saw Delilah looking with disgust at the trail of muddy footprints on the white tiled floor. She carefully stepped over and around them, not wanting to defile her gold shoes. I saw a small clump of mud clinging to the back of the left one and smiled, feeling mean.

Fritha, breathless, came in just after I did. She silently pulled me back out the door. She looked around. I could see she was shaking. "Sarah, someone saw me coming home from Shig's last night!" she whispered. I'm going to get a demerit!

"Who was it? Did you see?" I couldn't tell if it was

rain or tears that were streaking her face.

"No, I couldn't tell who it was. I just know someone saw me."

"Maybe not, Fritha," I told her, making my voice as calm and unalarmed as I could. "Sometimes the forest plays tricks on me and I think I see things that aren't there. Maybe that's what happened to you."

Her blue eyes were huge and round and I saw her chin begin to tremble. "No! I saw someone. I did. It was just too dark to see who it was."

"Well, maybe whoever it was couldn't see you clearly either." I put my hand on her arm. I saw Thorn turn the corner and head in our direction. "We have to go in. Don't worry." I didn't have time for more than that before Axel arrived and we all went into the classroom together.

Nothing was said about Fritha or anyone else during class that morning, but Fritha did not seem to relax. Instead, I thought she grew more tense as the morning wore on. I noticed that she took no notes at all, though she normally was almost religious about writing down whatever she heard come out of Russell's mouth.

On the way out, Lyric caught up to me when we were out of sight of the Main Cabin. "What's up with Fritha?" she asked. "She's been acting spooky all morning."

"Someone saw her leaving Shig's last night. She's

sure she's going to get a demerit." We walked fast, skirting puddles and little quagmires of mud.

"Russell usually saves the real juicy stuff for Meeting, the bastard. He loves to let people suffer."

I glanced behind and saw Axel using the path for once. I just had time for a quick, "Meet me in the Bathhouse when you've finished your lunch."

Lyric nodded and we split off to go to our cabins. I wondered if Axel had seen us. But then, I didn't really care. I was thoroughly tired of having to act like a teenager who had been grounded.

I knew no one would be gathering in the woods that day, so I had planned to work on my journal. I ate my lunch, or at least the part of it that didn't contain ham. Whose decision was it to include ham all the time? I was getting a little tired of cheese sandwiches.

While I ate, I mulled over how therapeutic I had found writing to be. Once I had gotten past the idea that it had to be perfect right from the get go, I found myself pouring out things that I hadn't even realized were in me.

But that would have to wait. I had a bit of laundry to do. I didn't really have enough for a load, but one of my optional hours in the Bathhouse was just after lunch on Monday. Or was it Tuesday? Again, I didn't care. They could regiment all they wanted. I was happy enough to go to Class, Monday Dinner and even Meeting, but the niggly little rules got old *very* quickly.

Lyric was there when I arrived. She was loading a washer with only a couple of pairs of socks and a t-shirt so we combined her laundry with my jeans and shirts. "They probably don't want our laundry fraternizing either," I said and she laughed.

"So what happened?" she asked when we had started the wash. We sat on the small folding table. Of course, Bleusette and Russell wouldn't have thought of putting in chairs for the Colonists waiting for their laundry.

"I only know that she saw someone who appeared to be watching when she left Shig's. She doesn't know who it was, but it should be easy enough to find out."

"Probably Delilah," Lyric said. She dragged a roll of Life Savers from her pocket and offered me one. The next one in the roll was orange, my favorite, so I took it. "She loves to snoop."

"So does Arturo," I said.

"Yeah, but he wouldn't tell on Fritha. It might be Cyr. He snoops and then he tattles to Russell. He thinks it will get him into the golden circle.

It made me laugh to think of Delilah, Axel and Thorn as the golden circle. The Entourage, yes, but there was nothing golden about any of them with the possible exception of Delilah's shoes.

"How are we going to find out?" she asked.

"Don't worry. I have my ways."

By that evening, Fritha was nearly frantic. She ate almost no dinner and didn't say a word to anyone. Bleusette chattered endlessly about Lawrence Fawcett and it was a relief to escape even if it was only for Meeting.

I saw Fritha standing in the door of the Meeting room and she seemed unable to take the step that would bring her in. Eventually, though, she had to move to allow Axel and Shig to enter. She sat down next to me. I gave her a smile that I hoped was reassuring but I think it was lost on her.

After the chanting had died away and the incense lingered in the air along with the smell of damp clothing, Russell stood at the lectern looking his most solemn. "I honestly thought I knew you, Fritha." He looked at her and she reacted by looking down at her desk. I silently willed her to look up, look him in the eye. Don't bow under his gaze. But she continued to stare, motionless, at the folder on her desk.

"You know, dearheart, that I must give you a demerit." He shook his head. No one else said anything. It was as if they were all intent on keeping Russell's attention from themselves. "Fritha, will you kindly recite rule number 18?"

Ha, I thought. *Even* I *know what rule number 18*

says. It was the only one I knew, but still...

Fritha mumbled something that sounded like "Fright shout" but it didn't matter. She could have said, "Fuck you," and Russell wouldn't have noticed. He was too intent on enjoying his task.

"Fritha was seen outside her cabin after ten o'clock last night," he announced to the class. His tone implied that she had at least murdered someone. "The rules at Whalesong are important to our careers, our well-being and our growth," he continued. I wanted to point my finger at the back of my throat in the classic, I'm going to throw up gesture, but I restrained myself.

"You can see that you deserve a demerit, do you not, dearheart?" he asked, sounding fakely kind and oh, so regretful.

Fritha nodded but said nothing. She had her gaze locked on her notebook. I saw a tear drop onto the folder. I wanted to reach over and shake her.

"Very well," Russell said and picked up a paper from the top of the lectern.

"Just a minute," I said. All of the heads in the room swiveled to look in my direction. "How do you know that Fritha was out after lights out last night?"

At first I thought Russell was not going to answer. I thought he was actually going to try the staring contest again, but he must have thought better of it.

"Suffice it to say, that someone saw her."

"Who?"

Every head swiveled again to look at Russell. Even Fritha lifted her head and looked at him.

"I don't believe I need to reveal that to you." Did he put a tiny bit of emphasis on "you?" I thought he did.

"I'm wondering who told on Fritha, because that person should be getting a demerit as well, since he or she was out after lights out too." I hoped like hell it wasn't Strom. But if it had been, he likely wouldn't have told Russell. I was fairly certain it was someone in the classroom. Sure enough, I gave each of them a quick look and Cyr's face was beginning to glow pink. Russell showed his hand by giving Cyr the briefest of glances too.

"Miss Augustine, I will refrain from awarding you a second demerit. I think you have much to learn from us and would hate to see you turned out at this point. However, I will thank you to mind your own business."

I was about to ask him what rule I had disobeyed by asking a simple question, but I thought I had stirred up enough disquiet for the evening.

This time he didn't even attempt the staring contest. He picked up the paper he had been reaching for.

He had had the last word, but I felt like I had won.

FIFTEEN

Wednesday, May 16, 1984

By Wednesday, the rain had dribbled away. The bump on my head from the previous Thursday was gone and my knees had healed but my jeans never would. It turned out that attack was not the last time someone would try to intimidate me, although I couldn't think of a single reason why anyone would want to do so. The previous night, I had seen the silhouette of someone outside just as I had reached my cabin. I couldn't be sure, but I thought it was Thorn. The size was right. I had discovered, through the background checks I had conducted, that Thorn had once been arrested for sexual assault. Worse, he had spent time in prison for assault with a deadly weapon. It is my opinion that people who use weapons fall into the cowardly category and Thorn struck me as just that type. Why he would want to frighten me, I didn't know. If it was him, however, he was going to have to do a much more thorough job if he thought I could be chased from the island.

In Class that morning, Russell paced in front of the window then came to rest in front of his desk. "Your characters must be alive!" He punctuated each of the last three words by pounding his fist on the gleaming oak. It was unlike him to express himself that way. His voice was naturally strong, but he usually saved any loud displays for Meeting.

"Your characters must have a life beyond the pages!" he thundered. His high forehead was becoming moist. "Real people do not stand like wooden images, doing nothing but mouthing words to one another. They move, they roll their eyes, they spit, they scratch, they pick their teeth. They have pasts. They have secrets. They have comedies and tragedies. These things show in their faces. Make your characters real."

I made a few desultory notes, but Russell's premise seemed pretty basic to me. Over the past several days I had learned much about writing and it was beginning to intrigue me. The idea of building an entire world and peopling it with characters and shaping it with plots was fascinating. I began to envy them all for their imaginations and industriousness. I briefly wondered if I would be able to shape my journal into anything readable. The idea gave me a little thrill and that afternoon, I put a fresh sheet of paper into my typewriter and let my own imagination take a tentative peek out at the world of possibility.

* * *

That night it was time to speak to Easy again. It was always so awkward, stilted and unsatisfying. It seemed like months since we had enjoyed a normal conversation. I wanted to tell him that it felt like being in a reform school for fourth graders. I wanted to tell him that I felt ready to stage a giant jail break and get everyone out before it was too late. But I could tell him none of that.

"Easy," I said as soon as he answered the phone. Bleusette looked up and scrutinized me. Maybe she thought that "Easy" was some sort of code word. I smiled at her and she looked back down at whatever she had been doing. If she only knew.

"Did you get the book?"

"I did. Thank you so much for finding that for me. I always wanted to read it." I had received Russell's book only a few days after I had requested it. Russell had opened it "by mistake" he had said. Apparently, though, he had not even bothered to thumb through it since it wore a jacket for *Love Story*

"I'll just bet you did," Easy said, laughing. Bless Easy for figuring out the book least likely to attract Russell York, or me, for that matter. If Russell had looked at it closely, he would have seen that it was one of his own books, and though he may have encouraged the reading of it, I was unprepared to give him any fuel for discussion of his own work not to mention an explanation of why it wore a *Love Story* dust jacket. I had simply wanted to read something of the great York and to see if everyone was right or if they were full of shit. Too, the gambit had proven my theory that not only did Russell York and Bleusette Huntsman control us all with what and how we wrote, they listened to our phone calls and opened our mail as well.

"So, did they open it?" Easy continued.

"Yes, they did," I said cheerfully.

"That's unconscionable," he said. "They screen your calls, open your mail and I'll bet there are a dozen other things that I don't know anything about yet."

"Oh, indeed there are!" I said, but I didn't want to talk about that. I had another task for Easy now. A task that I should have competed prior to leaving for the island.

"Anything else I can do for you?"

"As a matter of fact, there is," I said. "I have a song running through my head." I tried frantically to think if I had used this same ruse in front of Bleusette before. I probably had but suddenly, I didn't care. I needed Easy to investigate something and it might be difficult getting it across to him.

"Okay," he said. "What do you need?" He sounded

tired. I felt a stab of guilt. He was so tireless in his helpfulness to me, I hoped I wasn't taking advantage of him.

"I wonder if you can look this up," I said. I slid my gaze to Bleusette. She was very elaborately not looking in my direction, but I could almost see her ears swiveling like a dog's.

"The title has something to do with...It's a woman's name." *Oh, Jesus,* I thought. *He is never going to get this. There are only a trillion different names for him to guess.* I didn't want to say it because I was almost certain that Camille had been known to Bleusette. And, using a specific name would put her on the alert more than she already was. "You have so many records, I know you must have a copy of this one."

He must have heard my frustration because he laughed softly. "Calm down. We can do this. Is it another book?"

"No, no. Some woman sang the song."

"You don't want me to look up another book. Is it a record?

"No," I said.

"A woman? Check into someone?"

"Yes, that would be perfect,"

"And, tell me how many syllables am I looking for in her first name."

"Oh, just two."

"How many in her last name?"

I laughed. "Same here."

"So two. Let's start with last."

"You know I can't go to church while I'm here," I said.

"Church?" he said after a moment of thought.

"Uh...Yeah, the Catholic church..." I looked at Bleusette. She had begun to openly stare at me.

"The name of a Saint?"

"No. Uh-uh." I sighed in frustration. "I was remembering the last time we played chess. That was so much fun."

I was getting downright frantic and I thought Bleusette could see it.

"Chess? Chess pieces? Two syllables." He mulled it over for only a second or two. "Bishop?"

"Wonderful! I love it here." I smiled in Bleusette's direction and she went back to shuffling papers.

"Somebody Bishop..."

"I miss that caramel sauce," I said, wondering if Bleusette didn't think I had gone insane. On the other hand, I really didn't care.

"Carmel? Kamilla? Camelia? Camalla?"

I sighed. "No, not really.

"It's okay, Chey. Don't worry. We'll get this."

Suddenly I missed him so much it hurt. It seemed like so long since I had heard anyone say my name!

"We had a lovely meal tonight. I wish you could have been here," I said.

"Dinner..." he said. "Is it the name of a food?"

"Uh uh." I was beginning to feel like this was a lost cause.

The meals here are all good," I said, hoping I hadn't put too much emphasis on the second word.

"Meal?" He had picked up my intention. "Is that it?" He thought while I agonized. "Meal, meal," he murmured. "Camille?" he asked suddenly.

I laughed out loud. "You are so right! And, you're a genius."

"So you want me to check into the background of a Camille Bishop. She been in trouble?"

"Oh, I don't know. Maybe."

"Well, that shouldn't be so hard. I can let you know next Wednesday what I've found out. You okay, though? Any trouble?"

"Oh, no. Not at all." I wasn't about to tell him about the attack in the woods even if Bleusette hadn't been listening to every word. In spite of his promises, I was sure that he wouldn't be able to resist charging to my rescue had he known.

"You saying you aren't okay or that there isn't any

trouble?"

"It's no trouble at all!"

"Do you think this Camille Bishop had any dealings with Whalesong? Was she a participant?"

"That, I don't know for sure but I think so."

We chatted about nothing for a little while longer, then I reluctantly hung up. I almost thought it would have been better not to talk to him at all. It made me homesick every time. But he was providing me with valuable information that I wouldn't have been able to get otherwise.

SIXTEEN

Thursday, May 17, 1984

The previous Tuesday, I had read again without Kegan's manuscript going up in flames. The criticisms remained harsh and tension seemed to be growing. It felt as though Russell and Bleusette were almost eager for it to happen. They began to say things like "You won't find your true writer's potential until you release the hold this book has over you." And, "You know what must be done. You must break your bonds."

The week had been a productive one, at least. I read Shig's novel, *A Light in the Sky* during that week. It was so engrossing, in fact, that it took me just a couple of days to finish it. I had found it to be as good or better than any science fiction novel I had read and I considered myself a serious sci-fi fan. I felt a bit awkward telling Shig how much it had affected me, sure that he would think I was piling on the praise simply because I knew him. As a consequence, I don't think I conveyed to him how much I truly enjoyed it.

Another book I read with interest was *Velvet Wings and Mud,* the last novel that York had written (under his own name anyway) and found Russell's writing, as Shig had said, brilliant. I wondered why a talented writer like him would not have published any other works since. Except for the book of short fiction that he had written under a pseudonym and a novel or two that Lyric told me he had written, also with a pen name, he had no other works that I knew of. And why would a noted writer not use his real name? Why had he stuck himself on this little island determined to burn the really good manuscripts of his students and half-heartedly encourage the mediocre ones? There *had* to be something more to it than that and I was determined to find out what.

When I had started my notebook for the Whalesong case, I had made a page for each of the students and the two principals. So far, beyond privacy invasion and being an asshole, Russell York was not guilty of doing anything illegal that I knew of, with the possible exception of sexual harassment. Neither, I thought, was Bleusette. But I wanted to know these people. I wanted to know how they had come by the power that they so firmly believed they possessed. And I wanted to know the colonists as well. I wanted to figure out what drove them to this place and this situation, willingly letting this despot-like person have so much sway over them. It was a difficult job in any case, made harder in this one because of the restrictions.

Russell York seemed to believe he had a sort of priestly power over us. If I believed in such things, I might say that satanic power was closer to the truth. It seemed to have gotten a hold over him and, once rooted, had never let go. And he had infected the others with it. They had all but let it strangle them, as well. They seemed to have lost all objectivity and all ability to write on their own volition. For some of them, notably Fritha, every word, every paragraph, every page came into being only after assurances from York.

I reread the section about Lyric. She was a feminist and seemed reasonably self-assured. More so than Fritha, anyway. She had told me a little bit about herself; that she worked as a patient coordinator at a doctor's office. She had had one novel published but seemed a bit disappointed that its sales had not quite met her expectations. I wondered if she had expected publication to equal fame.

Bleusette had handled the sale of Lyric's first book and presumably would handle her current one as well. That is, if Lyric did not follow through on her plan to scout a new agent at the conference. Now, Lyric was writing a feminist novel that had been greeted half-heartedly at best by the R & B duo. Russell and Bleusette had initially been discouraging about *Pauline's Red Hat*, although I had noticed them tapering off lately. I seriously doubted that Bleusette would be interested in selling it.

Lyric had lied when she said that she had come to Whalesong after being inspired by *Velvet Wings and Mud*. I couldn't imagine why she had lied about that, but, then, everyone has his or her secrets. After Easy had gotten back to me with the scoop about Camille Bishop, I would hope to have a little better read on Lyric.

Delilah was an open book to me. She was arrogant and dramatic. She followed Russell's every move, every word with slavish devotion. In spite of her ass kissing, I sensed that she did not like Bleusette at all. I didn't have to touch Delilah to know that she was deeply jealous of Bleusette; would love to live in her home, wear her clothes, have her husband. Delilah was convinced that she was a superb writer, and she may well have become one if she would make the effort. She seemed content, however, half-heartedly writing the bawdy novels she produced. She apparently did not care whether she was taken seriously or not and seemed unwilling to put in the work necessary.

Fritha was even more transparent to me. Some of it she had told me and some of it I had gotten just from touching her. That is my gift, after all. I was determined to be a bit more touchy-feely with that crowd. They might think it weird, but I would tell them that I felt a need to connect with people and that's how I did it. The truth was always best.

Fritha wanted to be a writer more than anything else. She still lived with her parents and they discouraged her at every turn. I could see why she would be attracted to Whalesong. Russell York was nothing more than a surrogate daddy who let her write. Unfortunately, he wanted her to write something other than what she was inclined to write. She was used to doing things the way the dominant male in her life insisted. I thought that if she couldn't break away from her parents, she could never hope to break from Russell and Bleusette, assuming she ever wanted to do that.

Shig Takano had no agenda as far as I could tell. He seemed to know the score and was willing to work with it for the privilege of using Whalesong as a get-away once a year. From what little physical contact I had had with him, he seemed to be as open and honest as he appeared.

I had talked to Cyr Antonio briefly and he had struck me as a friendly enough young man, if a bit intense. Also, he was a snitch. I got the impression from him that he was attending Whalesong because of Russell, whom he considered his literary idol. I had noticed that he often went overboard on his agreement with whatever Russell said. And I had heard that he was always willing to throw the other colonists under the bus if it suited his purposes. He had proved that theory by tattling on Fritha. It seemed to me that he would very much like to be considered a part of the three elites whom the rest of us called The Entourage. Sometimes he seemed to belong in that group and sometimes not. Perhaps,

I thought, he had once aspired to be the up and coming young writer who had taken the world by storm when he was only in his twenties, but was slowly becoming jaded.

Arturo was a man of dreams. There was not much action in him. He loved to be known as a writer. His novel, *Auntie Sonya is Dead*, was probably not a potential best seller, but I thought it was definitely sellable.

I also knew that Arturo Kuppendapper was not who he said he was. I didn't believe, though, that there was any nefarious reason for his deception. I thought he simply wanted a more interesting name than John Smith or whatever it really was, and that he had carefully built his own persona around being a writer. Much as he had affected a beret to make him feel more so, he had essentially clothed himself in Arturo Kuppendapper. To me, he seemed harmless. He was simply enjoying himself.

Axel Meredith was an enigma to me. I believed that he was having an affair with Bleusette. If not an affair, they had taken flirting to a new high. His writing, the fantasies I had heard in Meeting, were what I would put into my category of mediocre. Bleusette and Russell seemed to pay little attention to them. Russell, in fact, didn't seem to like Axel very much. Jealousy? Bleusette shot down Russell whenever he wanted to criticize Axel's writing. If Axel and Bleusette were having an affair, did Russell know about it? If he did, why did he tolerate it?

There was so very much that I had yet to find out.

If Axel was an enigma, Thornton Swift was the opposite. I had that guy figured out from the minute I met him. He liked to think of himself as a "man's man," whatever that was. Bleusette seemed taken with him and I wondered if Axel's hold on Bleusette was in jeopardy. Thorn's writing was not what I normally like and I didn't feel qualified to evaluate it. He didn't make much impression on the rest of the colonists. Neither Bleusette nor Russell seemed to think his work was any more important than Arturo's. They simply ignored it.

The last person on my list was Bleusette. She seemed not to care about Russell, nor about the students nor about the books she handled as an agent, few as they were. Except for her erstwhile representation of Lawrence Fawcett, what she seemed to care about most was her image. She appeared to be concerned only for the way people perceived her and had little use for the others in her circle.

I spent the afternoon on my notes and journal becoming so absorbed that the gong startled me. I grabbed my jacket and pack, opened the door and almost stumbled over my dinner, forgotten on the doorstep. I quickly peeked under the metal cover, grabbed the dinner roll and pushed a mouthful of roasted green beans into my mouth. I slid the napkin wrapped cookie into my pocket, then gave the fried chicken leg a fling into the forest. The mashed potatoes and gravy got dumped under the porch. Then, late, I hurried off to Meeting.

That night, I was asked to read again. I was surprised. I had read only a few days before. Pressure, it seemed, was to be applied.

This time, *The Book of Signs* received so much criticism, I thought it might burst into flames on its own out of sheer embarrassment for existing.

"You can do better than this!" Russell bellowed. "There is no excuse for this." His tone reminded me of his mood that morning. He was loud and aggressive. Not the usual Russell.

I saw Arturo about to say something but I caught his eye and gave him the briefest of head shakes. Fortunately, he subsided. He didn't need to get kicked out of Whalesong because of me. It would be for nothing really since I wasn't even the writer. And, I was beginning to think, Whalesong may not last that much longer anyway. There seemed to be a tension building and I was afraid it was the kind of tension that may eventually blow everything apart. Little did I know.

Rather than let Russell see my face and read defiance or anything else on it, I bowed my head. It seemed to be what he wanted.

Bleusette stood and said, "You understand, Sarah, that Mr. York is acting on your behalf. He doesn't *have* to take on students. No, he is a successful author. He not only knows what he's talking about, he wants the very best for you all." I had looked up after she had begun to speak. I wondered what she read in my face because she stopped her little lecture.

Fritha was asked to read next. The reluctance was raw on her face, but she obediently began to read.

As usual, the story transported me to another world at another time. Fritha had a charming way of making the characters in her book feel like people I had known all my life. They had become real to us all, I thought.

Shig seemed as caught up in Fritha's words as I was. For once, he was not staring at his desk, but gazing at Fritha as if he too was wondering how such an insecure, timid person could transform herself into the genius world maker she was.

I watched as Lyric's eyes filled with tears when Fritha brought her characters to life and then eased a beloved faery child into death.

Arturo nodded and smiled at a witty phrase, seemingly not caring what Bleusette and Russell thought of his reactions. Normally, we were all cautious to keep our true feeling from them. I began to think I should warn Arturo to be careful.

Even Delilah looked stricken when an unexpected turn revealed a heartbreaking truth.

Axel doodled on his notebook, listening as raptly as the rest of us. Even Thorn, for a change, stopped his posturing and paid attention.

Cyr seemed as caught as we all did. His facial expressions changed from grief, to elation and back again with each scene that Fritha read.

Fritha herself seemed to become stronger with each line. Her voice grew surer and her words clearer. I was proud of her.

Bleusette and Russell listened as well. They seemed almost eager, though both, at times, shook their heads in apparent disappointment. It seemed only for show, to me, because I knew that Fritha had created a masterpiece and, I believed, so did they.

When she had finished, the room went silent. The faint lingering scent of the incense hovered in the air. A fly or a bee beat at the window behind the brazier. Somewhere outside, a bird called then went quiet.

Bleusette's voice cut through the calm and shattered the peace Fritha's work had created. "Oh, Fritha, dear," she said with a regretful sigh. "I just don't know how we're going to convince you." She shook her head and looked at Russell who stood and moved toward the lectern.

"Fritha, dearheart, you know what you must do. You understand what your duty is."

Fritha's lips tightened and she looked down at her desk, ruffling the edges of the papers she had just read from.

"We want the best for you," Russell said. "You know that. Now, I'm not going to make any comments on this piece because you know my feelings. You know that I think you should be writing a romance, or perhaps a vampire saga. The next time we ask you to read, we will expect the first chapter of some new work." He glanced around the room at us. "Are there any comments?"

No one responded. Russell's eyebrows lifted in surprise. "What? No one has anything to say? You do understand that this is a critique group and that the purpose is to offer suggestions and comments."

Still the colonists stayed silent, as though we had, by unwritten agreement, decided to stage a protest. *Good for them*, I thought. *Good for them all!*

Then Delilah cleared her throat and broke the spell. "I thought there was a problem with the viewpoint in one area," she said and looked to Russell as though for validation.

"I think there are many, many more problems than that," he said.

"I thought it was wonderful," I said. I saw Lyric, Shig, Arturo and even Cyr nod. "I think that Fritha is one of the more talented writers here."

"Sarah, dearheart, there is no need for you to insult the other writers," Russell said.

"I'm not insulting them. Fritha's being talented takes nothing away from them. I think they *all* realize how good Fritha is. And I think you do too."

"I don't understand you, Sarah," Bleuestte said, standing. Her outrage had made her face go red.

"Oh, I'm sorry," I said. "Is there a rule that says we are not allowed to disagree? I must have missed that one."

I saw the warning look that Russell shot to Bleusette. So did she, apparently, because she sat back down, though her anger was still clearly visible.

"And do tell me, dearheart," Russell said in a condescending voice. "What did you find so—how did you put it? Wonderful?"

"As I looked around the room," I said. "I could see that everyone was moved. Everyone was engaged. Everyone was listening. Including you. Fritha's writing has captured all of us. Isn't that its purpose? To capture us and make us feel?"

None of the others glanced my way. But I saw a few tiny, covert nods.

Russell carefully composed his face, but I could not only see but feel the heat of Bleusette's anger.

"You are new here, Sarah," Russell said, his voice controlled and tight. "You do not understand yet, the import of what we are doing here."

I started to say something, but he interrupted.

"Silence!" he shouted. Then he stood over me,

trying again to stare me down. He had no more success this time than he had the last. Finally, he said, his gaze still locked with mine, "Meeting is adjourned."

* * *

After Meeting, we gathered at Shig's. Fritha came along but only after some browbeating by me. I honestly think she was a little afraid to go against my inclination. I only wished I had that much power all the time. I was interested to hear what the others said about her work and I thought she should hear it too. Maybe if we heaped enough praise, it would water down Russell's and Bleusette's opinions for her and give her some perspective.

After we had gathered at Shig's cabin, there came a discreet knock. We all looked at each other in alarm. Shig opened the door to find Arturo standing on the minuscule porch.

"Art!" Shig said, standing aside to let him in. "I'm glad you could join us this time."

Arturo rarely attended our little conclaves. I personally thought he was shy. I had gotten that impression from him a few times. It may have explained why he seemed reluctant to offer his book for publication.

"I wanted to make sure Fritha heard how much I loved her reading tonight," he said. His accent was barely there. It seemed to me it got stronger with bravado and slighter with sincerity. I could have hugged him.

We settled on the floor as we always did. I wondered how outraged Russell and Bleusette would be if they could have seen the five of us. Almost every night, at least two, sometimes three or more of us gathered in one cabin or another or during the day, in the woods. Of course, that would be blatant infraction of the rules and we had broken them so many times, none of us would actually be in attendance. We would have been thrown out long ago. How, I wondered, would Whalesong continue without any writers to attend?

"Yes, Fritha," Shig said. "I thought that piece you read tonight was wonderful."

"We all did," Lyric said "You heard it. Even Delilah didn't make that nasty little expression she does."

"She said it had a viewpoint problem," Fritha said, looking like she had found herself on a highway with headlights coming straight for her.

"Pfft!" Lyric spit out.

Shig made a rude noise too.

"You know, we all know, that doesn't mean anything!" I told her.

"I know that the next step is for them to get me to

burn my book," Fritha said, her lips tightening in an effort to keep them from trembling. A single tear did gather in the corner of one eye.

Shig reached over and got a tissue off the futon side table and handed it to her. "That may be," he said. "But they can only get you to do it if you let them."

He turned to me. "I had to admire what you did tonight," he said.

"I'll be lucky if I'm still in Whalesong next week," I said, cheerfully enough.

"What I love," Lyric said, "is you didn't break any of the rules. Russell is furious because he can't legitimately put a mark on your record and give you one of his all-important demerits. There aren't any rules about being open with your opinion. They are just used to people always going along with whatever they say."

"Tell me this," I said. "How many manuscripts generally get burned in one term?" They all looked surprised at the question.

"Sometimes none," Lyric said and shrugged.

"Sometimes one," Shig added. "I don't think I've ever seen more than one. Maybe one every one or two years, I'd say."

I nodded. "If I let my manuscript be burned, then pretty much everyone else's is safe this term, right? Two would be a little excessive, don't you think?"

"Unless they decide to have a regular bonfire and burn two or three of them," Lyric said. "Besides, we wouldn't let you do something so utterly crazy."

There was a chorus of protest.

"No, we wouldn't," Shig said. "But I think Sarah has more to say. She looks like a woman with a plan. Let's listen to her."

"Shig warned me, right after they started getting the least little bit harsh with the book that I should copy it. Of course, we don't have access to a copier, but I did retype the whole thing. I wouldn't really let it get burned. They would just think it was the last copy."

"But they make us swear that all of the copies are handed in," Fritha said. "All of them."

"Well, I would tell them that the manuscript was the original and the only copy."

"You would lie?" She asked, her blue eyes going round. *Poor little innocent*, I thought.

"You should do that, too, Frith," Shig said. "You should retype your novel or at least the first few pages of it, then hand it in."

"They check the whole manuscript," Lyric said. "Before they burn it." She looked around. "At least, that's what... Or it looks that way, anyhow."

"Have you ever seen them burn a manuscript?" I asked.

"Yes, Kegan's," Lyric said. Shig, Arturo and Fritha all nodded. "We all saw that."

And I saw them burn Jim Winthrop's novel a couple of years ago and maybe one or two before that," Shig said.

"Did they riffle through each page and look at it?

"Bleusette feeds it into the brazier a few pages at a time. Yes, I think she does look at it."

I shook my head. "I'm having trouble figuring out why they do it. I don't understand why they can't let us all write what we want and let us succeed or fail."

"They do it for us," Fritha said. "They're trying to guide us. They want us to be the best writers we can be."

"But, Fritha," I said. "They can guide us without destroying our work. You know that your book is good. We've all told you that. Russell York isn't the only critic in the world. Why is he the last word that you'll listen to?" Shig and Lyric were both nodding.

"He's a writer!" she said as if that explained everything.

"Well, so is Shig. We all are." *Well, I'm not really, but I can't exactly tell her that,* I thought.

"But he's been published," Fritha said. She looked at us. "Okay, I know, Lyric and Shig have been published too." She looked like she was about to cry again.

"What Sarah is saying," Lyric said, "is that Russell and Bleusette are not the only authorities. They don't have the last word in what you do. You have it."

"You do not have to surrender your manuscript, Fritha," Shig told her. "They can't force you to."

"If I go back home and I've been kicked out of Whalesong," Fritha said, crying in earnest now. "I'll never be a writer. My dad will have won." She stood and looked at each of our faces. In a moment, she was out the door and headed back to her own cabin.

"I'll go," I told Shig and Lyric and followed Fritha.

"What did she mean, her dad will have won?" I heard Shig ask as I went through the door.

Fritha had not turned the lights on in her cabin. I opened the door and looked in. It was dark and cold. I could hear her sobbing to my right and knew she was either sitting or lying on the futon.

I didn't fetch the lantern and light it, though I thought about it. It was after ten by then. There was no need to get her further alarmed about breaking the lights out rule. Instead, I moved to the stove and stoked it with some of the wood she had stacked nearby. All the while I spoke to her in as soothing a voice as I could.

"Let's get you warmed up, honey," I said. "Then we can talk a little bit until you've calmed down."

She had settled into hitching sobs by the time I

sat down next to her and put my arm around her shoulders. She leaned into me and began to sob again. I let her for a little while and then leaned back and looked at her in the gloom.

"Fritha, tell me about your father," I said. I honestly didn't think she would. But poor Fritha had been instructed in what to think and do for so long, that she automatically obeyed.

"My father once told me that I was the stupidest girl on the planet," she said. Her voice sounded calm as though she was telling me that he liked to wear striped ties.

"Do you believe him?" I asked her.

"He's my father," she said, and looked at me in astonishment. "Why would he say that if it wasn't true?"

Because he's obviously a jackass, I thought but didn't say.

"What did your mother say about that?"

"My mother thinks that women would be better off if they let themselves be guided by men. She wants me to get married and have some children. She thinks that would make me settle down and forget about writing."

Oh, Jesus, I thought. "I don't think you're stupid, Fritha." I told her. "I think you're smart. A stupid person could not write the beautiful stories you write. They're quite wonderful."

She looked astonished again. "Do you really think so?"

"Of course, I do! You know I do. You heard me tell Russell and Bleusette so. Shig and Lyric and Arturo all agree with me. You heard *them* say so. Besides, you got one of your folktales published in a prestigious magazine. They don't publish bad stories. They publish only the very best ones."

She murmured something I couldn't get.

"And stupid people don't get Marketing degrees in college," I said. "Your father thought you were smart enough to do that, apparently."

She nodded. "My mom thought it was a waste of time, just like my writing. She thinks that women who go to college are 'not-very-nice-girls.'"

"Well then, I'm a 'not-very-nice-girl' and so are sixty percent of the female population. You don't believe that, do you?" I had pulled my sixty-percent statistic out of thin air but she didn't need to know that.

"No." She sat up and looked at me.

"What exactly *is* a 'not very nice girl?'" I asked her, more to keep her talking than anything else.

She shrugged. "I've never been sure," she said. "She teases her hair, I know that. She has her ears pierced. She gets tattoos and wears make up. She swears. She calls boys. She wears things that are too short or too low in the front. She wears two piece bathing suits." She shrugged again. At least, that's what my mother told me when I wanted to do any of those things. All my life I've been compared to the 'not very nice girl'."

"She sounds like someone I wouldn't like," I said.

"I don't like her either, but she's become like a companion to me. I live with her every day. I'll never get away from her." She wiped her face with her hands, not so much, I didn't think, to wipe away tears, but to somehow wipe away that image of the 'not very nice girl.' "The funny thing is, I've always tried to be good," she went on. "When I was little, when I got older, now. I've always tried. I don't feel like a not-very-nice girl. Well, sometimes I do."

I had to stifle a laugh. "When do you feel like a not very nice girl, Fritha?"

"Oh, when I don't do what people want me to do. When I go against what my mother and father say. When I write."

"I think your parents are wrong. And I think your parents are wrong about more than just that. I think you should start believing in yourself and not what Russell or Bleusette *or* your parents tell you."

She nodded. "You're right. I know you are. It's just...It's... I live with them."

"That's temporary, though, isn't it? You won't be living with them forever. You have a job. As soon as you can, save some money and move out."

"My mom says that if I move out on my own, I'll get into trouble."

"Trouble? What kind of trouble?" *What was wrong with that*? I wondered. Trouble was my middle name.

She shrugged. "The kind not very nice girls get into."

"What? You mean pregnant? I seriously doubt it. You're a smart woman. You wouldn't have any trouble at all. She's wrong again. Besides, a little trouble never hurt anyone. It hasn't hurt me."

She actually laughed then. It was shaky and a little moist sounding, but it was a laugh, nevertheless.

"Speaking of which," I said, standing. "I should get back to my own cabin or I'll be in more trouble than I already am."

"I admire the way you and Lyric and Shig don't seem to worry about getting into trouble," she said. "I'm going to try to be more like that."

"Good girl!" I said. "I hope you do." I put my hand on the door latch, then turned back to her.

She stood with the open door of the stove backlighting her with an unearthly aura. "I understand how Lyric feels when she talks about Moki," she said. There was a dark note in her voice when she said it. I waited to see what else she would say. "Sometimes, I would like to kill them too."

SEVENTEEN

Monday, May 21, 1984

The buzz all weekend was that Meeting the following Monday was going to be different from our regular routine. That was more than fine by me. That week only, Dinner would follow Meeting which would be foreshortened and limited to only one reading.

All week, Bleusette had been nattering on and on about a doctors' appointment she had on the mainland. I had noticed that Bleusette was hyper focused on her health. She talked often about her many allergies and the various illnesses and surgeries she had had. This time, I recognized the doctor's name when she said it and knew he was a prominent allergist whose office was in downtown Seattle. The appointment would cause Russell and Bleusette to spend the night on the mainland, leaving us colonists on our own for an entire night. I suspected it was also a chance for the couple to spend an evening out, have dinner in a nice restaurant, perhaps see a show or dance. Not only did I feel like the folks were leaving teen-aged me alone for the weekend, I knew that I could actually get something accomplished for a change.

After Bleusette had done her dog and pony show with the candle and incense, we were given an elaborate set of instructions for that night and following day.

"Simply because Class and Meeting will be cancelled tomorrow, does not mean that fraternization will be allowed," Bleusette had added to Russell's admonitions. "I wouldn't be going if this wasn't of vital importance to my health." I felt a strong urge to roll my eyes but didn't. "We expect you all to produce. There will be no slacking off in your writing."

"You will be watched," Russell said in his most ominous voice, while Bleusette nodded.

Really? I thought. *Who would be doing the watching*? I thought of Strom and wondered again why he had not told on us when he had caught us doing the forbidden fraternizing in the woods.

I was hoping that they would select me to read my manuscript that night. I was eager to implement a plan that had been percolating in my mind all week and I was ready to put it into motion. If I succeeded, then Fritha's manuscript might remain safely in her possession.

Instead of me, though, it was Fritha who was chosen. My heart sank. Fritha had been vacillating all week between bouts of heady independence and trembling uncertainty. I knew that at this point, her decision could go either way. Just the day before she had mentioned giving up writing altogether and getting on the next ferry for home. I thought I had talked her out of it, but in class that morning she had been stiff and robot-like. I didn't like her chances at all.

When she began to read, the room grew hushed at once except for her spellbinding words. She wove her world and peopled it with forest spirits, tricksy faeries and legendary creatures. We were rapt, once again caught in her web of magic.

When she had finished, Russell shook his head. "Are you still working on that?" he asked as though "that" referred to some piece of trash she had pulled out of the garbage can in the ladies' rest room.

Fritha hung her head as I silently willed her to be strong. To stand up to him. To tell him to go to hell.

"I won't say anything more about it, Fritha. You know my feelings toward this manuscript. You are fully aware of what you have to do."

"I know," she said. Her voice was barely audible.

"You know? You say that, but I don't believe you. I think you are being held back by the opinions of the rest of the colonists. The rest of the colonists who are *not* professional writers." He let his cold gaze sweep over us then come to rest for a moment, on me. "If you 'knew' then you would be ready to hand in your manuscript and go on to something more worthy of your talents." He let her sit in agonized silence for another moment, then asked, "Are you ready?"

She didn't say anything for a moment. She wouldn't look at any of us. I know that I was not the only one who would have given her a shake of the head had she met any of our gazes.

"Well," he said. "Are you ready?"

"Yes," she said so softly it almost didn't qualify as a voice. I heard at least one murmur from somewhere in the room. Lyric? Shig?

I wanted to stand up and shout "No! Take mine instead!" but I knew that an outburst from me would not benefit her at all. Instead, I would be harming her because I would no longer be allowed in the compound to try to help her. I needed to remain at Whalesong and finish my investigation. Now, more than ever. Nevertheless, it was hard for me to stay silent.

"What was that, Fritha?" Russell asked, but I knew he had heard her. He was simply putting pressure on the already sore spot he had created. At that moment, I hated him as much as Lyric and Fritha did. I wanted to jump up and twist the arm that reached out for Fritha's work until he fell to the floor in pain.

"Fritha?" he said again.

She picked up her manuscript with shaking hands and held it out to him. She was crying now, sobbing openly, not bothering to cover her grief filled face.

"Thank you, dearheart," he said and turned. Bleusette was behind the lectern by then. She had made her face blank but I could see the triumph burning in her eyes anyway. Triumph and, I thought, greed. She was every bit as gleeful as Russell. I wondered again what it was that made them do this. Surely, they knew that they weren't helping the writers. Somehow, I knew, they were only helping themselves.

"Is this the final draft?" Russell asked.

Fritha nodded.

"Do you have *any* others?"

She silently opened her pack and slid another stack of paper from it and hand it to him.

Bleusette made a great show of riffling through the pages of *Hildra the Queen*. She stopped here and there to peer at a page then continue. As she turned her back to us to feed the papers onto the coals, I watched her very carefully. I watched each movement, each tiny gesture. She seemed to be finding pleasure in her act.

Fritha cried silently as we all watched the pages light, darken, shrivel and fall into the glowing coals. We barely breathed. The room was silent except for the tiny rasp that the pages made as Bleusette slid them one, two, three at a time into the heat.

"Fritha has done the right thing, today," Russell said solemnly when the last page had been eaten by the fire. "She has taken the steps toward greatness at last."

Again, I wanted to stand up and tell him that he was full of shit but I kept quiet. I had something to do. If I was right, then the face of Whalesong would be changed forever.

EIGHTEEN

Monday, May 21, 1984

Dinner would be following Meeting that time and that time only. Russell had drilled this little tidbit into us. Russell and Bleusette would be getting on a ferry directly after dinner and wouldn't return until late the next night.

As if Bleusette's impending doctor appointment were not enough excitement for Whalesong that evening, she, seemingly not getting the attentions she wanted, had loudly declared that she was "deathly allergic" to tomatoes. At the same time, she physically recoiled from the slice that lay on her salad. I had actually seen the woman eating pizza and wondered what there was in the cooking process that made tomato sauce less lethal to her than raw tomatoes. Life, it seemed, at Whalesong was never dull.

Just when I thought she was through with her tantrum, she declared that she was going to speak to Jenna in the kitchen and rose from her place. We all sat, frozen, as her voice carried from the kitchen and the much softer murmurs of Jenna's voice responded.

"I believe that I have the salad without the tomato," Cyr said quietly. We all heard Bleusette's shrill voice clearly berating Jenna, saying that the woman had deliberately tried to kill her. He reached over and exchanged his salad for the offending one in front of Bleusette's plate.

Bleusette returned to the table and abruptly stopped when she saw the salad without the tomato slice. "Oh, I think not!" she said, looking around the table. "It won't help to take the tomato off. Even a trace of the acid..."

"I'm sorry, my dear," Russell said, interrupting her. "I believe it was a serving error, after all.

"I guess this dispels the myth that Russell does the Monday night cooking," Lyric murmured to me.

Bleusette glared at her but continued to cast disgusted looks at her salad. She had pushed it farther from her plate as though even the nearness of a non-existent tomato would cause her instantaneous death.

At last, we were allowed to settle down to dinner. We worked our way through our beef stroganoff which would have been quite good except for the hunks of meat. There may also have been an air of excitement at our impending freedom, limited though it was, if we were not worried about Fritha. She sat with her hands in her lap and her head down as though she was unaware that there was a plate of food in front of her.

At one point I realized again how much I had regressed. Here I was, eating food I didn't like, watched by "mom and dad" to make sure I cleaned my plate. Sis, in trouble, was being punished and made to sit at the table anyway before being sent to her room. Then I too would be going to my room and made to promise that I wouldn't talk to anyone. I was, essentially, grounded. How sad that my life had degenerated to this. I knew Easy would find it hilarious when I finally had a chance to tell him.

After I had slipped as many hunks of beef into my napkin as I could, I waited for a lull in the quiet conversation and groaned softly. Bleusette looked up and eyed me sharply.

"May I be excused to use the bathroom," I asked, trying as hard as I could to sound weak and shaky. I must have succeeded because Bleusette looked alarmed and nodded to me.

I made a show of rushing away with my napkin to my lips.

As soon as I was out of the dining room, I detoured into the Meeting room. I stopped and listened for a moment to see if I could hear anything from the dining room. Then I turned toward the lectern. There was nothing on top. The shelf under the top was empty too, as I had expected.

My next act was to inspect the brazier. The coals

were no longer glowing but heat still emanated from it. Toward the back, I spotted a corner of paper but it was too hot to reach over the coals to get it. I had to climb onto the window seat and snake around in back of the brazier without touching it. No easy feat and highly undignified as well! But I managed to pluck out the paper. I saw there were a few words remaining. It looked like the bottom right corner of a manuscript page. I quickly tucked it into my bra and climbed off the window seat. I headed toward the bathroom, dumped the meat as well as the paper napkin into the toilet and flushed it away. Then I got a tissue from the box on the counter, ran some water and went back to the dining room.

I returned wiping my forehead with the tissue to make it look like I felt better.

"Are you okay?" Lyric asked when I slipped back into my seat.

I nodded to her and glanced at Bleusette who was eyeing me carefully. Russell was calmly chowing down on his stroganoff.

"Perhaps you should go to your cabin," Bleusette said. "If you are ill..."

"I'm fine now," I told her. I made my voice sound strong and normal. She stared at me a moment but seemed satisfied.

As soon as dinner was over, I went back to my cabin, for once, being an obedient colonist and not speaking to anyone. I had a couple of things I had to do before I would be finished for the night.

First of all, I fished the scrap of paper from my bra. I had a momentary thrill of panic when it wasn't where I had put it, but only because it had slipped a few inches. I carried it to the futon table light and looked at it closely. There were only a few words. The top row said, "—mine. Tyrone and" and the next line read, "—e Rolex waiting. The". My first thought, of course, was, *hmmmm, I don't recall Fritha including a guy named Tyrone in her Nordic folk novel.* I was fairly certain that no Rolex appeared anywhere in it either.

Okay. If Russell and Bleusette weren't really burning people's novels, what *were* they doing with them? I tried to think of possible scenarios, but came up empty. They were stealing them, that was clear. But for what purpose? If they tried to pass them off as Russell's writing, they would be found out, wouldn't they? Besides, Russell had not published anything under his own name for years. A new book from him would be noteworthy. He had been a best-selling author in his day. He wouldn't be able to get away with passing off someone else's writing as his own. And if, suddenly, a Nordic folk novel by Russell York hit the bookstores...well, it simply wouldn't work. He had, presumably, been "burning" manuscripts for years. If he had tried publishing them, he would have been found out and he would be in prison by now, I was sure. Could it be he was selling them to someone? But, why?

I mulled it over and over but kept coming up

short. Perhaps my next task would help me find the answers.

At 11:00, I pulled on my black long sleeved T shirt. A minute later I was walking down the path with my briefcase/tool kit toward the Main Cabin. When I had retyped Kegan's manuscript, my lamp had been lit until after midnight, but Russell had said that my lamp was still burning at 10:30. I thought, therefore, if someone was patrolling the compound to make sure that we were all complying, it was likely at 10:30 or thereabouts.

All was quiet around me except for the sounds of rustling wildlife in the dark. Once or twice, I switched on my flashlight to orient myself, then quickly turned it back off. I was especially vigilant and kept watch in case my tracker came after me again. But I saw and heard no one at all.

The Main Cabin was dark and silent. I had expected the door to be locked and it was. I went around the house carefully looking for an open window or another door. I knew that if I found no other entry, I could pick the lock but I really didn't want to. In the back, the door was unlocked. Russell and Bleusette apparently thought the colonists weren't clever enough to look for another way in if they were bent on snooping. And, frankly, I couldn't imagine any of them doing it, with the possible exception of Thorn Swift, but he may not have had the motive I did.

The door led into the kitchen. I hoped that Strom wouldn't be in attendance, but I wasn't that worried about it. I made sure I made little noise and left the lights off. When necessary, I shaded the flashlight with my hand but kept it off most of the time.

The kitchen was modern and clean. It had a white tiled floor and counters, making it seem like a restaurant kitchen and it was, indeed, big enough. The cabinets were wood and, I thought, expensively made. I knew that a woman from the town, the hapless Jenna from that evening, made our meals. I wasn't sure if she made them in her own home and delivered them or if she came over to the York/Huntsman house to cook. The legend that Russell did the cooking for Monday Dinner had been dispelled at dinner that night.

I stood in the middle of the room for a moment to try to get a feel for the house in general and the kitchen in particular.

It was surprising really, how much I usually am able to learn from a house. People's bedrooms hold a wealth of information as a rule. Both psychic and physical. In the kitchen, I felt a vague unpleasantness. It was a kind of discouragement mixed with disappointment.

I looked in some of the cupboards and into the pantry closet, but it seemed normal enough. I spotted a stack of the boxes in which our breakfasts and lunches were packed and the covered trays on which we received our dinners. So Jenna did make them in this kitchen after all. I wondered if the discouragement I felt around me came from her.

There were canned foods in the pantry and the freezer was stocked.

Beyond the kitchen was a wide hall. To the right, I knew, were the two rooms where meetings and classes were held. The dining room connected the living room and the kitchen in the center of the house. Russell's study and Bleusette's office were to the left. The bedroom or bedrooms were upstairs and presumably there was also another bathroom as well. Some cabin.

I wasn't so much interested in the dining room or the Meeting and Classroom. I had been in them often enough to know that there were few secrets there, except perhaps, for partially burned scraps of paper.

So far, the overall impression of the house had given me feelings of deception. I knew there was something underhanded going on there. At best, there was dishonesty. At worst, depravity. I could feel an aura of secrecy everywhere I went in the house. I knew that at some point, I would have to go upstairs and snoop in the bedrooms, but I mostly wanted to leave, to abandon that negative space.

I decided to get the bedrooms over with first. The staircase, beautiful as it was, with its carved banister and newel post, seemed like a mountain. Each step made me feel heavier.

At the top of the stairs I stopped then peeked into each of the two room. Bleusette and Russell apparently occupied separate bedrooms.

Bleusette's room was French provincial. Everything was either white or gold. Frankly, I thought it looked like a prostitute's idea of luxury. Even the carpet was white. I slipped my shoes off at the door and stepped onto a thick pile that felt like my feet were sinking in up to my knees. The last thing I needed was to leave a trail of footprints. The air in the room wasn't stale, but it had a quality of un-freshness like the fragrance of a cheap perfume that was past its prime. I opened her closet and took a look at her clothing. There were lots of beautiful, hand painted, hand printed and embroidered jackets in a rainbow of color. There were a few designer suits and even a couple of expensive looking evening dresses. The same faint aura of unpleasantness lingered. I wondered if the couple had ever been truly happy. In some long ago day of youth, perhaps?

I didn't find anything noteworthy or remarkable about Bleusette's room. The book on her nightstand was *Pride and Prejudice*, a white leather and gold copy from some press that prints books more for show than for reading. I opened it and it actually creaked. Obviously, it hadn't been cracked in at least a decade, if ever. I opened the nightstand drawer to see if she had anything of interest. There was a package of tums, a small bottle of eye drops, a tube of KY Jelly and the usual detritus we all keep in our nightstands.

I gave the bathroom a pass. Well, I did peek in for a moment, saw that it was white and gold too and left with no more than a cursory look in the medicine cabinet. An inhaler, a prescription bottle of thyroid medication and some Dristan tablets were the only things other than the usual toothbrushes and mouthwashes everyone uses. At least she was being honest about having *some* kind of allergies anyway.

I moved out of Bleusette's room and headed across the hall to Russell's. His walls were a gorgeous shade of dark sage and he seemed to have taste a million times better than Bleusette's. He had one of those valet things that has a seat and a hanger for one's coat. The book next to his bed was *Rabbit is Rich* by John Updike and there was a bookmark in it so I thought Russell actually was reading it.

The aura in his room was a concentration of the miasma of unpleasantness I had found all over the house. I wanted to get out, but I still had a lot to do. I looked through his closet, his medicine cabinet, his night table but found nothing of interest. Still, there was that feeling that I kept getting from the house and both of the people. They *were* hiding something. They were up to something, and I didn't think it was a small something, either. I thought it was a something that would have big repercussions in the future.

I went downstairs again, glad to be out of the

intimate surroundings of the bedrooms. I glanced at my watch and saw that it was 12:30. I hoped that whoever did the wandering around the compound keeping tabs on the whereabouts of the colonists had planned to make only one trip that evening and had already done so. Before I had left, I had bunched up the blankets on the futon and put my wadded up clothes under them to make it look like I was sleeping. Unfortunately, I hadn't brought many clothes and didn't think it would fool anyone even if they didn't go inside.

I let myself into Russell's study. I had been in the room before, for phone night. The books on the bookshelves silently watched me try the drawers of Russell's desk. When I touched the wood, I got a sensation of deceit and avarice. The blinds were drawn so I made the decision to turn on the stained glass lamp on the desk. It was a beautiful thing of amber and ruby. Since working in Ab's shop, I had become familiar with stained glass and I recognized that lamp as being a well-made, expensive piece.

The top drawer in the desk was locked. It took me a few minutes but I managed to pick the lock easily enough. I found a typed letter addressed to someone named Bailey Attwood, stapled to an envelope with a return address in England. The Manchester Publishers apparently loved the novel that Bailey had written. The letter said *Boatman* was doing wonderfully and asked if he, Bailey, would be coming to Manchester any time soon. *Hmmm,* I thought. *Boatman*. I had never heard of it. The name Bailey Attwood, however, did sound familiar. I knew that Russell had read a short story to us in class one day. A story by Bailey Attwood, which, Russell had said, was his own pseudonym. So that would explain why Russell had possession of the letter. But it seemed to me that if Manchester Publishers knew that Bailey Attwood was indeed Russell, which they must, why had they addressed it to Attwood instead of Russell York? Curious. I took out my little camera and took a picture of the letter, knowing that I wouldn't be able to get it developed until I returned to the mainland.

A quick look into the other drawers revealed nothing remarkable except the middle one where there was a small bunch of keys and Russell's gun. I slid the drawer shut.

I switched off the lamp, relocked Russell's drawer with one of the keys and went over to Bleusette's office across the hall. I had been in that room as well. There was that same not-quite-stale-but-not-fresh aura in there too as well as the residual scent of stale incense. I wanted to get out of there as quickly as I could. I tried the drawers on her desk and, surprisingly, none of them were locked.

The top drawer held the usual junk; pencils, pens, paper clips, staples. Nothing, really. It seemed the desk of someone who plays at working. When I reached the bottom drawer, it slid open to reveal a thick manuscript. A familiar one. Fritha's.

I stood at the desk looking at it for a long moment. Why on Earth, would they steal manuscripts? It was obviously what they had done. Was *Boatman* a retitle of some manuscript they had "burned" in the past? Was Bailey Attwood really a pseudonym for Russell? How could they get away with publishing others' work? It seemed such a crazy idea that it was almost laughable. But I wasn't laughing. I flipped through Fritha's pages, then put the manuscript into my briefcase. I knew well that I was stealing and that I could get into a mountain of trouble, but I didn't care. What would the penalty be for stealing something that was already stolen? At any rate, I *would* get to the bottom of whatever was going on.

NINETEEN

Tuesday, May 22, 1984

The next morning, I once again felt as though we were all on Spring break. I got up early and went out into the woods to walk. A fine mist had settled in the treetops and it gave the forest a mystical, ghostly aura. I walked adjacent to the trail that ran all the way around the compound in one big circle. I hoped I was out of sight of anyone I might encounter along the way.

I had been walking for about twenty minutes before I saw Strom with his wagonload of breakfasts trundling along the path. He had stopped at Lyric's cabin, delivered her meal and was heading for Shig's. I made a quick decision and stepped out of the forest.

Strom, startled, stopped in his tracks. I waved and, smiling, went toward him.

"Good morning," I said.

He looked wary as he continued on his way. "Morning," he said. His voice was gruff as though he didn't use it often.

I caught up with him and we walked the path together. "I know I'm not supposed to be out of my cabin," I said. "But I couldn't resist the morning air. You won't tell on me, will you?"

He said nothing.

"I don't think I ever thanked you properly for not telling Russell and Bleusette about finding us in the woods talking," I said.

He still didn't say anything. I wondered if he perhaps he had trouble understanding English.

"I imagine you see all kinds of things go on around here," I mused.

He looked startled, as though he had been caught in some kind of infraction himself.

"Don't worry," I said. "You probably aren't supposed to be talking to me any more than I'm supposed to be talking to you. I won't tell on you either."

"Mr. York and Miss Bleusette don't like it," he said.

"I know they're pretty strict. They are with *us*, anyway. They don't strike me as easy people to work for."

He stopped the wagon in front of the short path to Shig's cabin. He looked at me as if appraising what I had said. Whatever he had seen on my face seemed to reassure him. He shook his head.

"Are you supposed to keep an eye on us besides deliver our meals?"

He nodded. He selected a box from his wagon and walked to Shig's cabin where he left it on the porch, knocked twice and headed back to the wagon.

"You are right" he said when he had reached me again. "I am supposed to report."

"Did you find anything to report last night?" I asked.

He looked at me for a moment. "I did not see anything," he said. "I was at home last night." He continued to watch me for another second, then continued on his way.

"Ah," I said and nodded. "Well, have a good day!"

I didn't follow him. I wondered if I had just earned myself another demerit. It didn't matter to me but I was interested in knowing just how much, if anything, Strom would report. And, since he had been at home last night, I wondered if someone else had been assigned to keep tabs on us intransigent colonists. Of course, there was always the possibility that he had been taking advantage of Russell and Bleusette's absence as we colonists were.

After I left Strom, I made one more complete circle. When I reached my cabin, I stopped to eat the breakfast that Strom had left on my porch, then set out again to walk the circle once more.

Just as I passed Thorn's cabin, I heard footsteps

crunching along the rocks, twigs and pine needles that littered the path. I stepped a little deeper into the dark wood and peered out from behind a tree. To my surprise, Axel came into view. He was moving slowly, as though he, himself, were spying. He stopped at the corner of the cabin and moved around it, trying to peer into windows. I could see from where I was that Thorn had hung clothing and a towel or two over the glass. Frustrated, Axel sat down on a split from Thorn's woodpile and seemed to be waiting.

I waited as well. Axel seemed to think that something was going on inside Thorn's cabin and I was just as curious as he was. We both abided, I sitting on a log with an almost straight shot to the cabin door and he at the side of the cabin.

Axel didn't seem to be the kind of person who would be sneaking and spying on his fellow colonists. It was different when I did it. It was my job. But he seemed out of place. He normally appeared quiet and dignified, wearing his ascot and tweed jacket. To me, he seemed more like a professor, not someone inclined to snoop.

About twenty minutes later, the door opened and Delilah stepped out. She looked both directions and then headed to the right, taking the trail toward her own cabin. Axel, waiting on the left side of the structure, immediately got to his feet when he heard the door and followed Delilah, no longer taking care to be quiet. I watched as he caught up to her. She turned on him, seemingly furious, said something then continued along her route. Axel grabbed her arm and spun her around to him. Without a word, she hauled back and whacked him across the face. I heard her say "bastard!" but I was too far away to catch any more. Of Axel, I could hear nothing.

Axel stood in the middle of the path and let her continue alone. At last, he turned and retraced his steps. For a moment, he hesitated and I thought he would confront Thorn in his cabin, but he continued past and disappeared from my view.

Well, I thought. *I wish I had known Delilah's cabin had been empty last night too.*

I continued my skulk through the woods for another hour but neither saw nor heard anything else.

The day had warmed. I went back to my cabin and changed into a T-shirt. I made some notes, though there was little enough I could add.

Delilah had most likely spent the night in Thorn's cabin. Nothing wrong with that. Axel must have known that Delilah wasn't home. Why else would he go looking for her at Thorn's? What had he wanted from her, though? And why the slap?

The main thing on my mind, however, was Fritha's manuscript. It still lay in the bottom of my case. I didn't quite know how I was going to handle it. I still needed to do much investigation to find out what on Earth was going on at Whalesong. I didn't want to present it to her because her entire demeanor would change and Russell and Bleusette would surely notice. They would be suspicious enough when they discovered the manuscript was missing. On the other hand, I didn't want Fritha to be so depressed. I was worried about her and I didn't think I was the only one. I had to find out what was going on before I could ease her mind.

I tried to imagine the conversation between Russell and Bleusette once they realized the manuscript was missing. Would they accuse each other of misplacing it? How long would it take them to figure out that someone had been sneaking around the cabin and had pilfered it? I thought the former scenario the most likely. Surely they would question Strom. I was fairly certain that he would plead innocent of any knowledge. And rightly. He claimed to have been at home. And, if he had been lying and had seen me, would he tell?

I couldn't seem to get Fritha off my mind. I decided to go to her and see how she was doing. As I went out the door, I picked up my lunch. On her porch, I picked up hers. Perhaps we could have lunch together. I knocked and called out to her. In a moment, she opened the door. I could tell, though, that she hadn't wanted to.

Fritha did not look good. She hadn't bothered to brush her hair and she had dark smudges in the pale skin around her eyes. Nevertheless, she let me in, took the container from me and put it on her futon side table.

"I thought we could take our lunches into the woods. It's a gorgeous day," I said.

"Oh," she said with a sigh. "You go. I'll just stay here. I don't feel much like eating anyway."

"Fritha," I said "I want you to come with me." I said it as authoritatively as I could. I had found that sometimes Fritha responded better to someone who seemed to be commanding her, rather than leaving it up to her. "Come on." I picked up the lunch box and handed it to her. "Let's go."

I was only mildly surprised when she obeyed me. It was no wonder she did whatever I told her to do. She, apparently was well used to following directions.

It was cooler in the woods and off the trail. The mist was gone and in places the sun filtered through the canopy of leaves making patterns on the forest floor. There were birds everywhere.

We found Shig and Lyric in their usual spot. They were silent as we approached, but didn't look alarmed or ready to flee.

"We figured it was you," Shig said and moved over on his log so I could sit down. They had their lunches with them as well.

Fritha sat next to Lyric but made no move to open her lunch box.

"This is great, isn't it?" I said. "All morning I've felt

like I'm on vacation."

"Enjoy it," Fritha said lifelessly. "It's all over tomorrow." She put her lunch box down onto the forest floor. "I think I'll be leaving tomorrow."

"What?!" Shig said. "And disobey the rules?"

Fritha looked up startled. "What?"

"Rule number 1. Surely you know that one," Lyric said.

"*I* don't know," I said. "What does Rule Number 1 say?"

"'You will be required to sign a pledge to remain the entire month and attend the four day West Coast Writers Association Conference at the end of the four weeks,'" Shig supplied. "We all signed it."

Fritha shrugged. "They won't care if I leave. They got what they wanted."

"I think you'll feel better in a day or two, Fritha," I said.

"I won't have my manuscript back in a day or two," she said. From anyone else it would have come out as a snap at me, but Fritha seemed so broken she was unable to produce any anger.

"No, but you can write something else just as wonderful," I said, thinking of her manuscript resting in the bottom of my briefcase. I wished that I could tell her it was safe, but I couldn't yet, not until I figured out what to do.

"So they can burn that one too?" She looked at me with her blue eyes blank.

"No, because you wouldn't show it to them. You can find a decent agent and get it published. I have every confidence in you."

"So do I," said Shig.

"And I," Lyric said.

Fritha stood. "You guys are so nice, but I know that I'm not going to be able to publish anything. If I were, they wouldn't have destroyed the manuscript. I'm going to go back to my cabin. I didn't sleep well last night and I want to take a nap."

We let her go, though I knew that we were all worried about her. I knew that now she wouldn't leave the island. The rules, for Fritha, were iron clad. She wouldn't disobey them.

"Whalesong is like an addictive drug to her," I said after she was gone. "It acts as a drug on all of us. It sucks us all in and has its way with us."

"No!" Lyric said, rather more forcefully than seemed necessary. "It isn't addiction at all. You don't know what you are talking about." Her face had gone red and I thought there was embarrassment mixed in with her anger.

"I'm sorry, Lyr," I said. "I only meant that she can't seem to stop coming even though it gives her great pain. She knows as well as we all do that this is not a healthy environment. Why are we here?" I had been surprised by her outburst. What was the secret that Lyric was hiding?

"We're here trying to do the best we can to achieve our goals," Shig said.

"But we can't achieve our goals by being restricted in who we talk to, what we eat, when we sleep, what we write. My God!"

"We can achieve our goals after Saturday by finding ourselves agents and publishers," he said.

"Then will you stop coming to Whalesong?"

He shrugged. Lyric gave a forlorn laugh. Her anger had seemingly drained away.

"I didn't think so," I said.

The day got warmer and soon it was uncomfortable in my cabin. I propped the door open and opened the window over my desk but there wasn't much breeze. This would be one night when I would have welcomed the chill of the meeting room.

Russell and Bleusette would be returning late in the evening. With the windows open, it was likely that I would be able to hear the van when it arrived. The thought made me a little depressed. Vacation had been nice while it lasted.

I spent the afternoon working on my journal. So far, I had included detailed accounts of two of my cases. I was pleased with the result but I knew I would never present them to Russell or Bleusette. I still had a plan for Kegan's manuscript. Besides, I couldn't let on who I was. Not at this point anyway. Maybe never.

It was getting late when I rose and stretched. I needed to get out into the cooler air of the woods and walk one more time to iron out some of the kinks.

The moment I opened the door, I knew that someone was nearby. It wasn't something I had seen nor heard. It was simply a sense that someone was watching the cabin and me in particular.

I pretended not to notice while carefully keeping to the path. Whoever it was, he or she was not very skilled at tracking. I heard twigs snapping in the woods on the left side of the path, then the sounds moved to the right. I walked for a while, singing under my breath to lead the tracker into believing that I was unaware of him or her. Then, halfway between Cyr and Delilah's cabins, I abruptly stopped and turned around.

"Thorn, you can come out," I called. "I know you've been following me."

He stepped out of the woods then, not ten feet from me. He wore a sheepish grin. "I wasn't following you," he said. "I was just taking a walk in the woods, like you. I didn't want to scare you."

The lie was so blatant, I could feel it without even

touching him.

"Uh-huh," I said. "Well, I'm heading back now. Have a nice walk."

I continued to walk past Delilah's and as soon as the path made a turn, I ducked behind a tree. He was so clumsy I would know it at once if he was continuing to follow. He didn't. Instead, he stopped at Delilah's door and knocked. She opened it, but apparently was no longer in the mood for a tryst. They seemed to be having words. Not loud enough words for me to hear, but the body language said it all. At last, he handed something to her and turned away from her door. For some reason, I had the impression it was money.

TWENTY

Wednesday, May 23, 1984

Tension seemed to be high everywhere in the compound the next day. I could feel it crackle in the air like electricity. I wouldn't have been surprised if all of our hair began to stand on end.

In class that morning, I felt Russell's gaze on me at every turn but convinced myself that I was being paranoid. Russell talked on and on about voice. I paid little attention.

Even Delilah seemed jittery that day and I wondered if something was going on that I had missed. She fidgeted with her pen until she flipped it onto the floor and Russell finally looked at her instead of me. Thorn's knee bobbed up and down endlessly. I both wanted and didn't want to reach over and put my hand on it so it would stop. Fritha sat like a robot. Her eyes were wide and round. She had a small pile of manuscript pages in front of her and I wondered what she had written. She had told me the day before that she was okay with giving up her work. She was starting on something new and with the right critiquing she was sure it would be saleable. It sounded to me like she was reciting a rote-learned lesson. Frankly, I thought the purpose of the whole charade was so that Shig, Lyric and I would get off her back.

Axel clicked his pen until Lyric nudged him, then he began to drum his fingers on the desktop. Lyric herself kept biting at her cuticles until I wanted to scream at her to stop. Even Shig looked tense. I saw the muscles at the corners of his jaw tighten and relax, tighten and relax. Perhaps they were all anticipating the Writers Conference that was to start on Saturday. I knew they were all excited about the conference. They had talked of little else for a day or two. I myself was antsy, eager to get away from the compound, hopefully with the mystery of Whalesong solved before having to face anyone from the conference. Cyr and Arturo were the only ones who didn't seem to be nervous.

The lecture that morning was on dialogue. Russell spoke about giving each character his or her own voice. He stressed that no two characters spoke the same way. He mentioned acting out the dialogue to hone it until it was ready to use. He touched on accents and the words that writers used to indicate who had spoken. I hoped that Delilah was listening. Perhaps she would get the idea that 'exclaimed' was not the only way to do it. That 'said' was perfectly fine.

After class I headed back to my cabin with my lunch. I took deep breaths of the cool, fragrant forest air and tried to force myself to relax. I knew that the only thing that would calm me down was yet another walk in the woods.

So, after lunch, I took the cookie from the box and muttering to myself, I shared it with the wild creatures. A bite for me, a few crumbs for them. In a few minutes I came upon Lyric and Shig sitting on the same logs I always found them on.

"Is it me, or has everyone gone crazy?" Lyric asked.

Shig nodded. "I noticed it too. What is going on?"

"Where's Fritha?" I asked them. I was still worried about her. She wasn't acting right, even for someone who had thought her manuscript destroyed. I needed to touch her, to find out how she felt, to reassure myself.

"She had some laundry to do, she said. She should be along in a few minutes."

"So, why *is* everyone acting nuts?" Lyric pressed. "Did you see Russell at Class? I thought he was going to explode. He almost had steam coming out of his ears. He's mad about something."

"Mad?" I asked, trying to look as innocent as possible. Maybe I had been caught, although he had said nothing in Class. Of course, he usually saved any really upsetting stuff until we were in Meeting. "I didn't notice that he was mad."

"Then you must have been sleeping," Lyric said. "I think it's affecting everyone. Probably everybody thinks he or she is the target of whatever his wrath is about. I don't think I did anything. Anybody else commit some unforgivable sin?"

"I don't think I did anything," Shig said. "Fritha did what he wanted her to do, so I don't think it was her. What about you, Sarah? Did you spray graffiti on Russell's desk or something?"

"Maybe he's mad at Bleusette," I said.

"Could be," Lyric said and looked at Shig. "Could be."

"Could be what?" Fritha said. She hadn't warned us that she was approaching and we had been too wrapped up in our puzzlement to notice her.

"Jeezus at the spinning wheel," Lyric said. "You scared the shit out of me."

"Sorry," Fritha said. She looked normal except for some dark circles under her eyes. I put a hand out to her and drew her down onto the log next to me. I felt a morass of hopeless defeat. More than that. It was a flood. Huge and bottomless. She was in danger of drowning.

"You okay?" I asked her in an undertone, though I

knew she wasn't.

"I'm fine," she said. She had an unnatural sparkle in her eyes and her voice sounded high and tight.

"You don't sound like it," Shig said.

"I'm fine! I wish everyone would stop looking at me like I suddenly turned into a freak!"

Shig raised his eyebrows but subsided. Lyric cleared her throat.

"I'm sorry," Fritha said stiffly. "I'm trying to be normal." She burst into tears. "I just want to be normal." She sounded anything but.

"Who said you weren't normal?" Lyric asked her.

"Oh, no one! Why doesn't everyone just leave me alone?!"

She got up and walked back in the direction of her cabin.

"The three of us looked at each other.

"Should I go after her?" I asked.

"Maybe not," Shig said. "She sounded like she wants to be alone."

"We're all keyed up," Lyric said. "Why don't you give her some space? Maybe we'll find out at Meeting why everyone has turned into raging lunatics."

* * *

The moment I entered the Meeting room, I could feel that the tension had ratcheted up a couple of notches. We settled at our chair/desks and I shuffled some papers so I didn't have to look at anyone. It seemed that everyone else was doing the same thing. We could hear that Bleusette and Russell were having a conversation on the other side of the door. Argument, more like. I heard Bleusette's voice chopping at the air and the rumble of Russell's in response. As hard as I listened, I couldn't understand what was being said.

In a moment, the chant began. It sounded like a death knell this time.

When Bleusette entered with Russell right behind her, I watched her closely. As always, she stood in front of the brazier for a moment, then lifted the incense and the candle from their respective boxes. She lit the candle from the brazier and touched the flame to the end of the stick of incense then placed it into its holder. Just before she turned to face us, she made a movement that we couldn't see then she turned and pinched the lighted candle with her thumb and forefinger, holding her fingers on the wick longer than necessary. She scanned our faces with an expression I would have said was accusatory, but that could have been my guilty conscience.

She continued to stand at the lectern until we realized that she was about to speak.

"Sarah Augustine," she said in a dramatic voice that she could have used for a scene from Shakespeare.

"We are aware that you were not in your cabin Monday night at 11:30 o'clock. Will you tell us all where you were?"

"I must have been sleeping," I said, trying my hardest to look innocent. "Maybe I didn't hear the knock."

Russell strode to the lectern to stand beside Bleusette. "We know that you were not in your room."

"How do you know that?" I asked. I heard Fritha gasp quietly. "Unless someone came into my cabin, you have no way of knowing if I was there or not. If someone did come in, I will have that crime investigated." *Ha! I should talk,* I thought. *At 11:30, I myself had been snooping in someone else's space.*

Russell's laugh startled me. "I assure you that no one came into your cabin."

"Then how would you know?" I debated about asking if Bleusette's "famous clairvoyance" had told her. I seriously thought about it, but fortunately I kept my mouth shut.

"Suffice it to say that I know. It is not allowed, as you are well aware. This is infraction number two. If there is one more, you will be ejected from Whalesong with no recourse."

"And, if we find out who you were with Monday night, my girl," Bleusette added, "He or she..." She paused slightly after the 'she' to indicate that I may be in even deeper trouble if I had indeed been with a 'she'. "He or she will also be in trouble." She glared at me. If she had been capable of murder with a look, she would have committed it right then.

The silence hung heavily over the room for another moment, then Russell whispered something to Bleusette. She continued her stare until she had seated herself in her usual spot next to the brazier. Then she shut her eyes and pressed her fingertips to them as if the stress of having such a recalcitrant student was almost too much for her.

I was curious to know who had ratted me out. I didn't think it was Strom. Of course, there were plenty of infractions committed at any given time in the compound. Someone, most likely, had taken the opportunity to get on Russell and Bleusette's good side. My suspicion was with Cyr. It wouldn't have been the first time that he had snitched while he, himself, was committing an infraction. I gave him a covert glance. He couldn't have looked more innocent if he'd had a halo perched on his head. That made me suspect him even more than I already did, although, how he had discovered the fact that I was absent from my cabin was a mystery to me.

Lyric was asked to read first and I relaxed somewhat and listened to her book. I continued in my belief that it was very well done. I could easily see her finding an agent at the conference and I wished her every good luck.

When Russell and Bleusette had imparted their tepid opinions and we had all handed our truths to Lyric, Russell came around to the front of the lectern.

"Sarah," Russell said. For a moment I thought he wasn't quite finished with his lecture. I sat looking at him, wondering what else he had to say. "We would like to hear what you have been working on," he said.

Startled, I opened my manuscript folder. "I'm still working on *The Book of Signs*," I told him. "Tonight, I will read from Chapter Eighteen." I had been doling out the chapters a few at a time as though I had been working on them during the day. Surprisingly, both Russell and Bleusette looked a mild version of eager.

I started to read and, as usual, I was instantly into the story. I always read the next chapter to myself a few times before presenting it to the colonists. I needed to make sure there weren't any names or words that I didn't know how to pronounce and I wanted to be familiar with it.

Each part that I read, convinced me more and more that Kegan Mercer had been a genius. This part of the novel was particularly poignant, dealing with the death of a beloved young woman. Each time I went over it, I was touched to my depths.

When I had finished, I looked around at the

listeners. Fritha wiped away a tear and I saw Shig swallow. Thorn looked down at his desk. Arturo gave me a furtive nod and a wink. Delilah, as always, looked bored, but this time I thought it was a bit forced. Axel didn't seem to be paying attention and Cyr raised his eyebrows and turned down the corners of his mouth in that expression you give when you are surprised as well as pleased. Maybe he felt a bit of compunction for having betrayed me.

"Sarah knows what I think about this work," Russell said. He looked at Bleusette. "What we both think. Are there any comments from anyone else."

Wow, I thought. *He isn't even going to give me any of the standard lines*—"You can do better than this" or "You will never reach your writing potential with this." Of course, his non-judgement gave no guidance to the others for opinions, although they all knew what he thought already.

"I thought it was wonderful," Lyric said.

"'Wonderful' is a vague word, dearheart," Russell said. "I hardly think that is constructive."

"Very moving," Cyr said. I was surprised. He didn't usually offer comments unless asked. He must have truly been moved. Either that or he really did feel guilty.

"Delilah, what did you think?" Russell said.

"Oh," Delilah began in that breezy bored way she affected. "I thought it was all *right*. But I hardly think there is a market for it."

Again, I was shocked. I had never even gotten so much as a "fuck you" from Delilah. She saying it was "all *right*" constituted the highest praise.

"Clearly, I have taught you all nothing," Russell said sadly. He stood at the desk, looking down at the floor in seeming dejection. "I am amazed at the attitudes here. It has been determined that this work is not at all right for Sarah. If it was, she would be better at it. It would have more verve. More *élan*."

I almost laughed. *Verve? Élan? What the hell? The man sounds desperate,* I thought.

"Sarah, my girl," Bleusette had risen from her chair. "Are you ready to hand this…this…work over to us? It seems that Mr. York has given you chance after chance to improve upon it and you have done a minimal amount of improvement. It, however, still doesn't work. It will never be sold." She stopped for a moment and I was impressed with the look of abject sadness she was somehow able to project. "I know, without a doubt, that this work will *never* be sold."

I tried to look sorry. It wasn't terribly difficult since I had just read the part of Kegan's work that was so moving that it made it hard to read around the huge lump in the throat. "I'm… I think I'm ready," I said and hoped my voice sounded properly contrite.

I heard murmurs of protest, but Russell silenced them with a look. Then he looked at me and I swear I saw a gleam of triumph in his eyes.

"But, maybe...Is there anything I can do to give it more verve?" I asked. "More *élan*?"

Impatience and triumph fought a battle all over Russell's face. "I believe I have given you several suggestions already, which you have chosen not to follow."

In my opinion, the loss of Fritha's manuscript had made them truly desperate. But, I wasn't going to make it easy for them.

"Let me have one more chance?" I asked. "Just one more? I think I can do better." I thought about adding a "Please, sir" but resisted.

He muttered and I took it as an assent. I looked up and Shig was staring at me. He and Lyric must have thought me crazy. I winked at him and his face relaxed.

TWENTY-ONE

Wednesday, May 23, 1984

It was my phone night and I was eager to talk to Easy but I lingered at my desk after Meeting. Lyric did the same.

"Do they check the cabins every night?" I whispered to her when Russell and Bleusette had gone.

"He probably had one of the Entourage check," she said. "Who knows?" She paused a moment and peered at me. "So where *were* you Monday night?"

"I think something is going on," I told her instead of answering. "I have to go. Bleusette won't wait for me long. You and Fritha be careful."

She stared at me, but I had no time to say more.

Easy was ready. "I don't know how you got this name, but Camille Bishop has had more troubles than I ever want," he said.

I had to sit passively, four short feet from Bleusette, with my face blank.

"Oh?" I tried to keep the interest out of my voice. I didn't want Bleusette thinking I was getting anything she would want to hear.

"The woman who reported her missing is Lyric Prentice. You know her?"

"Yes, I do," I said. "I like her very much."

"She a prisoner? I mean a colonist?"

I laughed. "Yes, indeed."

"She reported her roommate, Camille Bishop, missing in the fall of 1980. She, Camille, left one night after dinner and simply never came home. She was arrested about three weeks later for narcotics possession and released. About a year later, she was arrested again and that time there was a prostitution charge and another, more serious, possession charge. She's been in and out of jail for the past three years."

"Ice cream," I said.

"It's weird talking to you when you throw in things like that," he said. "Anyway, I talked to her mother. She lives in Everett. She said that Camille was, guess what? An aspiring writer. *And*, she went to Whalesong the year she went missing *and* she had her manuscript destroyed by the rulers of the kingdom up here."

"Oh, my God!" I said, unthinking. Bleusette's head snapped up and she stared at me until I smiled and shrugged at her.

"Her mom said she was devastated. Thought her life was over. She didn't see her again after that. Oh, and she won some kind of award at the West Coast Writers Association conference that same year for the novel that had been destroyed.

"But, then she still had the whole thing, right?" I asked, thinking the contest officials may have retained a copy of it.

"The novel, you mean? No. Apparently, you just send in a synopsis and twenty or twenty-five pages for the entry. So, she let them destroy the work, then got to the conference and they gave her an award for a novel she didn't have any more."

"Hot fudge sundae!" I said. I would have preferred "holy fucking shit!" but that was not possible under the circumstances.

"Well, after that, she never recovered. She started getting into drugs right after the colony and the conference. She went downhill fast, her mom said. I bet if you ask Lyric about her, she'd tell you."

"That's a whole other story," I said, hoping he knew what I meant. He did.

"You mean, she tells it differently?"

"That's right."

I knew then why Lyric hated Russell and Bleusette so much. I thought that Lyric and Camille had been more than roommates. I also thought I would feel the same if I were Lyric.

After a few more minutes of uncomfortable, one-sided conversation, I reminded him to pick me up at the ferry dock the following Wednesday. That reminded me that I had less than a week to wrap up what I had found out. I still had a lot to do. More, it turned out, than I thought.

* * *

I had been in my cabin only a few minutes, before there was a knock on the door. I thought it was Lyric coming to find out what she could about my shenanigans of Monday night. I almost said, "I was just on my way over to Fritha's." Good thing I didn't. Russell stood on my step.

He pushed his way inside and shut the door behind him.

"Russell, this is inappropriate, you being here," I said, suddenly tired. This was getting ridiculous. He might have thought he was king of the hill, but in my book he wasn't.

"I think we need to have a little talk," he said.

I didn't like what I saw in his eyes and I could smell alcohol on his breath. "No," I said. "You need to go." I opened the door. He shoved it closed again and leaned over me. I don't consider myself short but he was at least a foot taller. He put his hands on either side of my head and leaned against the door. Oh, Jeez. I was going to have to physically hurt him, and I knew he wasn't going to take it well. "I think you should leave right now," I said.

"Oh, really? And what are you going to do if I don't?" Did he honestly think I was flirting with him?

"If you don't, I'm going to have to throw you out," I said.

"Oh, you're going to throw me out, are you?" He started a smarmy chuckle and I kicked him in the knee, then grabbed one of his arms and twisted him around. He had been leaning and my move threw him off balance. My hand slid down his arm and before he could react, I had pulled his thumb so far back it almost met his wrist. With my other hand, I opened the door and cop marched him out to the step. I gave him a shove at the top and he sprawled onto the perpetual bed of pine needles that covered the front yard of the cabin.

"You will be sorry for that!" he said. I think he said something after that too, but I had slammed the door.

I fully expected him to try to come back in. The cabins were not equipped with locks, since we colonists were all so trustworthy. But after a few minutes, I peeped out the window and he was nowhere in view. I pulled on my jacket. I had to get over to Fritha's and make sure she was okay. I had been worrying about her all day. I couldn't tell her that I had rescued her manuscript but maybe I could reassure her. Also, I wasn't altogether sure that Russell wouldn't try her cabin next.

As I got closer to her cabin, I could hear Fritha's voice. I ducked back among the darker trees when I saw Russell hobble past and stagger toward the path leading to the Main Cabin. I ran to Fritha's door and tapped lightly on it.

"If you don't stay away from me, I'm going to kill you!" Fritha shrieked as she opened the door. The second she saw me, she broke into loud, raw sobs. I pulled her inside and shut the door behind us. I led her to the futon where we sat and I rocked her. I didn't think there had been enough time for Russell to do too much, but I needed to get her to talk.

"Did he hurt you, Fritha?" I asked.

"I'm going to get kicked out of Whalesong now," she wailed. If that was all she was worried about, then she was probably okay, I thought.

"I doubt it, Fritha," I told her. "You didn't do anything."

"I kicked him in the balls," she said, then sobbed

harder. I had to smile.

"Well, he deserved that," I told her. "I don't think there's a rule about that anyway. He's had a rough night. I threw him out of my cabin, too."

"I hate him. I hate her too. I hate them both. I hate this place." She stopped crying for a moment and looked at me then began again. "I've lost everything."

"Everything?" I said. "No, you haven't."

"Yes, I have. I've lost my manuscript. I'm going to lose my place here. I'm going to have to go home and tell my parents." She heaved a shuddery sigh. "At least they will be happy."

"Fritha, you don't have to tell your parents anything. You are an adult. What you do is a lot less their business than it was when you were a kid."

"But I live with them."

"Well, you don't have to. You know that. We've had this very discussion before."

"Oh, what's the use? I don't have my book anymore, anyway." The torment in her eyes was heartbreaking. "Do you know how many years I worked on that?"

"I know that you had at least one short story published. I know you are a wonderful writer and you should keep writing."

"I worked on it for four years. Now it's gone."

She began to cry again. "You were smart not to surrender your manuscript," she said. "I wish I hadn't.

I debated how much to tell her. "Fritha," I said. "I think you could reconstruct that book. Do you have any of the notes? Or an outline? I have a way...I have an eidetic memory," I lied. "I heard much of it. I could help you. Please, believe me. I think we could rescue it."

She watched me while I spoke but I got the feeling she believed me. She seemed to consider what I had said and apparently wasn't going to ask me any questions.

More than once, though, she needed reassurance. "Do you really think we could do that?" she asked again and again.

"Yes," I said. "I do. In the meantime, Russell York should be reported to the police."

"How? It's not like we have portable telephones," she said, and, from that, I thought she would be all right.

TWENTY-TWO

Saturday, May 26, 1984

I kept my head down for the rest of the week. It was a little easier to avoid Russell after the conference opened on Saturday, but prior to that he relentlessly tried to get me to give up the book. I had no intention of handing it over now, even though Kegan's copy was safely stashed in my briefcase. Two "burned" manuscripts in one term seemed unprecedented according to Shig. I knew I was right. Having discovered that Fritha's was missing, they were now concentrating on mine so the term wouldn't be a total loss. Whatever the reason, I had something they coveted and if I gave it up I would have no hold over them at all. They wanted it and I wanted to stay at Whalesong until I found out what was going on. I figured I could break every one of their silly rules and still not get ejected as long as I held something they so desperately desired.

Russell never said anything about the encounter with me or with Fritha. Apparently, he was more afraid of Bleusette's wrath than angry at us.

* * *

All classes and Meetings were suspended for the conference. After breakfast, we took the van to the hotel and listened to seminars, chatted up other writers, agents and publishers. I noticed that most of the colonists were a bit shy about approaching the rulers of the publishing world, though. I, on the other hand, not being a writer, had nothing to lose, so I felt much more comfortable with them. For the colonists, it must have seemed as though they were on a weekend long job interview.

I wanted to get a look into the other cabins but I knew I never would at that point. After the conference was over, we would all be going home. The compound was just a little too far from the hotel for me to pop back and forth to snoop and still make my appearance at the lectures and classes so I settled in to enjoy the conference. There were lots of people milling about the huge conference area so I didn't think it would be too difficult to avoid David should I even see him.

Meetings, seminars and speakers filled the morning and more speakers were scheduled for the evening. Bleusette had talked of nothing but the introduction she would do later. I knew she had a speech prepared and that she had been practicing.

Anyway, the morning was a million times more interesting than spending it listening to Russell prattle about structure or conflict.

I spoke to Jannie Wicks, one of my favorite true crime writers. She was personable and friendly. We chatted briefly about Diane Downs who had murdered two of her children and wounded another just a year before. Later I saw Delilah watching me carefully as I was speaking to Deborah Scottsfield, a well-known agent. We had been in the buffet line rhapsodizing about our favorite cheesecake toppings. Apparently, Delilah thought I had more nefarious intentions.

Early in the afternoon, I saw Jack Maynard who was making it a point to talk to everyone no matter who they were. He had written a book, he told me, called *So You Think Your Life is Bad.*

Perhaps he thought I was a publisher or an agent because he gave me the "pitch" for his book. On the other hand, I think he gave it to everyone, just in case.

"This is a book that everyone should read," he said. "It will make them feel better no matter how awful their life is." He handed me one of the postcards he had had printed with a picture of the book and an excerpt on the back. "I've had cancer eight times," he said. "And I broke my back twice."

I tried to look less skeptical and more sympathetic but he wasn't really paying any attention to me, he was scouting for others to approach.

"How has your sales pitch worked so far?" I asked him.

"Not that good. Just because a book is self-published," he said, "doesn't mean it's not a good book. Everyone is acting like this is a terrible book but it isn't."

Well, he wasn't selling me, but what did I know? "Don't worry, sir," I told him. "In the future, self-publishing will be a respected way of getting your book in print."

He stared at me from behind the lenses in his round black glasses. "Are you psychic or something?"

"Yes, I am," I told him and left him with his mouth shaped into a little O that perfectly matched his glasses.

I decided to approach Donald Whatcom who was a New York publisher. I had heard that he was respected and that if you could get him to notice you, then you pretty much had it made. I had listened in the class when Russell had taught us about writing a good pitch and I had actually written one for *The Book of Signs* that I believed was a good one. I put my name on the sign-up sheet and when my turn came, I gave him the pitch. Mr. Whatcom had acted interested, so I told him a little about the backstory of the book and the man who had written it. Then I shook hands with him. In doing so, I discovered that he truly had been intrigued and I vowed to give the pitch to Claire Mercer when I returned the manuscript and, perhaps she could get a little satisfaction by having Kegan's work recognized. I hoped so.

A woman approached me just as the last seminar for the afternoon was ending. Mariah LeRoy told me that she had heard that I was the new girl at Whalesong that year and she wanted to know what my experience had been.

"This is your first session, right?" she asked. I got the impression that she was feeling me out so see if I was the newest member of the Entourage.

"My first and my last," I told her. I saw her instantly relax.

"Why is it your last? Didn't you enjoy it?"

I laughed. "I have to say that I love the other writers but I'm not wild about the way the place is run."

"Well, that's what I wanted to know," she said. "I wanted to warn you to get out while you can. I was there for three years. It was two years too many. Have they told you yet that you can do better work than what you are doing?"

I nodded. "They want me to surrender my manuscript. In fact, I just pitched it to Donald Whatcom and he wants to see some of it. Did it happen to you?"

"Donald Whatcom?! That's great!" She seemed genuinely pleased. "Yes," she said and laughed. "I had mine burned in fact. The very same manuscript that just won the Potlatch Poetry Prize at the Portland Writer's Camp last month."

"Intriguing," I said. "Congratulations! Did you submit a duplicate to Bleusette and Russell?"

She nodded. "I gave them an earlier version. I was lucky I had brought it with me. I had been debating about it and I'm so glad I did. They burned it, candle, incense and everything. Even though you know it's not the actual manuscript, it gives you this horrible doomed feeling to see it go up in smoke."

"I can imagine," I said. "I recently watched them burn one of the other writers' manuscripts and it was devastating to all of us, I think."

I asked her for her contact information. If I found out that my theory about the "destroyed" manuscripts was correct, I would be getting in touch with her very soon.

She pointed to her card. "It's Mariah LeRoy. That's pronounced 'le-roy' with the accent on the last syllable. The entire three years I was there, Bleusette called me Miss Lee Roy with the accent on the first. I hated it and she knew it."

Later, when I was waiting in the coffee and tea line, I was surprised to find Delilah beside me.

"Hey, Delilah," I said as if we were old pals. I had probably spoken directly to her twice in the whole time I had been at Whalesong. I grabbed a cup and headed for the tea urn. She followed.

"I think it's perfectly terrible the way you are disrespecting Bleusette," she said, getting right to the point.

"Disrespecting? What are you talking about, Delilah?"

"I saw you talking to Deborah Scottsfield earlier. I know what you are up to and I think it's awful. Your work isn't so good that she's going to be interested in it anyway. Russell doesn't even like it. Neither does Bleusette."

I put some sugar in my tea and stirred it, trying to look thoughtful. "You know what? I don't care what Russell and Bleusette like or don't like. Nor do I care what you like." I said it with a pleasant smile and a friendly voice but I think she got the message.

"And, I saw you talking to Donald Whatcom!" She was sounding outraged by then. "Do you honestly think your book has a chance with him?" She said 'book' as though she was talking about something she had fished out of a toilet.

"He did say he was interested and would like to see the first few chapters," I told her.

"He did not!"

"I assure you he did." I picked up a napkin and

left her standing in front of the tea urn with her empty cup. I did not tell her that Mr. Whatcom had said he hoped to see me again before the end of the conference.

I found a seat in the second row of chairs. It was almost time for the keynote speaker and I was ready to sit down, enjoy my tea, listen to Lawrence Fawcett and think about what I was going to do next.

Soon the speakers table filled and I spotted Jim Hitchens, a mystery writer I admired as well as Lawrence, Jannie Wicks, an agent and Bleusette. The others were either speakers or introducers but I didn't recognize any of them. I let my mind drift when the speaking began.

Lawrence Fawcett was to be the second speaker of the evening. I saw that Bleusette already had the brazier going and her boxes of tricks nearby. There was, apparently, going to be a chant and incense show. I should have known.

At last, the chanting began and everyone stopped speaking.

Bleusette stood and swept to the lectern. She was wearing a deep purple dress with a lavender jacket which was printed with a gorgeous peacock design. I hoped that her flowy sleeves wouldn't come too close to the flame or a disaster would ensue.

She stood facing the audience for a moment with her head bowed and her palms placed together as though she was praying. Then she turned her back to us and took out a candle and an incense stick. She lit the candle in the brazier and put the stick in its holder before touching the flame to the end of the stick. She made that hesitation I had noticed countless times before in Meeting then turned to the audience. She pinched the flame with her thumb and index finger leaving her fingers on the wick for several seconds.

As she looked out over the audience, her face paled and her eyes seemed to grow hazy. She looked surprised and pressed her hand to her chest, blinked a few times and made a wheezing sound. She stood still for a moment, then, in seeming slow motion, she dropped the candle and collapsed behind the lectern.

The collective gasp from the audience seemed to paralyze them all. No one rose. No one breathed. I stood and headed toward her, and that seemed to galvanize the audience. Others rushed toward the front of the room and to Bleusette's side. I knelt next to her and felt for a pulse in her neck, trying to remember my CPR training. But there was no pulse. Bleusette was dead.

TWENTY-THREE

Saturday, May 26, 1984

The next sound was a piercing scream. Delilah pushed aside onlookers and knelt by Bleusette.

I turned to Janet Jeffries who was standing nearby looking terrified.

"Please go find a phone and call for an ambulance," I told her. She turned and instantly disappeared into the surging, horrified crowd.

Delilah put her head down. "'O proud death!'" she said in a loud, sepulchral voice. "'O proud death,'" she said again, more quietly, still crouching in the way. She turned her face upward and seemed to be waiting for something. One of the bystanders to take a picture perhaps? I tried to get her out of the way so I could straighten Bleusette out onto her back and attempt CPR.

"What the helll?" I heard someone say behind me.

"Hamlet," another voice answered.

A moment later, Russell had pushed through the crowd and stood looking down at his wife's body and me seeming to manhandle it. Delilah came to life and stood, then rushed to Russell. "Don't look," she said. "She wouldn't want you seeing her this way."

A man in a Hawaiian shirt pushed through. "I'm a doctor," he said. "Let me see what I can do."

He quickly knelt next to Bleusette and pressed his fingers to her neck, searching for a pulse. He shook her, rather roughly, I thought.

"Ma'am, can you hear me," he shouted.

He felt her neck again, then began compressions, alternating them with mouth to mouth resuscitation. After a few seconds he stopped and tried again to find her pulse. Apparently, he felt nothing for he resumed compressions. "Has an ambulance been called?" he asked, breathless.

I nodded. I looked up at the crush of people who were closing around us. "Please step back," I said. Some of them did, but others looked too stunned to even hear me.

After a few minutes, I took over for the doctor. He continued the mouth to mouth while I did the tiring job of trying to keep Bleusette's blood flowing. Then, in a few more minutes, he resumed. At last, he bent over Bleusette for a few moments, then stood, found me again and shook his head slightly.

"Can you tell what happened?" I asked him.

"The Medical Examiner will have to determine that. But she's dead all right."

I looked around. Mariah LeRoy was standing nearby, her hand pressed to her mouth. "Mariah, please go find a phone and call the sheriff, then will you recruit someone to make sure no one comes in or goes out?" I said. "Everyone else needs to step back." Most everyone did but Delilah and Russell continued with their tragic tableau.

"Delilah, Russell, both of you step back," I said. "Everyone, take a seat please and we'll wait for the Sheriff." Again, most of the onlookers complied but Russell and Delilah stayed, he looking at Bleusette and Delilah trying to shield him from the sight.

I carefully stepped around the body and looked at the brazier, the boxes of incense and candles, the lectern. Nothing seemed to be unusual about any of it.

I turned and spotted Fritha. Her face was utterly white. With her white blonde hair and her skin turned ashen, she looked like a ghost except for those blue upon blue eyes that had gone round in horror. "Fritha," I called to her.

She moved her gaze to mine. I grabbed her by the shoulders. For a second, I was jolted by the sense of guilt that emanated from her. "Fritha, go get my briefcase for me, will you?" She stared at me, uncomprehending. I gave her a gentle shake. "Fritha!"

Then I saw Shig elbowing his way through the bystanders who had been creeping forward again. “Shig, please go get my briefcase from under my seat in the second row.” I pointed. “Then will you take Fritha toward the back and find a seat for her?”

In a moment he was back with my case. I opened it and slipped on latex gloves. I saw him steer Fritha to a seat. He said something to her and then came back to me.

“What can I do?” he asked, eyeing Bleusette’s still form.

“You can go to the front of the building and wait for the Sheriff, then bring him back here.” I looked into his face. “Thank you, Shig.”

I looked around and asked two men to please try to keep the crowd of people back. To persuade them to find seats. Seemingly grateful to be of some help, they turned and began to herd the shocked and frightened onlookers back toward the rows of chairs.

I took pictures of the area. While I did that, I instructed Lyric who had appeared beside me to find some blank paper and some pens and see to it that everyone present wrote down their names, addresses, phone numbers and what they had seen, heard or otherwise knew.

I bagged the candles and the copy of Bleusette’s speech that she had written out on index cards. I initialed, dated and noted the time on it all, leaving it in place for now. As I bagged the box of incense, the overly sweet smell assaulted my nose and threatened me with a bout of sneezing. I carefully pulled the burning piece out of its holder and snuffed out the smoking end with a drop or two of water and started to put it into an evidence bag as well. Then I stopped, struck by something and gave it another reluctant sniff. I looked at the stick closely before I sealed the bag. I thought I knew, then, what had killed Bleusette.

* * *

After what seemed a very long time, the buzzing crowd had quieted somewhat and many of them were busily writing on the paper that Lyric had handed out. I heard a stir at one of the doors into the auditorium and saw Shig and a stocky man in a uniform approach.

When they had caught up to me, I stripped the glove off my right hand, shook hands with him and introduced myself as Sarah. From the momentary contact, I could tell that I could trust him. He looked about my age, maybe in his forties. He had an impressive moustache and kind looking brown eyes. I asked Shig to keep an eye on the scene of Bleusette's death and make sure no one touched anything, then I steered the sheriff back behind the table out of earshot. I wasn't quite ready to come out from undercover to the colony.

“My name is Cheyenne Bruce,” I told Sheriff Con Bradley. I’m a private detective. I’ve been working undercover at Whalesong for the last month. The people there know me as Sarah Augustine and I would prefer being Sarah for another day or two if you don’t mind.”

Bradley seemed to understand my urgency, because he nodded and muttered the name Sarah Augustine. “I’m glad to see that you know what you’re doing,” he said. “I radioed for the coroner when Ms LeRoy told me that this woman was dead.”

“I have reason to believe that this may not be from natural causes, Sheriff,” I told him. “Until we know, I think we should be careful with the scene.”

He took off his hat and rubbed the top of his head. “This is a hell of a thing,” he said. “We’re so short-handed right now, the last thing I need is a death to investigate.” He seemed to look me over. “Our force is pretty small as it is. We’re all there is for the three small islands in the group. If you’re a licensed investigator, I sure could use your input.”

“If you’d like, you can check with Perce O’Dell at the Seattle Police Department,” I told him. “He will vouch for me. I’ve worked with SPD before on a consultation basis.”

“O’Dell? I know O’Dell. We went to Wazzu together!” Wazzu was Washington State University. He seemed overjoyed and a little relieved. I guess he had decided I wasn’t just some crackpot after all.

"Hell, I can deputize you and you can take over most of the investigation if you're willing," he added. "I don't think it will be too complicated."

"I'd like it if you would get official confirmation from Perce before I do that," I said, smiling. "We want everything to be on the up and up. This may be murder."

He looked over at the scene. Someone, the doctor I thought, had covered Bleusette's face with a linen napkin. Delilah was still hovering around Russell who was now seated on the floor with his head in his hands.

"I kinda doubt that it's murder," he said slowly. "It happened in full view of all these people."

"That doesn't mean it wasn't, Sheriff," I said. "Anyway, you don't want to take that chance."

He eyed me. "What do you know?"

"Only that more than one person wouldn't have minded seeing her dead."

He nodded and moved off into a corner to do some covert radioing. I appreciated that. I didn't want to blow my cover now when I was so close to getting some answers. I turned back to the scene of death that I was coming more and more to believe was a crime scene.

In a moment, Bradley was back, a grin covering his face. "They patched me through and I talked to O'Dell myself. Great guy," he said. Then we turned our backs to the crowd. Half of them were watching us curiously and the other half seemed to be chatting amongst themselves. In another moment, I was a Deputy of the San Juan County Sheriff's Department.

Bradley announced to the room at large that no one would be allowed to leave the island until cause of death was determined and maybe even longer. There were groans and some mild argument, but surprisingly, no one seemed to object as much as I had thought they might. Maybe the sleepy little island was ready for something interesting to happen. Sheriff Bradley had said "until the cause of death is determined" but I knew that the cause was the least of it. If it turned out Bleusette had died of simple heart failure and there was no foul play involved, fine. I didn't care what happened. I could go home, make my report and never return to Klallam Island. If, on the other hand, it was murder, as I suspected, I would be stuck here along with the conference attendees and the Whalesong colonists until I found out the answers. I thought I already knew the how. Now I needed to find out the who.

TWENTY-FOUR

Saturday 26, 1984

At long last, everyone who had witnessed Bleusette drop dead had written a statement of one kind or another. Some of the statements were laughably short. "I wasn't looking," or "I was in the men's room," but most of the potential witnesses had actually been looking at her as she turned from the brazier and with the chant as a background had fallen dead in front of their eyes. Of course, everyone would have to be interviewed at some point.

We had secured the scene and processed it as well as we were able considering our lack of help.

Sheriff Bradley had assigned two of the conference attendees to stand guard over the scene and poor Bleusette's body until the Medical Examiner arrived. Meanwhile he and I repaired to one of the conference rooms. Together we made up a list of questions so that we could weed out some of the attendees—those who truly had nothing whatsoever to do with Bleusette Huntsman. One of the questions was "Have you ever spoken to, been represented by or in any capacity had any dealings with Bleusette Huntsman?" If the answer was yes, then more in depth questioning would be required. If the answer was no, then those people could wait until they may or may not be needed.

By the time the Medical Examiner had come to remove Bleusette's body, I had spoken with the organizers of the conference. Madeline Hawcroft was the Event Coordinator and Jaime Streeter was the President of West Coast Writers. They told me that the manager of the hotel had convinced them not to cancel the rest of the conference. Since everyone would have to remain until the investigation was finished, they might as well have something to do in the meantime.

Bradley was still convinced that Bleusettes death was from natural causes but in my mind, it was murder. To me, the most likely group of suspects were the colonists. More than one of them had a motive for wanting Bleusette dead. Lyric, in revenge, perhaps for the loss of her partner due to Bleusette's manuscript destroying antics. Fritha, who had felt so very guilty when I touched her, possibly had more motive than any of the others, since she had had her manuscript "destroyed" just days before. I thought Russell was a viable suspect as well. He was clearly having a fling with Delilah. And Delilah herself, who, despite her theatrics, possibly wanted Russell to herself. I still thought Shig was innocent and I thought Arturo was as well. I was unsure about Cyr, Axel and Thorn, though any of them could have had a motive of which I was as yet unaware. There were some people who had been attending the conference who, as former Whalesong colonists, may have had motive too. And then, there was Strom. He had as much motive as any of the colonists and, I would venture to guess, the opportunity as well.

* * *

By 9:15 that night, the ME had arrived, removed Bleusette body and the conference attendees had retired to their rooms. I had heard that the hotel had had to make extra space available for the few who had planned to return to the mainland or nearby islands for the night. Of course, the management didn't mind. A buck is a buck even if the guests are reluctant.

Private security guards had been hired by the hotel. One was assigned to see to it that no one entered the room where Bleusette had died. Another was stationed at the one ferry terminal and Sheriff Bradley was making plans that the ferry be grounded for the time being.

One voice ran into another as soon as we boarded the van to head back to the compound.

"Oh, my God," Lyric said. "Can you believe this?"

"What's going to happen now?" Fritha asked.

"What a frightful evening!" Arturo said.

Shig opened his mouth and closed it without saying anything.

Thorn yawned and slid into his classic nothing-ever-fazes-me pose.

Axel stared stonily out the window while Cyr muttered, "Great. Just great."

Delilah, apparently still with Russell, was not on the van. When Strom parked in front of the main cabin, I saw lights inside and had to assume that at least Russell was at home.

Lyric, Fritha, Arturo, Shig and I all headed in the same direction. We were all tired but way too keyed up to sleep.

"Where on Earth did you learn to do all that stuff you did, anyway?" Lyric asked when we had settled on the floor and futon of my cabin.

"Yes," Shig said. "I was impressed. You seemed to know exactly what to do."

"I've had some police training," I told them. "I told the Sheriff that and he asked if I could help since they are terribly short-handed right now.

"What happens now?" Fritha asked again.

"Well, I think we'll just keep right on with the conference. The management has decided it will continue," I told her.

"I meant, what happens to...to Whalesong now?"

That, of course, no one knew. They talked about the possibility of the colony continuing but I didn't think that was likely. Given what I suspected about Russell's dealing with the stolen manuscripts, I would be surprised if Russell didn't end up in prison.

Promptly, at ten, the compound lights went off. Fritha gave a little scream of fright and reflexively jumped up to leave for her cabin before she was caught.

"Relax, Fritha. You're not breaking any rules," I told her. "Believe me." She didn't, apparently, because in another moment, she was out the door.

"I'll go see about this," I told the others, and followed Fritha out.

I took my flashlight and trekked to the Main Cabin. Clearly, Russell was still trying to control the colony. He didn't seem to realize that, with the loss of Bleusette, Whalesong was in danger of falling apart. In a way, I felt sorry for him.

I wasn't very surprised when Delilah answered my knock. She, however, looked taken aback.

"You're supposed to be in your cabin," she said.

"And so are you. I need to speak to Russell."

"He's worn out. His wife died today, in case you hadn't noticed. I'm seeing to it that he is being taken care of."

"I'm sure you are, Delilah. Here are your choices: you can wake him and have him turn the power back on in the compound or I will arrest you for impeding a criminal investigation and awaken Russell myself."

"What criminal investigation?" Her drama act had suddenly vanished. "There isn't a crime, here. Bleusette died from...from a heart thing. Attack. Anyway, you can't arrest me." She turned to go and I clasped her upper arm. Immediately, I knew that she was guilty of something. Of course, that wasn't a surprise at all. It could have been that she felt guilty for being so brazen in her attraction to Russell mere seconds after Bleusette's death, guilty for being relieved that Bleusette was out of the picture, or for having murdered Bleusette herself.

"Actually, I can. Sheriff Conroy Bradley deputized me this evening and I have the authority to arrest you."

"Deputized?" She began to look scared. I wondered of what.

"Someone has to investigate this death. I have a background in police procedure and investigation," I told her as vaguely as I could manage. "Now, get those lights back on. I have work to do and I won't be stopping at ten o'clock because Russell thinks we are all a bunch of children."

I gave the door a truly admirable slam on the way out.

Just as I reached the door to my cabin, the lights

blazed back on. I smiled to myself.

I opened the door to find Shig, grim faced and looking as tired as I felt, still there. Everyone else had gone back to their cabins.

"You seem to have more power than I ever expected," he said. "What did you do?"

"I have a feeling many of the restrictions are null and void from now on," I told him.

He looked at me silently for a moment, then said, "Sarah, what's going on?"

I briefly debated with myself then made my decision.

"I'm going to tell you. For now, I would appreciate it if you would keep this just between us."

He nodded.

"First of all, my name is Cheyenne Bruce, not Sarah Augustine. I am not a writer. I'm a private investigator."

He laughed. Clearly, he did not believe me. "Yes, and I am Prince Fujimoto of the Second Dynasty."

I didn't say anything. I knew that in a moment he would see that I was being straight with him.

"What...why..." He rubbed his face with both hands. "Truly?"

I nodded. "Kegan's family hired me to investigate what is going on here at Whalesong. They think that Kegan committed suicide because of Russell and

Bleusette. They believe that Whalesong is a cult and that Russell and Bleusette control the colonists. At this point, I'm inclined to agree with them."

He tried at first to brush off what I had said. "It's not a cult. We can go whenever we want to. We aren't brainwashed," he said, as if almost to convince himself that it was true. Then he looked at me and I saw anger bloom on his face. "You mean you lied to us all?" he said.

"Yes, I did. I'm very sorry I had to do that. I had to find out what was happening here."

"So, did you find out?" he asked. His face had gone red and his eyes blazed.

"Not everything. But some, yes. I believe that Bleusette was murdered and I think it was done by someone in Whalesong."

The anger disappeared. Incredulity had taken its place. "One of us? I'm sure...I know you're wrong, Sarah." He put both hands to the sides of his head. "Or whatever you said your name really is." He stood and paced in the small room. I let him. He needed to work off some of his confusion.

"Call me Sarah," I told him, keeping my voice soft and calm. "I need you to continue to know me as Sarah. And, yes, I'm convinced that one of the colonists killed Bleusette."

"Why are you telling *me* this? What if I'm the person who did it?"

"I don't think you are. In fact, I'm sure you aren't."

"You can't seriously think that Lyric or Fritha had anything to do with it," he said. "That's just crazy."

Actually, I did think that one of them could be guilty but I didn't want him to know everything just yet.

"I know you didn't do it. And I'm pretty sure Arturo didn't. That's *all* I know right now."

"It...It just isn't logical to think one of them killed someone."

"I'm afraid we drove off the logic bridge several miles back, Shig. There are things going on around here that you may have trouble believing when you hear about them. Unfortunately, I can't tell you about it until I'm sure. For now, I know you didn't kill Bleusette, and I'm going to need your help."

"But *how* do you know?"

"Well, did you?"

He sat back down and I put my hand on his arm. He was as innocent as I was. More, in fact, innocent than I.

"No," he said.

"There. You see?" I smiled at him. "You don't have any motive, for one thing. You keep your head down, work on the novel that's most important to you and leave the Stupid Warriors as your cover."

"Well, if it isn't me, who is it?"

"I don't know that yet. I have ideas, but I can't tell you until I know for sure."

"So, why *are* you telling me all this?"

"Because I need your help."

"My help? Why me? I'm not...I don't know..." He covered his eyes. I could tell he was exhausted too. "I need a minute to digest this."

In a moment, he looked at me again. "I'm just an ordinary guy who came here to get away from everyday life. From chaos. And here I am right in the middle of a huge mess. How on Earth could *I* possibly help?"

"For one thing, I need another body to help me question people. And I need another pair of eyes and ears."

He thought for another long moment. "Okay," he said. "I'm willing. What do you want me to do?"

"I'd like you to help me question people. I would like you to keep your eyes and ears open.

"Okay," he said, sounding doubtful. "I'll do what I can, but I don't know how much help I'll be."

"For now, please keep this whole conversation a secret. Tomorrow, I may ask you to interview some people. It will be just preliminary stuff, for now. We need to get the autopsy report back and see what killed Bleusette, though, I'm pretty sure I already know."

"That doctor who tried to revive her said it was probably a thunderclap heart attack," he said.

"If it was, then fine. It may have been a heart attack, but there may be more to it than that." I thought for a moment. "Do you have an appointment with anyone at the conference tomorrow?"

"Yeah. I'm seeing Janet Jeffries at 2:00 and I'm not going to miss Guy Loring's seminar at 2:30. I've got a pitch session with Donald Whatcom at 4:20. Why?"

"I need you to try to keep Russell occupied somewhere other than the Main Cabin. I need to get in there."

It was his turn to think. "Do you think Russell did something to...make Bleusette die?"

"I don't know, but that isn't the reason I have to get in there. I think that Russell and Bleusette were involved in some illegal activity. I need to look around at some things and I may need to make some phone calls."

"That's illegal too, isn't it? If I do that, I won't be an accomplice or an abettor or...?"

"No. I've been deputized by the sheriff," I started to tell him. "Okay, it isn't entirely legal. Officially, I would need a warrant. But I've done it before. I know," I said, putting up my hand when he started to speak. "I know having done it before doesn't make it right again, but I need to confirm my suspicions.

I think the Mercers are right when they said that Russell and Bleusette were doing something they shouldn't be doing." I looked at him, straight into his eyes. "Can I count on you? You won't be doing one thing that's illegal. I promise. I'll take care of all the unlawful stuff."

It was a moment before he nodded.

* * *

It had been determined that the colonists would attend the seminars, speeches, classes, lectures and appointments as usual. The hotel management was most anxious that the conference continue and that things seem normal.

Behind the scenes, they were anything but.

Shig, Sheriff Bradley and I made sure that everyone filled out the questionnaire that we had handed them. We had almost two hundred people to question. With the initial survey, I was able to weed out a few people who had never heard of Bleusette Huntsman. I tried to speak to each one and to shake hands with them as well, so that I could determine whether or not they were telling the truth.

It was surprising, really, how many others did know her, had heard of her, had studied under her husband's teachings or who had been rejected by her. She wasn't, apparently, well liked. Not liked at all, as far as I could determine. Story after story, of Whalesong, rejection and discouragement cropped up and those were set aside for more in depth scrutiny.

Shig and I had determined that he would approach Russell at the conference and ask for a meeting with him. He would say that he required some advice now, for his Samurai novel and he wanted recommendations for representation. That should keep Russell occupied for the hour I needed in the Main Cabin. I checked and found that Delilah, the only other person who was likely to be in the Main Cabin, had hurriedly made an appointment with one of the other agents now that hers had passed on. Shig and I carefully coordinated the times, so that I was sure to be alone for as long as I needed and I wouldn't cross paths with the mythical Jenna who did the cooking.

TWENTY-FIVE

Sunday, May 27, 1984

At 12:15, after I had seen Russell enter an empty conference room with Shig, and had seen Delilah waiting for her turn with Deborah Scottsfield, I grabbed my case and walk-jogged back through the woods to the compound.

By the time I arrived at the Main Cabin, I was warm, breathless and out of sorts. I entered the Cabin from the back door and went straight to Russell's study.

I really was not fond of snooping in other peoples' homes and it was as illegal as hell. I'd *still* be in prison if I had had to pay for all of the times I'd done it, but sometimes it was necessary. Normally, I just looked and got the sense of the building and the people who lived or worked in it. My job was to investigate and part of my investigation technique was to feel. I needed to handle furnishings and walk among belongings in order to get impressions of them and the people who lived with them.

* * *

I knew that *Boatman* could be a shortened version of something else. Since The Manchester Publishers had mentioned *Boatman* doing well, I had to assume that it had been published. If so, Russell would have a copy of it. I looked through his bookshelves and finally found one called *The Boatman of Scarborough* that was bound in a deep blue leather with gold lettering and page edges. The author's name was Bailey Attwood – Russell York. I thumbed through it, reading bits here and there, but I didn't have time for a serious perusal. I didn't know Russell's writing well enough to tell with a quick glance if the writing seemed like his.

Next, I tried the file cabinets. The cabinets were made of polished teak and were quite lovely. Only the bottom one was locked. I had found the small cluster of keys that I knew were in the same drawer that held the gun.

The top few drawers held manuscripts that corresponded to the bound copies he had on his bookshelf. There were only two or three authors' names among them.

The bottom drawer held several manuscripts as well. They all had different names. I found one called *The Boatman Returns*. This one was by someone named James Winthrop. I remembered hearing Shig mention that name as a former colonist who had had his manuscript destroyed. That was interesting, not to mention incriminating. I took photos. Then, I took photos of the title pages of the other manuscripts where the authors' names, addresses and phone numbers appeared. I shut and locked the drawer and turned my attention back to the bookcase. I found a copy of *Upper Ipswich* and another of *The Time Keeper's Trial* which roughly matched the names on two of the manuscripts. I quickly snapped a shot of the bookshelf. Then I locked up the place and gave it another glance to make sure I hadn't left anything behind.

It had taken me a little over half an hour. The rest of the afternoon would be taken up with interviews. I was not looking forward to it.

* * *

About 5:45 after the conference had finished for the day, I went back to the Main Cabin and knocked. Delilah, once again answered the door. This time, when she saw me, she attempted to shut the door, but I pushed it open and stepped inside.

"Russell is too devastated to speak to you now," she said. "He isn't seeing anyone."

"Delilah, you have no authority here. I'm afraid this is official business this time. Right now, I need to speak to Russell."

Delilah glared at me a few seconds then she ran upstairs. In a moment she was back with Russell.

"Miss Augustine, what is the meaning of this intrusion?"

"I have something to say and everyone needs to hear it. I would like you to sound the gong to bring the others here to the meeting room, I would like us all to gather there as it's the biggest room in the compound."

Russell stepped back and allowed me to enter, though the forbidding scowl on his face was enough to turn anyone away. "What 'official business' do you have that's so important?" he asked.

"This is official *police* business, Russell," I said. It wasn't really police business as such. The ME's report had not yet been returned and it was only I who suspected that Bleusette had been murdered. I would feel pretty foolish if the report stated that she had died from natural causes, but I would worry about that if and when it happened.

Delilah all but growled with rage.

Russell had looked outraged until the 'official police business' part and then he looked just confused.

"Police? Are the police coming here?" he asked.

"Don't worry," Delilah said. "She has some delusion that she's part of the police department or something. I'll get rid of her."

"This is not your house, Delilah," I told her. "Russell, this is official business. I am helping the Sheriff's office to investigate Bleusette's death."

"But it was a heart attack." He turned to Delilah. "You told me it was a heart attack."

"I believe the ME's report will indicate that it was murder, Russell," I said, cutting through Delilah's shrill explanation. "Please, would you sound the gong? I would like to discuss this with everyone and I do not want to have to repeat myself.

Russell silently went to his office and in a few moments, there were voices on the porch.

"Delilah, would you let them in, please?" I asked. It was all I could do to keep a semblance of a smile plastered onto my face. I had seen and heard way more of Delilah in the past days than I wanted to.

"I most certainly will not! You get out of this house immediately!"

Russell put his hand on Delilah's arm. Muttering, she went to the front door.

In a few moments the chairs in the meeting room were filled and I was standing at the lectern. Russell sat in Bleusette's chair near the cold brazier and Delilah reluctantly had taken one of the remaining desk chairs.

"I've asked you all to come this evening so I can explain something of what is going on." I still wasn't sure how much I was going to tell them but I plunged ahead.

"The Sheriff's office has deputized me to help with the investigation of Bleusette's death. I have some background in investigation." I saw Shig look down at his desk. Fritha looked frightened like she did most of the time these days. Lyric and Delilah looked defiant, Thorn bored, Arturo more interested than I had seen him look all month. Axel and Cyr appeared to not care one way or the other.

"I will need to question each one of you over the next day or so. I would like this to be cleared up so that we can all take the Wednesday afternoon ferry back home like we had planned to do."

Russell started to get up. "Please sit down Russell," I said. "You can't go anywhere right now."

"I most certainly can. I will not be 'questioned' by some amateur detective who fancies herself a professional. I am leaving."

"No, I'm afraid you aren't. You can either speak to me here or we can call Sheriff Bradley to speak to you. He, of course, would want to question you on Whidbey Island."

"I want to speak to my solicitor," he said. He was doing a splendid job mirroring Delilah's affronted expression.

"Fine. When we are finished here, you may call him or her and when he or she arrives, we will talk then. But we will talk."

"Right now," I continued with my gaze still on Russell. "I'm trying to get to the bottom of Bleusette's death. You all probably know by now that the ferry is not running any passengers from the island. I'm afraid you all have to stay here until this is cleared up. In the meantime, you are free to attend the conference and go anywhere on the island you wish. You simply cannot leave the island. The lights out mandate," again I stared at Russell when I said this. "is *not* in effect." Reluctantly, he nodded. "Further, be assured that you are free to stay in your cabins and have your meals provided as you have paid for them until the end of the conference." Again, my gaze came to rest on Russell, and, again, he nodded, though he looked as though he would rather eat dirt.

I explained to them that Bleusette's death was being investigated pending the Medical Examiner's report and that I was helping in the investigation. Also, they were not under arrest or anything of the sort but that when I questioned them, they all had a right to have their attorneys present. I would merely be taking more in depth statements from them. They all, except for Russell, agreed that they would speak to me.

"I suppose if I refuse and demand an attorney, you'll think I'm guilty," Delilah said.

I didn't say anything. I saw Russell frown at

her and, after a moment, even she insolently and defiantly agreed. We set up rough appointment times that would not interfere with the appointments they all had with agents or publishers at the conference.

Surprisingly, there were few questions. I believed that everyone was still in a state of shock.

When they had dispersed, I went back to my cabin. I saw no one on the way and thought they were probably gathered somewhere discussing the turn of events. I was glad to be alone. I needed a little time to think and sort out what information I had already.

After I had filtered out some of the witnesses' statements, I added the questionnaires that Shig, Bradley and I had collected from the conference attendees. I had dismissed some of them as well. Very few really. It seemed everyone had heard of Bleusette.

I had been surprised to find that the great Lawrence Fawcett, who had once been represented by Bleusette, had actually attended Whalesong for one term. I would be interested in hearing what he had to say.

My heart almost stopped when I had read Guy Loring's responses. He had indicated that he had once queried Bleusette as a potential agent for his first novel, *Last Train, Leaving Now.* Bleusette had turned him down out of hand. Her response had been that she didn't "believe a man so physically damaged would be able to withstand the pressures and demands of being a famous author", which she, of course, would have made of him.

Wow, I thought. *If that isn't incentive to commit murder, I don't know what is.* Of course, it wasn't really, but it did put Guy Loring on my list of suspects. That meant that at some point I would have to confront him. In the back of my mind, I may have thought that I could avoid talking to David altogether. If he only had said that he had never seen or heard of Bleusette Huntsman in his life, I could possibly have escaped. But no.

Another one of the questions I had added to the survey was "Have you ever attended the writers' colony known as Whalesong?" The fourteen people, including Lawrence Fawcett, who had answered in the affirmative, intrigued me. One was Mariah LeRoy and I had already spoken to her about her experience. But the others had been unknown to me and I was most interested to seek them out.

The conference was to last through the first half of Wednesday. The award luncheon would be the final event. Even so, unless this rat's nest had been cleared up by then, none of us would be leaving.

And even if the murderer of Bleusette had been discovered, there still remained the problem of the stolen manuscripts.

TWENTY-SIX

Monday, May 28, 1984

The next morning, I awoke early, took a walk and came back to find Strom leaving my breakfast at the door. He glanced my way, gave me a curt nod in greeting then turned to deliver Axel's breakfast. There were only a few meals left in his red wagon.

"Strom," I said. "Strom, wait!"

He stopped and turned back to me. He seemed surprised. I knew he wasn't used to interaction with the colonists. He stayed behind the scenes and we rarely saw him. He had, though, proven himself to be somewhat aligned with us rather than with Russell. I hoped that would help me to get honest answers from him.

As I approached him, he dragged his cap off. His tousled hair was white. "Something wrong with the meals?" He wore his perpetual scowl.

"No, no, nothing at all. I wonder if you would be available after you've finished your delivery to speak to me a little. It's about Ms. Huntsman's death."

"It's a bad business," he said, shaking his head. "Bad business."

"Yes, it is." I looked at my watch. I had made an appointment with Axel at 8:00. Most of my day was filled with interviews with the Colonists and the conference attendees. "Tell you what; when you deliver the lunches, deliver mine last and then we can talk for a few minutes. Would that work for you?"

"I have to wash Mr. York's car this afternoon," he said.

"Mr. York will be happy to let you put it off for a half hour. I won't keep you longer than that. Please stop by when you've delivered all the lunches and we'll talk."

He gave me a glum nod and resumed his trek along the trail. I watched him as far as I could. It didn't look right, a grown man pulling a toy red wagon of breakfasts.

At 8:00, I knocked on Axel's cabin door. He appeared in his usual attire of shirt, slacks and ascot but I got the impression he had just awakened. His thinning hair was combed but his eyes were puffy. He stepped back and ushered me in without saying anything.

"Axel," I said. "I won't take up too much of your time, but I have some questions to ask you. I know you're probably eager to get to the conference."

He nodded and looked resigned. "Yes, I have an appointment with Peter Saling at Saint Martin's before lunch." He had folded up his futon and gestured for me to sit on one end. I did and opened my case to retrieve my notebook and pen. He sat down at the other end and stared at the far wall, seeming to be deep in thought. He stretched his long legs out before him.

"Where were you when Bleusette died?"

"I was in the audience." He sounded surprised and gave me a quick glance. "You must have seen me."

"Were you watching when she did her chant and incense thing?"

He nodded.

"So you saw her collapse."

Again, he nodded.

"Do you know what she died from?"

"I believe it was a heart attack." His eyes opened wider and he turned his head to look at me. "You mentioned last night that you thought it was murder, but I hardly think so. It isn't possible to kill somebody that way, is it? A heart attack... That would be natural causes."

"I have reason to think it was something else. Do you know of any allergies that Bleusette had?"

"Oh, yes," he said. His smile was small and I

thought forced. "She seemed to be allergic to several things. At least, that's what she said."

"You don't think she really was?"

"Well, no." He chuckled sadly. "Not really. I believe she may have had allergies but she wasn't allergic to everything she professed to be, no."

"Like what?"

"She claimed she was allergic to peanuts and that she was allergic to bees. But she said she had allergies to tomatoes as well. She made a big fuss but she wasn't really allergic to tomatoes. She just didn't like them. And cinnamon. I don't know why she said she was allergic to cinnamon. She liked it."

"So you were pretty close to her, yes? You knew her pretty well, it sounds like."

That's when I saw Axel's defenses slam into place. "I...I knew her. We all knew her, didn't we?" A dull red had begun to creep onto his face.

I watched him closely. "Axel, were you having an affair with her?"

"I hardly think that's any of your business," he said, making a move to stand.

"Sit down, Axel. It's a legitimate question," I said. "Like I said, this is an investigation."

"All right. Yes, I was conducting an affair with Bleusette. However, that doesn't make me a killer."

"Where did you meet to 'conduct' your affair. Did

she come here, to your cabin or did you go to the main cabin."

"I hardly think this is relevant!"

"Bleusette's actions became relevant on the day of her death, Axel," I told him. "All of our actions did."

He sputtered a bit more, then settled down. "She came to me. She said that Russell didn't know anything about what she was doing. They...they slept in separate rooms, apparently."

"You don't think he noticed all the signaling between you two going on in Meeting?"

This time, he looked startled. Clearly, he had thought no one had ever noticed.

"You said you saw her die. You were with the rest of us. How did it make you feel?"

"It made me extremely upset," he said. I knew he was telling the truth. I could see it in his pale brown eyes. He stopped talking for a moment.

"In that case, Axel," I said. "I'm very sorry for your loss."

"Thank you," he said. "I cared for Bleusette. I know that she was hard for some people to get along with but she was a very special woman. I would never have killed her."

"What is your relationship with Delilah?"

That took him by surprise. The pupils in his eyes dilated and his face grew pink. "I know Delilah as well as any of us do, I suppose."

"You have no romantic attachment to her, then?"

He crossed his arms. "I assure you, I have no interest in Delilah." I thought that was a blatant lie. He had sat vigil outside of Thorn's cabin seeming to know that she, eventually, would emerge.

"You knew, though, that she had spent the night with Thorn," I said, still watching him carefully. The surprise I saw in his face wasn't from the fact that she had slept with Thorn, but from the fact that I knew about it.

He bowed his head. Then, a moment later, he raised it and nodded.

"How did that make you feel?"

"I am not interested in Delilah," he said, putting a slight emphasis on the "not".

"Axel, shortly after I saw you waiting outside Thorn's cabin, I saw Delilah slap you. Can you tell me what that was about?" I seriously hoped that he wouldn't soon realize that some of my questions had little to do with Bleusette's death, but, in my defense, I felt that all of the dynamics of the Whalesong colonists was potentially pertinent.

The red on his face deepened. "Delilah was angry at me," he said.

I waited.

"She had...made an advance."

"And you refused her."

He nodded.

"But that wasn't why she slapped you, was it?" I asked him. I was pretty sure the proposition had not occurred along the trail on the way back from Thorn's cabin. Axel had caught Delilah unawares.

"She slapped me because she said I was spying on her."

"Why *were* you spying on her?"

"I wasn't really..." he said, hesitating. "I had gone to her cabin to talk to her about something and she wasn't there. I was worried about her. When I passed Thorn's cabin, I heard her voice and I stopped."

"What did you want to talk to her about?" I asked.

He looked at me, obviously thinking. "That isn't relevant."

"It may be."

"It isn't," he said. I thought I saw a flash of fear on his face, then it was gone.

"What are you afraid of, Axel?"

He looked down at his lap, seemed to make a decision then raised his head. "Delilah threatened to tell Russell that I was...with Bleusette if I wouldn't... do what she wanted."

"Which was what? Sleep with her?"

He said nothing.

I knew that he was holding something back and that there was more to the story. Nevertheless, I plowed ahead. I didn't think I was going to hear all of it right then.

"Do you have any idea who might have wanted Bleusette dead?" I asked him. "Let's assume for a moment that I am right and someone killed her. Who do you think would do that?"

"I think I would ask Thorn that question," he said.

"Why?"

He shrugged "Intuition?" The shrug, the word and the coy look were so unlike him that I almost laughed. He was hiding something for sure.

I stayed quiet. After a moment, he looked at me again. "I have no idea who might have killed Bleusette," he said. "No idea."

I waited again but it seemed he had nothing further to say.

* * *

When the ME's report came back, I was not surprised. It had been determined that Bleusette had died from Anaphylaxis. The autopsy report showed an "'empty heart' attributable to reduced venous return from vasodilation and redistribution of intravascular volume from the central to the peripheral compartments." There had been no sign of any coronary disease.

Bleusette *did* have a real allergy after all. She had been allergic to peanuts. Someone knew that and had been willing to use them to kill her.

I had already noticed that the stick of incense she had handled had been coated with peanut butter then wiped clean. On all of the sticks on the top row in the box, the wood had looked darker than those on the lower layers. By lifting it to my nose, I could detect the unmistakable smell of peanut, though it wasn't noticeable at a distance of a foot or so. I had noticed too, that the hesitation Bleusette always made prior to pinching out the candle's flame was to give her a chance to wet the tips of her forefinger and thumb by licking them. It made her show of slowly pinching out the flame ever so much more dramatic. To me, the amount of peanut butter residue left on the wood handle of the incense didn't seem like enough to have caused someone to die.

"It only takes a trace," the Medical Examiner had told me when I had called him from the hotel. There had been documentation, he said, of someone dying from kissing another who had eaten peanuts moments before. He said that Bleusette's had been a severe reaction. It happens, he had told me regretfully. "It doesn't happen often, but it happens."

Perhaps the person who had killed her had only wanted to make her ill temporarily. But for what purpose? To frighten her? Again, why?

There was more than one person who disliked Bleusette and would be glad to see her off the island in one way or another. I knew that Delilah Duncan would have been eager to see Bleusette out of the way. She was, I believed, having an affair with Russell. Yet she had spent the night with Thorn. Why? She made a great show of mourning Bleusette but I had seen her instantly turn to Russell and now, it seemed, she was even staying at the Main Cabin.

Was Russell as eager to rid himself of Bleusette as Delilah was? He had gone to Fritha's cabin more than once, hoping to use his power over her. He had come to mine as well. He seemed to have no allegiance to any one woman. But was Russell a killer?

Axel and Bleusette had had something going on between them. Had she rejected Axel? Had she turned her attentions to Cyr or Thorn? I was sure that Axel had been lying when he said he had no idea who might have killed Bleusette.

My next appointment was with Cyr. I didn't get much from him. He was much more interested in Russell York than Bleusette.

"Bleusette flirted with me a little after my phone call one night," he admitted to me with an embarrassed laugh. "I pretended that I didn't understand her meaning, but I did all right."

"But you weren't interested?"

"No," he said. "She's a little..." his gaze flew to mine. "She's a little older than I am."

I agreed. She had at least twenty years on him.

"Can you think of anyone who would want Bleusette dead?"

He looked like he was seriously considering the question. He cocked his head to one side and said, "Fritha"?

"I asked *you*," I said.

"Okay, Fritha," he said more definitely. "Bleusette burned her manuscript. I'd be pretty pissed off if someone did that to me."

"Enough to kill them?"

"No, probably not," he said. "I don't know that I've ever been *that* mad."

I was pretty sure Cyr had nothing to do with Bleusette's death. He hadn't known about the allergies when I had asked him about them. I gathered that he didn't pay much attention to the details of what went on around him. Not a good habit if you want to be a writer. But I didn't say anything.

I had one more interview before lunch and then I would talk to Strom.

Lyric looked nervous when she let me into her cabin.

"My God, Sarah, you don't think I had anything to do with this, do you?"

"I don't know anything at this point," I told her. I steered her to the futon and sat down next to her. "I have to talk to everyone. After I finish talking to everyone in Whalesong, I have to speak to the conference people."

"Do you really think Bleusette was murdered?" she asked. "It's unbelievable."

"Why is that? It seems to me that there were more than a few people who didn't like her. I know that you were one of them."

She looked at me as though I had gone insane. "I didn't like her. Can you think of anyone who did? But I wouldn't kill her. I don't like either one of them. What reason could I possibly have for killing *her*?"

I looked at her. I liked Lyric and I hated to open old wounds for her but it had to be done. "I think that you might have wanted some satisfaction after what she did to Camille."

At the sound of the name, Lyric's face went paler, something I had thought impossible in a person with dark skin.

"How did you find out about... her?"

"That doesn't matter. Could you tell me about it?"

"I don't usually like to talk about it," she said. "She was my... my roommate."

"I got the impression she was something more than that," I told her gently.

She looked down at her lap, then up at me. "She was my partner. I...We were in love."

"And what happened?"

"She came to Whalesong," she said as if that was answer enough. "This was before I ever came here. I guess you already know that. Bleusette and Russell did what they do. They made her destroy her manuscript."

I waited.

"When she came home, she was devastated. She wouldn't eat, she couldn't sleep. She certainly couldn't write." A tear rolled down her cheek and then she began to sob softly. "She left. I didn't know where she had gone, and I thought something had happened to her. I thought she'd gotten hurt or... something."

I put my hand on Lyric's. She was telling the absolute truth. I wanted to cry myself.

"I reported her missing, and, at first, they couldn't find her. We...her mom and I found out later that she had gotten into drugs. She got into trouble for that. Then she got arrested for prostitution. I never saw her again." She was sobbing in earnest now.

I put my hand on her arm. "I'm so sorry, Lyric," I said and waited for her to calm.

"It seems to me that would make you want to get

revenge of some sort," I said after a moment.

"Of course, I did! But if I was going to kill, I wouldn't stop at one of them, I would kill them both."

"Do you know how Bleusette died, Lyric?"

"She had a heart attack, they said." She blew her nose and wiped her eyes. "Wasn't it a heart attack?"

"The coroner determined that it was an allergic reaction," I told her.

"To what!? I thought she was just blathering when she talked about how she was allergic to everything."

"I can't say, but that's what they determined."

"Well, I didn't do it," she said.

"Can you think of anyone who would?"

She looked at me for a long moment. "I would say that *I* would, except I didn't."

"Where were you when she died?"

"I was right there, watching," she said. "I saw the whole thing. She just...dropped. I thought she had fainted."

"Did you notice anyone hanging around the lectern prior to her chant and incense thing?"

"No, they had it all set up before-hand." She seemed drained. I didn't think I would be getting much more out of her.

"It will be cleared up in a few days," I told her and patted her hand before I stood.

"If I had known she was really allergic to something, I might have been tempted," she said. "In a way, I wish I *had* known. Only, like I said, I wouldn't have stopped with just her. I would have killed them both."

About that, I knew she was telling the truth.

Strom sat on my porch step with me while I ate my lunch.

He was clearly reluctant to be there. He kept looking around the way Fritha always did.

"I'm not supposed to talk to the colonists," he said. "Mr. Russell will have my hide if he catches me."

"Don't worry about Mr. Russell, Strom," I said. "Besides, this won't take long."

He continued to look nervous. He twisted his flat cap, put it on the step next to him then picked it up again.

"What all does your job entail?" I asked him.

"I do the yard work, and the repairs for the house," he said. "I deliver the meals my wife fixes for the students." He sighed. "Whatever Mr. Russell and Miss Bleusette ask me to do."

"Your wife cooks the meals?" I asked. "She's a wonderful cook."

He gave me a little smile. It was the first one I had ever seen from him. “I will tell her you said so.”

“And you keep an eye on the students and report to Mr. Russell, don’t you?”

“I don’t like to,” he said. “I don’t like spying on anyone.”

“But Mr. Russell makes you do it?”

He nodded. He started wringing his hat again. “Sometimes, I don’t tell him what I see, but he says that if I don’t tell him the truth, he will fire me. And she...”

I waited for a moment, then asked, “She what?”

“She is not a nice lady,” he said.

Well, that came as no shock. “In what way?”

“She is not nice to my wife,” he said. He looked at me as if to decide whether he should continue. “Once she hit my wife with a wooden spoon when she thought Jenna gave her a tomato in her salad.”

“My God, Strom!” I said. “Why on Earth do you stay?”

He shrugged. “We need the jobs. There aren’t very many jobs on an island as little as this one.”

"Why don’t you move then? Go to the mainland or one of the larger islands?”

“This is our home,” he said.

I didn’t think anyone needed a job that badly, but

I had to presume he was right that the opportunities on the island were limited. Besides, we were getting off track.

"Where were you when Miss Bleusette died?"

"I was here. I am usually here."

"Where was your wife?"

He looked surprised again. "She was at home."

"Do you know how Miss Bleusette died?"

He shook his head. "I heard it was a heart attack, but then they said that it was something else. Allergies?"

This time *I* was surprised. "Where did you hear that?"

"I think I heard Miss Delilah and Mr. York talking about it."

"Where were they?"

He shrugged. "It was when I picked up Jenna, I heard."

"When was that?"

"It was yesterday." He thought for a long moment. "Yes, it was yesterday," he said.

Yesterday, the ME's report had not yet arrived. I was most eager to speak to Delilah and, at some point, Russell.

"Okay," I said. "How do you feel about Miss Bleusette's death?"

"I feel okay," he said and looked at me. His eyes were almost as blue as Fritha's. "I am not sad."

He, apparently, wasn't the only one.

"Who do you think killed Miss Bleusette, Strom?"

"Me? I..." He stopped and looked completely blank. I wondered how many times he had been asked for his opinion at Whalesong. I would bet that this was one of the first.

"If I had to choose one, I would say Mr. York. Those people, they don't treat each other nice."

"How do you mean?"

He stepped up the hat wringing. "I don't think I can say any more," he said and stood.

I let him go, then. I thought that he had plenty of motive, but I wasn't sure that he would have jeopardized the job he so desperately needed. I thought he knew a lot more than he was saying.

TWENTY-SEVEN

Monday, May 28, 1984

The Memorial Service was held in one of the hotel's conference rooms. Bleusette had been affiliated with no particular church and the small one in the village of Klallam was too small to accommodate the number of people who would be attending. The hotel management, still deeply concerned that someone had died on their premises, had graciously accommodated Delilah's demands for the space. Bleusette, she had told them, was an agent beloved by the writing world.

Bleusette herself could not have timed her death more perfectly. She would have loved the thought of so many writers, agents and publishers paying homage to her, though most of them came out of curiosity or likely attended only because they happened to be there at the time.

Delilah had taken over the show. She made sure that Bleusettes chants were playing and the air was filled with the incense that Bleusette had loved.

Russell sat woodenly in the front row, looking uncomfortable and strange in a slightly out of date black suit. Delilah was beside him, hovering really. She was wearing a black dress that came to well above her knee. It too was somewhat out of fashion, though it looked well-made and expensive. I had to wonder if she had brought it with her to the island. If so, for what purpose? Perhaps it had actually belonged to Bleusette, I thought. Clothing which fit Bleusette would have been much too short for Delilah and that dress obviously was. I felt mean for thinking such things, but still… Delilah's gold shoes made an odd contrast to the dress and the situation.

Delilah murmured to Russell while the rest of the mourners filed in. At last, she stood to deliver the speech she had written. It was filled with dramatic pauses, quotes and moments of inability to speak at all. I don't think she fooled anyone. The excited sparkle in her eyes must have been visible all the way to the back row.

We colonists sat in the row behind Russell and Delilah which remained empty but for them. Delilah had told us with a straight face that Russell needed the extra space for his profound grief.

Various writers, agents and publishers stood to momentarily utter cursory statements as Delilah called upon them. Only a few demurred and refused, saying that they hadn't known the deceased at all. I thought it was interesting as well as telling that Delilah called on none of the colonists. Perhaps she was afraid that one or two might actually tell the truth.

I sat between Shig and Lyric, with Fritha on the other side of Shig and Cyr on the other side of Lyric. Arturo sat next to Cyr. I spotted Thorn, looking bored as usual in a row farther toward the back. I didn't see Axel at all.

We silently listened as Delilah prattled about the good Bleusette had done and her accomplishments, both real and imagined. At one point, I glanced over and saw Lyric roll her eyes and I was certain I heard a derisive snort from Arturo. Russell had apparently heard it too as he swiveled his head around and gave Arturo a glare.

At long last, the memorial service attendees dispersed to their respective classes and meetings. It was time for me to resume my interviews. I wasn't looking forward to the next one on my list.

I had arranged to have all of the colonists' interviews in their own cabins in order to minimize distractions and interruptions. Strom was using the van as a shuttle going between the compound and the hotel at regular intervals so we were able to come and go as needed.

Thorn let me into his cabin reluctantly. He clearly wanted me to think that he was unconcerned and above all the ruckus from the past few days. His faux blasé attitude put me instantly on the alert.

He had not bothered to fold up his futon and I

wasn't inclined to go anywhere near it. I pulled over his desk chair, removed the pile of clothing that hung there and sat down. He had no other place to sit but on the futon.

"How well did you know Bleusette, Thorn?" I asked him.

He gave me an indulgent laugh. "I knew her pretty well," he said. "Pretty well."

"How so?"

"You mean was I having sex with her? Sure, I was. I think all the men here were, weren't they?'

"No, I don't think so. Why do you think that?"

He looked flummoxed. What did he think? That all women thought all men wanted nothing but sex?

"Well, I heard she was sleeping with Meredith."

"Axel isn't the only other male in Whalesong. Where did you hear that?"

He shrugged. "I don't know. I heard she had the hots for that Cyr guy too."

"Did Delilah tell you that?"

He shrugged again and didn't seem inclined to answer. I let it go. I could come back to it later.

"Where were you when she died?"

"I was sitting there, watching, man."

"How did that make you feel?"

"Hey, I've seen people die before. Plenty of people.

Doesn't bother me."

So much for the "Any man's death diminishes me" business, I thought.

"Did you see anyone hanging around the lectern or the speakers' table prior to the speech?"

"No. And I wasn't there, if you thought I was."

"I didn't say you were. I'm simply trying to find out what happened."

"She had a heart attack, didn't she?" He suddenly seemed to remember something and got up from the futon to retrieve a large plastic bag of pepperoni from an open gym bag on the floor. He reached in and extracted a stick, then chewed it with his mouth open.

I didn't answer his question. "Were you aware of any allergies that Bleusette may have had?"

"Allergies? No. I mean, she talked about stuff like tomatoes and cinnamon, but I never paid any attention to that stuff."

I knew at once that he was lying. I didn't even have to touch him to get it. The man was like a large print book; you could see his content from anywhere in the room.

"Hey," he said. "Why don't you join me on the bed here? You don't have to be so standoffish."

"Thanks, no," I told him.

"You women around here are pretty cold," he said.

"Except for Bleusette. Man, she was something."

"Is Delilah cold too?"

"Oh, no! Delilah's one hot dish." He actually smacked his lips.

"Have you been sleeping with her too?"

He gave me a "Well, duh!" look and shrugged.

"Are you married, Thorn?"

He laughed as though that was the most ridiculous thing he had ever heard. "No way! I'm married to the craft."

"The craft?"

"Writing."

Yeah, I thought. I'd read his work and heard some of it in Meeting. It was spare and completely lacking in color, flavor, anything that would give it interest.

"So, you want to know if I killed Bleusette, don't you?" he asked smiling.

"Did you?"

"Kill her? Maybe."

"Look, Thorn," I said. "I'm trying to conduct an investigation. It doesn't help when you try to deflect my questions, tease, change the subject. Can you just answer my questions?"

"Sure." He laughed. "Okay, I didn't kill her. Satisfied?"

I ignored him. "So you said you were sleeping

with Bleusette. How do you feel about her death?

"Fine. She didn't mean anything. I wasn't in love with her or anything. I can't afford to get involved with just one woman." He stretched his arms out and put them in back of his head. To me, that was a classic move. This guy was always performing. I couldn't and didn't believe much of anything he said. I did put him at the top of my list of suspects, though.

"You don't seem terribly broken up about her death," I said.

"I'm kind of relieved, really. She could be a little pushy."

"Pushy? How?"

"Oh, you know. Demanding." He laughed, a little shamefacedly, I thought. "I guess I couldn't leave her alone, either."

"So you were somewhat obsessed by her?"

"Pfft...! Not me. You should talk to Cyr. She talked about him *all* the time."

"Did that make you jealous?"

"Oh, hell, no." He frowned harder.

I thought he was lying about that, too. Neither did I believe that he had a regular thing going with Bleusette. In fact, I thought he had never laid a finger on her. His eyes flicked to the wall over my right shoulder.

“I wouldn’t blame you if you were,” I said. “After all, Cyr’s a good looking guy. Pretty young, though.”

“Humph!” was all he had to say about that.

“So, her death made you relieved,” I said.

“I told you I didn’t kill her.” I thought he was beginning to get angry now. *Good*, I thought. Angry people sometimes slip up.

“Do you have any idea about who might have killed Bleusette?

“You know who you should look at,” he said. “You should be asking Lyric. That woman hated Bleusette.”

I was surprised. Clearly, he had been thinking about this.

“Do you know why?”

“No,” he said. “But everyone knows she hates her. And Russell too.”

“One more question, Thorn,” I said and stood up. “Were you having an affair with Delilah as well?”

“Naaaww,” he said, letting the word drag out. He looked like he had something more to say.

“I happen to know she spent the night in your cabin one night. What were you doing, playing Mah Jong?”

“Ma what?” he said.

“Never mind. She did spend the night here,

though."

"Okay, yeah. She did. But, I don't know. She's not really my type."

I didn't think Bleusette was his type either, but I didn't say anything. I held out my hand to shake his. He put his hand into mine and immediately I knew, though it came as no surprise, he had been lying about almost everything he had said and he knew more than he let on. Much more.

Delilah was next on my list. She didn't want to let me in. I told her that we could sit on the porch if she preferred, but that seemed to go against her sensibilities and she reluctantly let me into her cabin. The place had a stale smell as though no one had been there for a day or two.

"What did you think of Bleusette, Delilah?" I asked her.

"Why, Bleusette Huntsman was my best friend," she said. She did the thing again where she looked down her nose at me. It wasn't going to work this time either.

"Your best friend? Really?" I knew right off that she was lying. Her gaze constantly flicked to the right and the small muscles around her mouth tightened and relaxed.

"Yes, of course. Everyone knows that."

"Tell me about your relationship with her."

“I adored her. And she adored me.” She constantly flipped her hair around as though it would make her seem energetic and attractive. It didn’t. “We were very close. She helped me get my first story published. And every time I was making a new story, she was nothing but encouraging. I honestly don’t know what I’m going to do without her.”

“Maybe you can help Russell to cope,” I said, not really meaning to be sarcastic but sometimes I can’t help it.

“Russell, the poor, poor man.” She bowed her head and raised her hands to it. “I’m doing what I can for him.”

I’ll just bet, I thought but didn’t say.

“Where were you when it happened?” I knew, of course, because I had seen her in the audience waiting to hear Lawrence Fawcett speak.

“I was sitting in the audience. I saw it happen. It was the most horrible thing…” She turned her head and covered her eyes with one hand as though she were conjuring up tears.

“Do you know how she died?”

She put her hands back into her lap. “The doctor said thunderclap heart attack.” She blinked her eyes several times.

“Are you aware of any allergies Bleusette might have had?”

She looked up again. “Oh, no. She didn’t have any

allergies. She was in wonderful health."

"Strange, being her best friend, that you didn't know she had allergies," I said, trying to sound like I was simply musing. "You and Russell were heard talking about her death possibly being due to an allergic reaction."

She looked elaborately blank. "If she had allergies, she never mentioned them. She was strong that way," she said, but she was starting to sound a bit unsure, I thought.

"I heard her talk about her allergies many times," I said.

"Oh," she said, laughing. "She was just being funny. She had a wonderful sense of humor. I loved that about her."

"Wasn't that what she and Russell went to the mainland for last week? She was visiting her allergist, I thought."

"Oh, no, that wasn't an allergist. That was a routine doctor's visit."

"No," I said. "She told us all that she was going to see Dr. George Marshall. He's quite a well known allergist in the Seattle area."

She shrugged. "Hmmm. Maybe she had recently developed an allergy." Delilah looked at me, almost defying me to contradict her again.

"Did you see anyone hanging around the speakers' table prior to the speeches?"

She looked genuinely dumbfounded when she shook her head.

"What do you think Russell will do now? Do you think he will keep Whalesong going?"

"I'm sure he will. Why wouldn't he?"

"Money," I said, trying for innocence this time. "It must cost quite a lot to keep this place running, I would think."

"He doesn't have to worry about that," she said, the confidence fairly dripping. "He'll get all Bleusette had."

"Oh, is there family money on her side?"

"She inherited." She flipped her hair again. "Yes, Russell will have all he needs. We may...He may go abroad. To forget."

"To England, maybe," I said.

She looked at me and I thought I saw suspicion in her

eyes. "Why England?"

"Why not?" I asked. "Can you think of anyone who would have wanted to kill Bleusette?"

"Axel," she said almost immediately. "Either him or Thorn. Or that little blondie...Fritha." She shook her hair out. "Honestly, she wanted to get back at Bleusette for burning her manuscript. Go talk to any of them. Or maybe that Chinese guy."

"Shig is Japanese," I said.

"Whatever. He's such a Mr. Goodie Twoshoes, I wouldn't be at all surprised if he did it." She laughed. "Seriously, though, I'd say Axel."

"Why Axel?"

She shrugged. "Oh, you know. They were having a fling. She told me all about it. I think she was losing interest. Maybe he was jealous."

I wanted to address the slap that she had given to Axel as well as the night she had spent with Thorn but since almost everything she had said so far was fantasy, I decided to leave it alone at least for now.

She shrugged again and stood, as if to shake off the whole interview. I guessed my questions were finished as well. Mentally, I put her somewhere near the top of my suspects list too.

Even before I got to Fritha's cabin, I began to dread the interview with her. She seemed so fragile. I wondered if she was capable of killing one of the people who had been instrumental in what she thought of as the death of her book.

"Oh, Sarah," she said when she answered the door. "This is the worst! I just can't believe it! Bleusette helped me get that story published in the *Three Penny Review* and now she's dead."

"You said you were going to look for another agent at the conference," I said.

"Well, it doesn't matter anymore, does it? My

manuscript is gone." She seemed to deflate then. It was as though the death had temporarily taken her mind off of the manuscript she believed had been destroyed but now the situation had rushed back on her.

"I have some questions to ask, Fritha," I said, after giving her a moment.

"I know you have to investigate, but I honestly don't know a thing. I was there. I saw it, but I don't know anything. Besides, it was just a heart attack, wasn't it?"

I ignored the question. "Did you notice anyone hanging around the speakers' table?"

"No, just Bleusette and her incense."

"I meant before that."

She shook her head. "You don't think someone somehow killed her, do you?"

"Yes, Fritha, I believe someone did."

"How?" Her blue eyes went round and her hands flew to her mouth. "You think someone gave her some drug that makes you have a heart attack?!" She looked around as if she expected to see a murderer skulking in her cabin. "That means someone at the conference," she said. "Or...Oh, my God! You don't think it was one of us?"

"I don't know what to think at this point. That's why I'm talking to people."

"But why would I..." She looked at me in horror.

"You think I killed her because she burned up my book, don't you?!"

I laid my hand on hers to calm her, but she yanked it away. "I didn't kill her. If I was going to kill someone, I would have killed Russell, not Bleusette."

"Bleusette was the one who burned your manuscript," I reminded her.

"Yes, but she didn't come to my cabin and try to have sex with me," she said.

She had a point. "To me, the loss of the manuscript supersedes the attempted rape," I said. "What about you?"

She sighed. "When I think about it, I think I would have probably killed them both if I had the chance. Her for the manuscript thing and him for the sex thing. But, then I don't think I could actually kill anyone."

"If you had to guess, who would you think capable of doing it?"

She glanced frantically around as if to find the answer hidden somewhere in her cabin. "I...I don't know. Maybe Cyr?"

I was surprised. "Really? Why Cyr?"

She looked miserable. "Well, he's always telling on people and trying to get them into trouble. I don't know. I guess it could have been pretty much any of us, couldn't it?" Her blue eyes looked huge as she stared at me. "I don't think I could do it even if I had the chance."

I tended to agree with her, but I had seen her inconsolable devastation after her manuscript had seemingly gone up in smoke. Much as I didn't want to, I left Fritha near the top of my suspects list too.

Arturo gave me nothing. Arturo was interested in one thing. He wanted to be known as a writer. I wondered briefly if he would be willing to commit murder to become known. I doubted it. If he had committed murder, he would be in a permanent prison, not just one that met four times a year.

He told me he had been getting a cup of coffee from the back of the conference room when Bleusette had died. He had not paid attention to the speaker's table at all, he said. But, rather, had been trying to think of an excuse for leaving. He told me that he held animosity toward neither Russell nor Bleusette. He didn't like the way they pushed people around and thought they had treated Fritha "awfully" but they had not done anything against him.

I could think of no reason for him to have wanted Bleusette dead. He seemed content with the status quo. He knew nothing about the allergies, beyond what she had said numerous times. His opinion was the same as Axel's, that she said she was allergic to everything when she probably wasn't allergic to much of anything at all.

Arturo's guess about who might have killed

Bleusette was "whoever is the least likely person."

"That would probably be me, wouldn't it?" I asked him. "Or you."

He laughed and nodded.

Since Russell had insisted that his "solicitor" be present while he was being questioned, I had to put off questioning him. He, after all, had plenty of motive for wanting Bleusette dead. We had all heard the loud arguments coming from the Main Cabin on warm spring nights. He knew his wife was having at least one affair with at least one colonist. And I couldn't forget what Delilah had said about Russell being the beneficiary of Bleusette's money. I was reasonably sure that he himself had been sleeping with Delilah even before she had moved into the main cabin. Then there was the fact that he had also turned his attentions on Fritha and me as well. Oh, yes, he had lots of motive.

TWENTY-EIGHT

Tuesday May 29, 1984

The next morning, I awoke to a long list of more interviews. This time, with the conference attendees, agents, publishers and editors. I was hoping it would turn out to be more interesting than my interviews of the day before, but I was convinced that the killer was one of the Whalesong ten.

My first appointment was with Lawrence Fawcett. I met up with him in one of the smaller conference rooms that the WCWA staff had offered us for interviews. He had an interestingly asymmetrical face and graying hair that I had seen innumerable times on book jackets. I knew that he was about my age, maybe early forties. I wondered what it must be like to be so recognized. I didn't think that I would like it.

"I'm sorry you have to take the time to do this, Mr. Fawcett," I told him. "I will take as little of your time as possible."

"Think nothing of it," he said graciously. His voice was deep and fruity. "I have never attended a writer's conference this exciting. And, believe me, I've attended a few. Ask away. As long as you don't ask me where I get my ideas, I'll answer anything you throw at me."

I laughed. "You don't have to worry then," I said. "The question hadn't occurred to me. What I am most interested in is your time at Whalesong,"

"Ah!" He looked up at the ceiling. "It was many years ago," he said. "I'd say back in the late sixties. I had had a couple of stories published and was looking for a place where I could get away from life and just write."

"Whalesong seems like an odd choice in that case," I said. "It's extremely regimented."

"Well, I didn't know that then. I was enamored with the idea of being led by the great Russell York. And I thought it was ideal that an agent was at hand. It seemed perfect. Russell and Bleusette were younger. Russell was becoming well known. Bleusette was quite beautiful. It seemed perfect to me."

"But it wasn't?"

He laughed. "I tangled with Russell almost immediately. After I had read a couple of chapters, he wanted me to turn my attentions to westerns of all things. He tried and tried to get me to hand over my manuscript and write something else. I wasn't about to do that. I was working on –well, it turned out to be *Crowded City* in the end. If I had given up on it for one reason or another, I certainly wouldn't have destroyed it."

I had read *Crowded City*, a classic in the historical thriller genre. "What was your relationship with Bleusette? You mentioned that she was beautiful. Were you attracted to her?"

"Oh, sure." He laughed again. A hank of his salt and pepper hair fell into his eyes and he idly brushed it away. "I was in my twenties. I was attracted to any female under the age of forty."

"She became your agent," I said.

He nodded. "After I left Whalesong, I found a publisher interested in *Crowded City*. I didn't know the first thing about publishing and knew I had to get an agent. Since I knew Bleusette, she seemed perfect." He laughed softly.

"But she wasn't?"

"No, she was fine. I… It turned out she wasn't the right agent for me, is all."

"And you never went back to Whalesong," I said.

"At the end of the term, I decided not to return. I wasn't so much interested in the instruction, though, God knows, I should have been. What I wanted was a way to write without distractions. I've since learned that there is no such thing. If you can't learn to write, distractions and all, you'll never be a writer."

"Good to know," I said.

"You a writer?"

"No, but I've dabbled.

"Well, if you want to write, do it. Don't dabble."

I nodded. "So, you pretty much didn't really know Bleusette and haven't seen her for at least twenty years. Did she ever mention anything about allergies when you knew her?"

"Allergies? No, I don't think so. The only time I was ever around her was at that damned Monday Dinner. She was there at the Meetings of course, but she didn't have much to say. Thankfully, she hadn't started with that incense and chant thing yet. That would have driven me straight out of there."

I laughed again. Just then, I caught a flash of color out of the corner of my eye and turned to see Delilah just ducking away from the open door. I wondered if she had been listening.

"I don't think I have any more questions for you, sir. I do appreciate your taking the time to do this." I put my hand out for him to shake. His handshake was firm and honest. The man was hiding nothing.

It was about a half hour later when I took a break in the ladies' room. I was washing my hands when Delilah came in and, from the expression on her face, I knew that she had something to say.

"I know you're a fraud," she said. "Don't think that you can get away with it."

Had she found out somehow that I was a private detective? How could she? I wondered.

"A fraud?" I said. "Whatever are you talking about, Delilah?" I watched her in the mirror. She couldn't resist her own reflection and she smoothed brows, flipped her hair in that annoying way she had and wiped the edges of her lipstick while she spoke.

"I saw you flirting with Lawrence Fawcett this morning. Don't think that you can get ahead by making plans with him."

"What plans would that be?" I asked her.

"Oh, don't be coy! He knows influential people. Lots of them. You won't get ahead by sleeping with him. He's gay. He won't want anything to do with you."

I laughed. She was still looking outraged when I pushed through the door.

* * *

By afternoon, I was exhausted from talking to writers, agents and publishers. I had eliminated most of the latter two, though. It was the writers who still remained on my list that I was most interested in. I was amazed at the amount of anger toward Bleusette that I had encountered. Either those who knew her were mad at her for accepting them as clients and then seemingly ignoring them or they were angry for the reason that she would not accept them. Neither of those reasons, however, seemed a motive for murder. Also, I wasn't sure how many people knew about Bleusette's allergies and in particular her allergy to peanuts. Axel knew. Thorn knew. Russell did too. Bleusette had made a sizable ruckus about her many illnesses and allergies and I knew that some of them were completely baseless. She had eaten foods often that she claimed she had allergies to and so no one took her complaints seriously.

I had finished up with what I had hoped to be my last interview of the afternoon. I stood, stretched and turned toward the door of the small conference room I had been using.

A man in a wheelchair was blocking the doorway.

For a moment, we simply looked at each other, saying nothing. My heart started to thud and my hands suddenly turned to ice.

"Cheyenne," David said at last.

"David." I thought my voice sounded remarkably calm.

"I had hoped this would never happen."

"Funny," I said. "I always hoped it would." He looked the same as I had seen him in Hawaii except that he now wore a suit and tie. He had the leg of his pants tucked up behind what remained of his left leg and the left arm of his jacket the same. He watched me closely with his remaining right eye.

He smiled and I was suddenly furious with him.

"You always knew the perfect thing to say," he said. "I only meant that I had hoped you would never have to see me this way."

"What way is that? Alive?"

"Cheyenne," he began but I cut him off.

"No, don't bother explaining to me why you let me think you were dead for twenty years. I hardly think that matters now, anyway. If you wanted out of our relationship you should have said so."

"I didn't 'want out of our relationship,' and I think you know that." He sounded like he was a bit miffed himself. *Good*, I thought. Although, what he had to be upset about, I didn't know.

He moved his motorized wheelchair closer and I sat back down. "I'm glad you're here," I said. "I need to interview you anyway."

"I didn't come in here for that," he said. "I came because I knew you were aware that I was here." He stopped and watched me. I don't know what he expected. It was as if I no longer knew him at all. I supposed I didn't. "If you have questions, go ahead and ask."

"You indicated on your questionnaire that you had had contact with Bleusette Huntsman at one time. Did you know if she had any allergies?"

"I didn't mean..." He sighed. "No, I didn't know she had any allergies."

"But you did know her? You indicated on your survey that she had rejected you as a client."

"Cheyenne, I don't want to talk about Bleusette right now."

I put down my pen and looked at him, making my face a perfect, I'm sure, study in patience. "What do you want to talk about?"

"I want to explain to you what happened."

I continued to look at him. I didn't necessarily want to hear some lame excuse as to why he had left to go to Vietnam and had been injured but never bothered to contact me again.

"I'm not the man you think I am," he said finally after the pause had gotten awkward.

"That, I know to be the truth," I said. "The man I remember wouldn't have let me think he was dead for twenty years. The man I remember knew that I loved him and would have been terribly hurt if he did something like that. Obviously, you are not the man I thought you were." I hadn't really wanted to let on how much he had hurt me, but I couldn't take it back at that point.

"I'm sorry," he said. He bowed his head.

"I would think so," I said, standing. "I'm very busy.

You won't mind if I leave you here."

"Cheyenne, wait," he said, and I stopped. It was David's voice asking me to stop. How could I not?

"When I landed in the hospital, they didn't think I was going to live. They didn't know who I was. I had lost my dog tags. *I* barely knew who I was. I was unconscious most of the time." He waited, apparently for me to say something. I didn't.

"When I finally got some sense back and saw how much of me was gone, I wanted to die. I was actually angry that they had saved me." He laughed softly. "I couldn't come back and let you hook yourself up to —"

"Oh, don't give me that 'half a man' crap!" I said, finally breaking my silence. "That's bullshit! You could have done me the courtesy of letting me decide."

"I understand why you're angry."

"No," I said. "You don't. I spent years trying to get over it. Years! I met men that I liked. Loved! But I didn't let them get close. Because of you." That wasn't entirely true, but I was too angry to care.

"Oh, really?" He said, getting angry himself now. "I came back about twelve or thirteen years ago and discovered you were married. So, instead of totally ruining everything you had built for yourself, I quietly went away again, glad that you had found someone. Don't give me that 'I never got close to anyone' line, because you don't marry people you don't get close to."

Okay. He had me there.

"So, is Mr. Chey here too?" He made a show of looking around.

"No," I said. "We're...not together anymore."

He watched me. I watched him. Oh, hell, it was David.

He must have seen my eyes change, felt my aura shift, something. "So, you're a lot more badass than you used to be," he said. "That star shaped scar on your cheek is a nice touch."

I had to laugh then, even though I didn't want to. "And you're a hotshot author," I said. "But don't think you're off the hook. You let me suffer needlessly for twenty years. It wasn't your decision to make."

"I know that now," he said. "And I'm sorry."

"Why did you come here, anyway?" I asked him. "I was told that you never make speaking engagements, you never travel. Hawaii is a long way from here. Why here? Why now?"

He shook his head in honest appearing bewilderment. "I can't say."

"What the hell is that supposed to mean?"

"I guess I felt, somehow...driven." He gazed at me with that curiously disturbing one eyed-stare.

"I can't explain it." He paused and I let him. He looked around. "What are you doing here anyway?" He asked. "I certainly never expected you to be at a writers conference."

"I've just spent the last month at Whalesong."

"Interesting." His right eyebrow went up. "Are you writing?"

"A little," I admitted. "I'm just starting to write."

He nodded. "I met a man yesterday who must be one of your contemporaries at Whalesong. Takao?"

"Takano," I told him. "Shig Takano."

"I have to say I was impressed with him. He came up to me after the seminar. Didn't ask me to read his work or even ask for an autograph. Said he just wanted to meet me and shake my hand. The more we talked, the more interested in his work I was. How good of a writer is he?"

"In my opinion, he's excellent."

"Glad to hear it," he said. "I gave him the name of my agent and told him to contact her. She's actually here and he said he had had a session with her." He took a slim notebook out of his jacket pocket and held it out to me. "Write his name down for me, would you, and I'll tell her to be on the lookout for his work."

"Yes, he had a meeting with her yesterday," I told him, writing Shig's name in his notebook. "It would be wonderful, though, if you could put in a word about him."

"Will do, Chey," he said, looking at the name I had written,

It almost undid me hearing my name again from his lips. Between that and his kindness toward Shig, my icy anger melted away completely.

We talked for awhile longer and I began to feel more and more like myself. But I realized that David was not the same man, though, occasionally, I heard notes of the old David in his laugh, saw flashes in a passing expression. Somehow, he was less innocent, less loving than he had been. He was hardened. It shouldn't have come as a surprise to me, I suppose, given what had happened to him. It made me sad to think that my David was gone and there was another in his place. But at the same time, I felt released from something.

At last, I stood. "I have to be getting back," I said and started to turn away.

"Where did you hear that I never make speaking engagements?" he asked as if what I had said had only just then sunk in. "And how did you know that I live in Hawaii? I never include that in my bio material."

I turned back again. "I was in Hawaii," I said. "I read one of your books and I…I saw you."

"I…Was that in January?" He looked confused.

"Yes. I read this really great book and when I

finished, I happened to see the back flap of the dust jacket and there was a guy who looked nothing whatsoever like David, but I knew it was him, nevertheless."

"I felt that," he said slowly. "I felt you. That you were near. Not so strange, I guess. We used to have a connection. Maybe that's the reason I felt so drawn to come to this conference. When they sent the invitation, I actually threw it away, then fished it out of the bin." He shook his head. "I should have known. You still use your 'abilities'?"

"I do. I'm a private investigator. I was on Hawaii working on a case. That's actually why I'm at Whalesong, too. I went undercover to investigate something. When Bleusette was killed, the Sheriff deputized me."

I saw a sparkle of admiration in his eyes. "Like I said." His voice used to be so dear. "Badass. Supremely badass."

When I finally left David, it was nearing dinner, and I rushed to catch the van for the last trip Strom would make that evening. I hadn't asked David to join me. We could have hit the hotel restaurant and continued to catch up. I wasn't sure why I didn't want to, at first. It was as if some great sea-change had taken place in me. I had suffered over David for so long, it had become a habit. I felt as though I had gone through some kind of miraculous rehab where the cure was instantaneous. I felt lighter. A strange feeling, for sure.

Back in my cabin, I ate my dinner, still marveling at myself.

Suddenly, the sound of the gong filled the evening. I put the last bite of cherry tart into my mouth and grabbed my case. This was surprising, the gong ringing at 6:30. We normally had Meeting at seven but Meetings and Classes had been suspended during the conference. It would have been unusual, except that nothing at Whalesong was usual right then.

I made my way through the semi-darkness to the Main Cabin. I heard someone behind me and saw Cyr and Axel, looking confused and hurrying toward me. Shig and Fritha were right behind them.

The first thing I felt when I opened the door was a buzz of fear. That was even before I saw Thornton Swift standing over Russell York with a gun. Russell had a huge blood stain on the front of his shirt and it was clear even from where I was standing that he was dead.

TWENTY-NINE

Tuesday, May 29, 1984

Arturo was just inside the door with his hands covering his mouth. His gaze found mine and then he didn't move. The others crowded into the room behind me. Fritha made a frightened squeak and Shig said, "What the fuck?" I heard Axel's voice say, "Oh, hell!" and Cyr crossed himself. Thorn slowly raised the gun and pointed it in our direction. No one moved. Horror hovered over us like a cloud.

"Where's Lyric?" I asked then. "And Delilah?"

Just as I said her name, Delilah burst through the door. She shrieked and rushed to Russell's side paying no attention to Thorn or the gun. She knelt next to Russell and cradled his head into her lap. I heard her saying "Oh, you fool! You utter fool!" but I wasn't sure who she was talking to or about.

Thorn waved the gun at us and commanded us to shut up, though none of us were speaking.

"Sit down on the floor," he said. We did, still silent.

Everyone moved as quietly as possible, wanting, it seemed, to disappear into the background.

Thorn stood in front of us while Delilah wailed in back of him. I heard her repeating, "It was for you, my darling, for you!" over and over while she stroked Russell's hair.

"Yes," Thorn said, as though someone had asked him a question. "I killed him."

Fritha began her low moaning again, but I put my hand on her arm.

"Thorn," I said, "Why don't you put down the gun and we can all discuss this. There's no reason for you to hurt any of us."

"I'm in charge now," he said. "Not you. I don't have to answer any more of your questions. I killed Bleusette too and I'm going to kill you all. Don't think I won't."

"Thorn, man," Shig said quietly. "You won't be able to get away with it."

"Oh," Thorn said, waving the gun again. "I will 'get away with it.' Once I've killed all of you, Delilah and me will leave the island." He gave an indulgent laugh. "Don't worry about me."

"How are you going to leave the island?" Axel asked him. His voice was calm as if he were asking for directions. "There are no ferries."

Delilah still crooned to Russell. Thorn turned to glance at her, then back to us. "Helicopter," he said.

Clearly the man was delusional. "You said you killed Bleusette, Thorn," I said. "How did you do it? We haven't been able to figure it out." Of course, we had, but I wanted to hear what he had to say. I was pretty sure it had not been him.

"I poisoned her," he said grandly, still waving the gun wildly at us. I only hoped that he didn't accidently pull the trigger.

"You idiot!" Delilah shrieked at him. "What have you done? You killed him. I didn't want you to kill *him.*"

I glanced at Shig and was pretty sure he had heard it too. She had definitely put an emphasis on the word "him".

"What kind of poison did you use?" I pressed. At that point, I was both wishing that Delilah would shut up and hoping that she would keep talking.

"Arsenic," Thorn said. "I used arsenic."

"Ah," I said, nodding.

"You see why I can't let any of you leave this island alive, don't you?" Still holding the gun, he turned to Delilah and knelt next to her. I heard him murmur something to her but she shook him off.

"You fool," she said in a spitting hiss. "It wasn't arsenic."

"You said poison."

"Idiot! I said peanuts. Peanuts are *like* poison to

her. Now, look what you have done!"

"I was protecting you, 'Lilah!" Thorn said. "Helping you."

"You call this helping me?! You didn't help me!" she shrieked at him. "I came to you and asked you to help me, but no!"

"Let me see if I can help Russell," I said and stood.

"Sit down!" Thorn said, but his attention was still on Delilah, so I remained standing.

"Why did you kill him? Why!" Delilah's voice was rising and I thought she would be in full hysteric mode in another minute.

"I did it for you," he said. "For us. We can go away. We can open our own colony." He seemed to believe that this plan was actually viable.

"You fool!" she shrieked. "You've ruined everything! Everything! I asked you to do a simple thing, but no! You couldn't do it. You wanted to do it *your* way. Well, your way isn't working, is it? To think, I wasted sex on you!"

I took a tentative step forward and Thorn didn't seem to notice so I stepped even closer. I sensed someone behind me get up too. I put my hand in back of me to motion whoever it was to stay put.

As I got closer, Thorn finally noticed me and steadied the gun. The gleam in his eyes was alarming. I believed the man to actually be deranged. I stopped where I was, about three feet from him. I put my hands out to each side, first moving the fingers of one hand and then the other. He seemed to try to see both of them at the same time. I slowly moved into the ready stance.

The roundhouse kick knocked the gun from Thorn's hand and sent it spinning across the floor. Out of the corner of my eye, I saw Shig bend to pick it up.

I moved toward Russell. I didn't think there was any hope, but I didn't want to take that chance.

Delilah, her lips curled back from her teeth, shrieked and jumped to her feet, crouching over Russell like a jealous she-lion. "Don't you dare touch him! Don't you dare!

I stopped. "Delilah, let me take a look. He might still be alive," I said slowly trying for calm but she was having none of it.

"Why did you have to come here anyway? You've done nothing but cause trouble. You tried to take Russell, you flaunted the rules and ruined the term for everyone!" She was so furious she was spitting. Suddenly she whirled on Thorn. "And you! You couldn't even manage to get her to leave the island."

Thorn looked stricken. "I hit her as hard as I...You said 'don't kill her,' so I didn't."

"Delilah, you killed Bleusette, didn't you?" I didn't have to ask. I knew she had done it.

"I killed her, not Delilah," Thorn said. "*I* killed

Bleusette. *I* killed Bleusette!"

"No, Thorn, you didn't," I said.

"Peanuts," he said. "I gave her peanuts."

"You fool," Delilah said. She sounded almost regretful.

"You said poison," he whispered forcefully. "You said poison."

"Shig," I said. "Would you hand me the gun and go into Russell's study and call the Sheriff?"

He nodded and passed the gun to me, then moved around us in a wide circle. In a second, he was back with Lyric then he returned to the study and in another moment, I heard his voice at the phone.

"Lyric," I said. "What were you doing in there?"

"Hiding," she said, but I knew that she had been up to something more than hiding. It didn't matter. What did matter was getting this nasty mess untangled.

* * *

Sheriff Bradley had brought another deputy with him and they cuffed Delilah and Thorn and put them in the back of his car, then he came into the house. He had dark circles under his eyes and I sent Fritha and Arturo out to the kitchen to make coffee and a pot of tea.

“So, it was Delilah Duncan who killed Bleusette,” he said. It wasn’t a question. He had taken statements from all of us and everyone had heard her words.

“She smeared peanut butter on all of the wooden sticks on the top layer of the box of incense.” I said. “She knew Bleusette would be using one prior to the introduction speech. She wiped the peanut butter off carefully but there was still enough so that, when Bleusette licked her thumb and finger to pinch the candle out, she would get some into her system.”

“Risky way to do it,” he said. “It might not have worked.”

“Russell must have told her how allergic Bleusette was to peanuts. If it hadn’t killed her, it would have at least made her extremely ill. Then Delilah could try another time.” I sipped my tea. It was too hot and I put it back down.

“She first hired Thorn to try to chase me off the island,” I told him. “He hit me on the back of the head one night. When I didn’t leave, she demanded her money back from him.”

Bradley, writing in his notebook, smiled.

“Delilah then spent the night with Thorn and tried to hire him to murder Bleusette. With Bleusette out of the way, she could have the life she wanted. She could be the writer with Russell by her side and live the lavish life. Thorn thought that poison wasn’t manly enough for him, and he wanted to do it differently so Delilah demanded her money back again and decided to do it herself. After Bleusette was dead, he thought Delilah would want Russell done away with too so they could be together. But, in Delilah's mind, Thorn ruined it all by killing Russell."

The Sheriff shook his head. "Those love triangles can get pretty deadly."

"Besides that, there's another thing," I told him. "I believe that Russell and Bleusette have been stealing the Colonist's manuscripts for years and, after changing them a bit and adding a different author's name, selling them in England."

He shook his head and let out a low whistle. "That what you were here to find out?" he asked.

"No, not specifically," I said. "My clients wanted me to find out how Russell and Bleusette could brainwash the colonists into giving up their work. The real question was, *why* did they want the colonists to give up their work? So, yes, in the long view, I guess that was it."

"Well, you did what you came for."

"I was hired to find out what was going on," I said. "It turns out it was more than anyone had thought. They were running, if not a cult, at least an elaborate scam."

"What are you going to do now?" he asked.

I turned to look at him. He seemed genuinely

interested. "I'm going to go back home and see if I can right some of the wrong that Russell and Bleusette have been causing for years."

"That's a big job."

"Yes," I said.

We gazed out the window into the darkening woods.

THIRTY

Tuesday May 29, 1984

When I had returned to my cabin, I found all but Thorn and Delilah gathered outside the door. They were talking in low tones, kicking rocks and milling about.

"Is it a party?" I asked.

"It seems we all have questions," Cyr said.

"I'm sure you do," I said, and though I was exhausted, I asked them all to step into the cabin. Five of us filled up the small floor, while two sat on the futon.

"I guess it's time to tell you all what I have been up to," I said.

"I've given them a little bit of it," Shig said. "I hope you don't mind."

I smiled and shook my head. "My name is not Sarah Augustine," I said after a moment. "My name is Cheyenne Bruce, and I am a private investigator. I was hired originally, by Kegan Mercer's family to investigate Whalesong after he committed suicide last year."

Lyric cleared her throat. "My question is why didn't you tell all of us?"

That seemed to open the floodgates. Questions flew at me from every side.

"Calm down," Shig said quietly and they did. "Let her explain."

"I know you all are probably angry. I know I would be. I lied to you about who I was. I understand that."

"But you could have used your real name," Fritha said. "You didn't have to lie to us."

"I had to be under cover," I told her. "I'm a private detective. Do you think Russell and Bleusette would have admitted me if they had known that?"

She shrugged. "I guess not."

"That isn't the most important question," Lyric said. "What were you investigating?"

"The Mercers think that Russell and Bleusette drove their son to suicide because they essentially forced him to hand over his manuscript. The real question is, why did they insist on students handing over their manuscripts? You all know that they are the manuscripts that are the best ones. They left the rest of them alone." I knew I was disparaging Arturo's work and Cyr's too and Axel's as well. They had never been asked to hand over theirs. But Arturo didn't look ruffled at all. "I'm sorry, Arturo, Axel and Cyr." I said. "I don't mean to say that your manuscripts are not some of the good ones, but Russell and Bleusette never seemed very interested in them."

Arturo shrugged. "I always was grateful that they weren't interested in mine."

Cyr didn't say anything. I don't know what he was thinking.

"I don't think they understood mine well enough," Axel said. "It doesn't bother me. I'm with Arturo on that. I'm glad they left mine alone."

"The question I had was what happened to those manuscripts?" I went on.

Fritha's face went pink. "I know the answer to that one. They burn them. They burn them right before your eyes. The work you put so many hours on. The work you gave everything to. They burn them."

"Actually, Fritha, they didn't burn them," I told her. "After dinner on the Monday your manuscript was burned, I went into the Meeting room and found a little scrap of paper in the brazier."

"That was the night you were sick," Arturo said.

"Yes, only I wasn't sick. I wanted to get a look at the Meeting room. Anyway, I took the scrap back to my room and it had the word 'Rolex' on it and the name 'Tyrone'. I don't know about Tyrone, but I'm pretty sure your Nordic Folk novel didn't feature a

Rolex."

"Oh, my gosh!" Fritha said, covering her mouth with both hands. "What happened to my book, then?"

"I have it right here," I told her and reached under the futon table for my case. In a moment I had it unlocked and handed her back her book. She hugged it to her chest with tears streaming down her face.

"How did you get it?" Shig asked me. He looked worried.

"That night they were on the mainland, I opened the back door of the Main Cabin and snooped around in Russell's den and Bleusette's office. I found it in one of Bleusette's desk drawers."

No one said anything. They seemed to accept, without question that I had entered the cabin and snooped around. Maybe they thought that was what all private investigators do.

"What do you think was going on with the rest of the manuscripts?" Lyric asked.

"I'm thinking that they retyped the manuscripts with a pseudonym and sent them to England, Bleusette representing the author. They were published there with the stipulation that they were not to be released in the US. If a few of the copies actually made it to the US, the original author probably would never see them. They chose the very best books. They got excellent reviews in the

UK according to Manchester Publishers, and Russell made a great deal of money from them."

"That bastard!" Lyric said.

"I found a manuscript titled *The Boatman Returns*, by James Winthrop.

They looked at each other. "Yes, we knew James. He was here a couple of years ago," Shig said.

"Yes, it was two," Lyric added.

"Well, there was a letter in Russell's desk that said "Boatman" was doing well in the UK. I found a copy of *The Boatman of Scarborough* on Russell's bookshelf by Bailey Attwood. I would be willing to bet it's the same book with a few changes. I'm sure the names of characters, places and so forth have been changed. But the plots probably remain the same. I believe the books Russell stole could be recognized by the rightful authors."

"Oh, my God!" Lyric said.

"So Kegan's book, *The Way of Wonder*, could be in England right now in pre-publication under some other title?" Arturo asked.

I nodded. "Shig told me that they burn fewer than one manuscript per term. If they have been at this for at least twenty years, they've stolen lots of books. I will try to see to it that whatever books have been stolen are properly identified. If everything works out, at some point, the rightful authors will get their rights back and there will be restitution from the estate."

I heard Lyric mutter something. She looked as if she was about to cry. I didn't blame her. She had lost Camille and now it had been discovered that it had been Camille who had been defrauded. I wondered how many other tragedies would be uncovered that could be laid at Russell and Bleusette's feet.

"I'm glad you didn't give up your book, Sarah," Fritha said. "Oh, I mean...What did you say your real name is?"

"It's Chey, but you can call me Sarah if you want," I told her. "I kind of like it. It isn't my book anyway. Kegan's family gave me his manuscripts to study and to use while I was here. I'm not the writer."

"It's Kegan's work?" Fritha's eyes went round again.

"You know, a couple of times it occurred to me that your work sounded like something Kegan would have written," Shig said. "I thought you and he were both influenced by the same instructor."

Fritha looked at her manuscript and thumbed through it as though her child had been returned to her after several years' absence. At last, she put it into her lap and looked at me. "I can't thank you enough, Sarah...uh, Sarah."

"Sarah is fine," I told her again. "I know how horrible you felt when you had thought it was burned. I felt horrible for you. I know how I would feel if it were mine. I always felt disappointed and hurt when Russell used to disparage Kegan's work and it wasn't even something I had done. I, of course, had to add my own inept changes when Russell demanded them. But I always kept Kegan's work separate. I believe that it will be published one day. It's excellent."

"I thought your changes were good," Shig said. "I don't think you should say they're inept."

"No, your changes were top notch!" Arturo added. Fritha, Lyric and even Cyr and Axel nodded.

"I have to admit, that I haven't been sitting around twiddling my thumbs while you all have been working. I've been writing a journal."

"Whalesong has turned you into a writer!" Shig said. "I've seen more than one writer quit after a term here. This is probably the first time a non-writer has come here and turned into one. Maybe someday, you'll see it published."

Before they left, I told them that they should finish the conference. They had paid their money and had every right to stay in the cabins until it was over. I told them that I hoped they would find agents, publishers or whatever it was that they wanted most.

"I, myself, plan to speak for Kegan" I said. "Donald Whatcom is interested."

THIRTY-ONE

Wednesday May 30, 1984

The next morning, I slept later than I had intended. I found my breakfast, cold, still sitting at my doorstep. I gobbled it while hurriedly dressing. I needed to get to the Main Cabin to catch the shuttle to the hotel. When I arrived and saw that it no longer sat in the courtyard, I hefted my bag onto my arm and set out to walk.

The woods were lovely that morning. The birds didn't seem to mind my passing through their territory, but sang to me much of the way. I felt full of energy and purpose. The cloud which had seemed to hover over me since my return from Hawaii had dissipated. I knew that the few remaining wisps of it would soon be gone once I was back home and busy with my normal life –whatever that was.

At the hotel, I headed for the appointment desk to see if there was a slot available with Donald Whatcom. I knew it was unlikely but I was prepared to be pushy to get what I wanted for Kegan. There wasn't any availability, but I learned that the last appointment would be finished at 11:30, only an hour's wait. I wandered the conference area, speaking to two or three writers I had met. They didn't mention it, but I knew they must have heard about the events following Bleusette's death. One of them patted my arm and one gave me a brief hug. From both of them I felt a genuine, honest caring.

As I loitered, I again felt as though a weight had been lifted from me. For one thing, I no longer felt the burden of David. It was as if those memories had once had physical weight and I had been carrying them around with me for twenty years. But they had vanished in the past twenty-four hours.

At 11:30, I lurked around the door of the room where Donald Whatcom was holding his last appointments. When the last of the writers had left the room, I stepped inside.

He recognized me at once. "Come to bring me those manuscript pages?" he asked.

Surprised, I stammered. "Actually, I came to thank you for your interest after you heard my pitch and to let you know that I will be sending Kegan's work to you. I have them right here," I said. "But I thought you publishers didn't like to be inundated with manuscripts to haul back home."

"Normally we don't," he said. "But I was intrigued by what you told me about the young man who wrote this book. The pitch was well done and it did exactly what it was supposed to do. It interested me." He looked at me over the top of his glasses. "*Your* pitch? Did you write it?"

I had pulled the manuscript from my bag and begun to separate the first two chapters. "I did," I told him. "Kegan never had the chance."

"Here, why don't you just give me the whole thing?" he said. "And don't tell anyone! I'll be buried in manuscripts after the next conference if you do."

I handed him the stack of pages and he managed to fit it into his already full briefcase.

"That's a copy that has my name on it," I told him. "But Kegan wrote it. I'll be giving the original back to his family." I stopped for a moment, then went ahead. "Mr. Whatcom, I can't thank you enough for this. Kegan's family, I think, will get some measure of comfort from what you are doing."

"I can't promise anything, you understand," he said.

"That's okay," I said. "Just having you take it and look at it should give his wife enough encouragement to press on. I hope so, anyway."

"I'm eager to read it. And, I think you are doing a fine thing for Kegan's family, I might add. If *you* ever write anything, and I think you should, I hope you'll give me the honor of looking at that too."

I promised him that I would, though I doubted that he would ever see anything of mine.

* * *

Lyric, Fritha, Shig, Arturo and I had all decided to skip the awards luncheon. No one in the group had entered the contest anyway. None of us had seen Axel or Cyr since the impromptu meeting in my cabin the night before and we assumed they had either gone home or were attending the award banquet. We decided instead to have lunch in the hotel restaurant. We had a wonderful time. Once Fritha got loosened up with a couple of glasses of wine, she was surprisingly witty and kept us all laughing. Apparently, Fritha's 'not very nice girl' was quite appealing.

Later that afternoon, we once again boarded a ferry. This one, headed for the mainland. The five of us had managed to put together a hefty tip for Strom who silently chauffeured us to the dock. I felt sorry for the man who had been such a loyal servant for the dead couple. I knew they had not treated him with respect and we had all tried to make up for that. I hoped that whatever happened to the Whalesong compound, Strom would be a part of it so he could stay on his beloved island.

"Well," Shig said when we all stood on the deck watching Klallam Island retreat, "I guess I'll have to find me another writers colony."

"Not me," Lyric said. "I'm going to stay away from writers' colonies and writer's conferences for a while."

"You need to find a publisher for that novel, though," I told her.

"Oh, I will, I guess," she said, but she didn't sound very sure.

"I'm going to try to get mine published," Fritha said. "I had an appointment with an agent this morning and he said he was interested. He wants me to write a complete synopsis and send it and two chapters!" She did a little excited dance on the deck. Lyric looked at me with a raised eyebrow and I had to laugh.

While Lyric and Fritha were trying to convince Arturo to at least try to get his book published, Shig pulled me aside.

"I don't know what you said to Guy Loring or Janet Jeffries, but I don't think there are enough years in my life to thank you."

"I didn't do anything," I told him. "When I was interviewing Guy, he mentioned that he had met another writer from Whalesong. I simply said that your writing was excellent. Honestly. That's all I said."

"Well, I don't believe that, but whatever it was, I can't thank you enough."

"Actually, Shig, Guy Loring is an old friend of mine that I've known for more than twenty years. He'll believe anything I say," I said. "When I told him how great those Stupid Warriors are…Well! " I shrugged.

Shig laughed. "If I had known that you were buddies—"

"Shig," Fritha interrupted. "Come and talk agents with me." She turned to me. "I love being a writer!"

Fritha and Shig got into a conversation about their prospective agents. It was good to hear Fritha's voice with a lilt of excitement. Arturo moved to a protected area so he wouldn't have to be so careful of his beret. Lyric and I moved to a shaded part of the deck

"You aren't going to give up writing, are you, Lyric?" I asked her.

"I don't know," she said. She sounded dispirited. "I probably won't. It's just that the only agent I ever had was Bleusette. She wasn't a very good one but she was at least an agent. Now I don't even have that."

"Please don't give it up," I said. "You already have published one novel. That's something you can point to and say, 'See, I can do it!' If you give up, for the rest of your life, it will feel like Russell won. You don't want that."

"No, you're right," she said. She stared at the water glittering in the sunlight. "Sarah," she said, then looked at me. "Or, Cheyenne, I guess. Could I confess something to you?"

"Of course," I told her.

"I don't know whether I should tell you this or not." She looked worried and, I thought, shamefaced.

"If you're not comfortable, don't say it," I told her but I could tell she very much wanted me to hear what she had on her mind.

"The reason I was in Russell's den..." she said, then stopped. "I went over to the Main Cabin to kill him. To kill Russell," she said in a rush after a long moment. Her deep brown eyes stared into mine.

I waited for her to continue.

"I went to the Main Cabin. I don't know where Russell was, but I just walked in. I was intending to go into his den and get his gun out of the drawer and shoot him."

"But you didn't," I said, hoping to comfort her.

"I would have though." She looked down at her hands clasped tightly in front of her. "Before I had a chance to look for the gun, I heard someone else come in the door and I thought Russell had come back. I hid over by the file cabinets, in the corner, you know?" I nodded. "I saw Thorn come in and start going through the desk drawers. Then I heard him leave the room. I don't know where Russell was, but I knew that Thorn hadn't left the house. That window in the den looks out onto the front courtyard and he never went out the front door. I was afraid to come out. He had the gun, after all. Pretty soon, I saw Russell come up onto the porch and go in. Then I heard them shouting and the gun go off." Tears were streaming down her face now. I put my hand on her arm. I saw her rage at Russell and her fear. Something else, disappointment, I thought, was there too. Disappointment because her dreams seemed to be going up in smoke or because she hadn't been the one to kill Russell?

"I heard the gong and knew everyone would be coming, but I was too scared to come out. I didn't know if Thorn intended to kill us all."

"He said he was going to but then he got into that argument with Delilah," I told her.

"When Shig came in and picked up the phone, I must have made a noise because he saw me right away." She still watched me. "I *did* intend to kill Russell, Cheyenne. I did. I wanted to."

"I know," I told her. "I think I understand why."

She looked out over the water. "I guess you do," she said.

"You wanted to kill him because of what he did to Camille, didn't you?"

"Yes," she said. Her eyes seemed to be looking at something that had happened long ago. "I loved her so much," she said. "We…It…We wanted so badly to get married. Of course, we couldn't. But, even so, we were so happy. We both wanted to write and we had our future all planned."

Lyric turned her face to the wall. She was crying now. "She became a prostitute. Or at least she was. She's in prison. I loved her," she said, sobbing softly. "I still love her."

I put my arm across her shoulder. "I know you do."

"And there is nothing I can do for her. Nothing! I was going to kill him for her. At least then I would feel I had done something."

"But you didn't. That makes all the difference."

"How does it make any difference?" She was still crying but was once again watching the sun on the water.

"If you had killed him, you would have ended up in prison too. If you were in prison, there really would be no way to help Camille." I watched her for a moment. "Have you ever contacted her?"

She shook her head. She looked so dejected, I wanted to cry. "No. I think she made it plain that she doesn't want to hear from me."

"Don't be so sure. We don't really know what others think," I told her. "I think you should give it a try. You never know. It might do nothing. It might help. And, when she gets out, you'll be there to help her."

She nodded but didn't look convinced.

"As a writer, you have power. Writers have more power than many of them know. They can change minds and lives. You can still try to use your power to help Camille, and others too."

She seemed to consider what I had said. Then she nodded.

"I'm glad I told you," she said.

"The important thing to remember is that you didn't do it. You may not have even been able to kill him when it came right down to it. You'll never know. But you can believe that, if it will make you feel better."

She thought. "Actually, I think I like to believe that I *would* have killed him if I had had the chance. Maybe that makes me a terrible person, but that's the way I feel. I want to think that I would be willing to kill for Camille."

Shig and Fritha interrupted us then to say that the ferry was about to dock. We gathered our things and headed for the mainland and home.

* * *

Easy met me at the dock. After I had introduced the four people I had virtually lived with for the past month, they went their separate ways and Easy and I headed for his car.

"I missed you," he said.

"I missed you too," I said. "And telephones, and streets and people and traffic." I laughed. "I missed everything!"

"I missed having normal conversations with you," he said. "It's disconcerting to have you answer, 'linguini' when I ask you a question that has nothing to do with Italian food."

"It was like being in grade school with really strict teachers watching you every second. I never did figure out why the others put up with it year after year."

"It gets to feel normal after a while, I suppose," he said.

We drove in silence for a minute or two. I-5 was still wet from a recent rain. Whalesong seemed very far away. The silence was different than that on the island. The present silence was full of sounds. The roar of traffic, the sounds of planes, the music of radios coming from other people's cars would normally have seemed annoying to me. But not then.

"I read about some of it in the paper," he said finally.

"Really?"

"Why are you surprised?" He glanced at me. "It was a double murder, after all."

"I didn't see any reporters around," I told him.

"But then, no one had been allowed on or off the island for a few days so I guess that isn't so surprising. What did you hear?"

"Just that the man and woman who ran the colony were killed. They said the San Juan County Sheriff was on it. They may have mentioned a private detective from Seattle being on the case too, I can't really remember."

I laughed.

"That really was about all, though," he said. "You might have a few reporters hanging around your front door when you get home." I glanced at him and could see he was teasing.

"If I do, I think I can handle them."

Then he looked at me and smiled.

"There's probably something you did not read in the paper, though," I told him. "David was there."

Easy said nothing.

"I found out he was going to be there about midway through the month. I was hoping I could get the case cleared up then get home so I wouldn't have to run into him. Then Bleusette had to go and get herself killed and I had to question everyone. David was one of the speakers at the conference."

"Leave it to David," he muttered. I laughed and he glanced at me again, looking surprised.

"Anyway, he avoided me for a day or two, then,

when it was his turn to be questioned, we had to have a talk."

"You sound awfully blasé about having talked to the guy you have pined over for the last twenty years," Easy said.

"I know. I do, don't I?" I grinned at him.

"Okay, I think you had better tell me what happened."

"Nothing happened. I talked to him, he talked to me. I discovered that I had been 'pining' over the wrong David."

"What?"

"Well, David went to Vietnam and got seriously injured. He was changed by the experience. I stayed home and I changed too. Everything changes. Everything. In my mind, though, I had been thinking that David was exactly the same David that he was when he left. But he wasn't. He was different. I had to decide if I wanted to pine over the David he was or the David he is. It's the difference between the Bill Russell SuperSonics versus the Lenny Wilkens SuperSonics. It's Royal Blue versus Elvis Presley. It's Star Wars versus The Big Chill..."

"Okay, I get it," he said.

"Those things are very different from one another. One isn't better than the other, just different. It isn't that he's a bad David. He isn't. He's a perfectly fine guy. It's just that he isn't the one I knew. He's so different, he isn't even the same man. Probably the one I knew wasn't even the real David. I had idealized him. No one can stand up to that."

"I don't think I've ever heard you say his name so many times in the whole time I've known you."

I sat back in the seat and smiled. "I know, right?"

"I think I was right about what I told you before you left," he said. "I think this case did you a world of good."

THIRTY-TWO

Friday, June 1, 1984

Two days later, the late May sun streamed into my office through the glass doors.

Stella Mercer, calmer than the last time I had seen her, and Claire sat in front of my desk while JW once again seemed taken with the view of my front yard. They all appeared eager to hear my report.

They heard it with apparent mixed feelings. Outrage and elation clashed while they digested what I had to say.

"I will see to it that all of these authors are given the proper credit for their works," JW told me when I handed him the list of stolen manuscripts. Sheriff Bradley had sent me a more complete list once the crime scene had been completed as well as a thorough search of Russell and Bleusette's cabin.

"We can't thank you enough," Claire told me. "It can't bring back my husband, but at least his work will be recognized."

"Donald Whatcom was very interested," I told her

after I had explained that I had given him my copy of Kegan's manuscript.

"That alone was worth the price of hiring you, Miss Bruce," JW said.

"It was an interesting case," I told him. "I have to thank you for the opportunity." I didn't mention how much the case had helped me. "If something good can come out of it, all the better."

Claire looked at her father and mother-in-law. "May I tell her what you are planning, Dad?" she asked.

He nodded.

"Dad has plans to buy the property that Whalesong is on and open a writer's colony there," she said.

"I want to erase the past," he added. "My law firm will see to it that the York-Hunstman estate pays those authors what they are due and we will set up a foundation with the rest of their stolen wealth to benefit other writers."

"I think that's a wonderful idea," I told him. "It's a lovely setting and, in the right hands, it could be an idyllic place for aspiring writers." I knew they were happy with the outcome of the case and I was too.

After we had said our goodbyes and I had closed the door, I turned toward the future, looking forward to my next case. Thankfully, I was blissfully unaware of what awaited me.

Epilogue

Over the next few months, JW Mercer's law firm contacted the writers from Whalesong whose manuscripts were found in Russell's file cabinets. Of the sixteen authors represented, two had committed suicide, three, including Camille Bishop, had slid into addiction, and five of them had given up writing altogether. Few of them had seemed eager to speak about the weeks, months and sometimes years, they had spent at Whalesong. When it was explained to them that their work had been stolen and published in Great Britain under other names, some of them were eager for restitution and some only wanted to forget about what they considered a dark time in their lives. They were given the option of donating their share of the restitution to the Kegan Mercer Foundation and all but one of them did.

While you cannot erase the past as JW Mercer had planned to do, he had righted a great wrong and he had saved lives as well. He eventually did establish a writers' colony on Klallam Island in the buildings which had been Whalesong. The Kegan Mercer Writers Residence is staffed by a rotating crew of established, reputable writers who give encouragement and mentorships to their students.

In the years since the Whalesong case, Fritha had become a good friend to me. She sold her book and, at long last, with much heart wrenching and agonizing decision, moved away from her parents. She still struggled with her mom and dad issues and never married nor had children of her own. Sometimes I wonder what her path would have been had she been able to defy some of the authority that had been heaped upon her for her entire life. She continued in her marketing job, even though she disliked it so very much. And, though she went on to publish more books, she never seemed to be very self-assured or to enjoy their modest following. It was my belief that it wasn't just mother and father who had done this to her. I believe it was Russell, Bleusette and Whalesong as well.

Lyric, too, became a friend, but she moved to California and I rarely saw her. She had succeeded in getting her second novel published also. I heard too that, upon Camille's release from prison, she and Lyric connected and were together again, however I knew nothing more than that. I was touched to tears when I saw that Lyric had dedicated *Pauline's Red Hat* to both Camille and me. I was happy to be in association with poor, broken Camille whom I had never met.

I had another book dedicated to me as well. Had I taken Shig's advice and read the book he had handed me that night at Whalesong, I may have seen that David had dedicated his first novel 'To Chey-Bear. I will never forget you.' When I saw, after all those years, his affectionate name for me while we were together it almost broke me. I was glad, though, that I had discovered it after I had resolved my issues with David. I'm not at all sure of what my reaction would have been prior to that.

Shig Takano and I corresponded for many years and I followed his career with great interest as he became a prolific and respected science fiction writer. To me, his books were worthy rivals for Guy Loring's work.

Over the years, I lost track of the others.

In a way, the Whalesong case, though horrible in its outcome, helped me to heal. I felt that I was "over" David, though there are nights, still, when I wonder where my own path may have led had his decisions been different.

I am still tormented by my actions on Hawaii, but there is comfort in knowing that I have saved lives too.

Whalesong had been a peaceful dream. A place where writers could go and work and get instruction from the great master. Only the master turned out to not be so great. It must have been even more of a heartbreak when his students found out what York had been doing with their work. They were writers. I knew that whatever York had done with their spirits was nothing compared with the betrayal they felt at the fates of their manuscripts. The couple, Russell York and Bleusette Huntsman had been responsible for more than one life taking a dark turn and more than one life lost. Their legacy will be scars that will never heal.

Kegan Mercer's book *The Book of Signs* became a classic, used in literature classrooms across the country. It won several awards. I was pleased and humbled to note that more than one of my "edits" to the manuscript were included in the final published work. It's ironic that Kegan himself never was able to enjoy the notoriety his work generated. Again, I can't help but wonder what would have happened if he had not encountered Whalesong or if he had defied Russell and Bleusette's edict to destroy his work. If he had taken Shig's advice and submitted an earlier, unimportant draft for destruction, the world may have turned out to be a different place today.

It only takes one step along an alternate path to change everything.

Cheyenne Bruce

March 2020

ACKNOWLEDGEMENTS

Many thanks to my dear friend Barb Roberts
who is invaluable for many, many reasons.

Thank you to my husband, Guy, who is
the most patient man in the world.

Thank you to Gale Peck of Iceberg Strategic
Creative for the cover designs of all three books.

Lyrics from "The Letter" by Wayne
Carson Thompson

Heartfelt thanks to my readers. I hope you enjoy
these books as much as I have enjoyed writing them.

ABOUT THE AUTHOR

Lella Rae

Lella Rae is the pseudonym for Delores Peck.

Delores was born in Tacoma, Washington and has lived in the Pacific Northwest most of her life. She holds a Bachelor of Arts degree in the Humanities from the University of Washington, She lives in West Seattle with her husband, Guy.

BOOKS BY THIS AUTHOR

Always A Bad Sign, Cheyenne Bruce Mystery, Book One

When former screen star Magda St. Martin's husband, Jake, was found murdered in his car, Magda hired me to investigate the crime. I agreed only because five and half years before, I had failed to locate Magda's missing teenaged daughter. The case haunted me ever since.

Now, Magda had lost two husbands and a daughter under mysterious circumstances.

From the beginning, I realized that Magda, her secretary, Laurel Gold and her gardener, Rolf Edmondson, were lying to me.

As secret after secret was uncovered, I felt farther and farther from the truth until the final macabre moments.

Sign Your Life Away, Cheyenne Bruce Mystery, Book Two

I was in my car when the news came over the radio that Royal Blue was dead. Shocked, the world seemed to stop moving for awhile.

Once or twice in a lifetime there arises a star the brilliance of Royal Blue. The world would eventually become used to his loss, but, like the ripples on a pond, his essence would never really die.

I drove on that day, little knowing that with the passing of years my life would become entangled with the lives of those Royal Blue had loved. Though I didn't yet know the players, they were waiting in my future to affect me to the end of my life. And though the case was finished long ago, I dream about it still. In my sleep, I'm standing on the edge of hell with a madman.

THE SIGN OF THE RAVEN

Look for the fourth Cheyenne Bruce mystery coming in September, 2023.

In the summer of 1984 death stalked the cities, towns highways, waterways and forests of Washington State. The Pacific Northwest, by then, was all too familiar with serial killers. In the 70s, Ted Bundy had terrorized the area by charming and then killing young women. In the 80s, Gary Ridgeway, known as the Green River Killer, murdered and hid his female victims only to return and visit their remains again and again.

But, unknown to everyone, there was another killer lurking in the state during those years. One which remained unnamed by the press, undiscovered by the authorities. An unknown, free to pursue and eliminate whomever the killer wished. So skilled were the murders, they were not believed to be homicides at all, but natural deaths.

It was a strange, knowing what I knew but being unable to convince anyone else. Death seemed to lurk around every corner, to watch quietly and bide its time, waiting, waiting.

The setting, a peaceful town on the Washington Coast, became a scene of terror that summer and I headed into a case that would continue to haunt me for the rest of my life.

DISCLAIMER

Whalesong and Klallum Island do not exist anywhere but in my imagination.

Pegasus Book Exchange does exist in West Seattle as it did in the 1980s. It is truly a wonderful place.

I beg the San Juan County Sheriff's Department and the Seattle Police Department to forgive the liberties I have taken with their organizations.

Made in the USA
Middletown, DE
07 April 2023

28087547R00236